Our Haunted Home

Matthew Fodor

Copyright © 2024 Matthew Fodor

All rights reserved.

ISBN: 9798325931161

*For Kirsty and Reuben,
for giving me the time to learn how to do this.*

WINTER

CHAPTER 01
0 SUBSCRIBERS

"You must be Harry" the agent said, holding out his hand for Harry to shake. "Stephen" he said with a smile.

"I must be" said Harry. "This is my wife, Lisa."

"Hello" Lisa said, shaking the agent's hand. Harry could tell that she was unimpressed, and she had good reason to be.

The yard that they were stood in, which was far too small to be considered a garden, was comprised almost entirely of weeds. Thick, thorny vines interwove around angry looking nettles. Plastic bags and discarded crisp packets sat snared amongst the thorns. The driveway that this foliage framed was in an even worse condition still.

Cracked, loose paving slabs led up to a battered looking front door. Most of the paint had flaked away leaving only exposed and damp looking wood. The windows were dirty, their wooden frames holding up as poorly as the front door itself.

"Wow" Lisa said. "This isn't quite what I was expecting."

A roaring sound, distant at first and then frighteningly close, revealed itself to be a quad bike. It flew past the house at breakneck speed. Its rider wore no helmet. Instead, a black scarf was wrapped tightly around the man's face.

"Shall we look inside?" Stephen said hopefully.

"I think we'd better had."

"Don't look so worried" said Harry, placing a hand on the small of his wife's back. "I did warn you that it was going to be a bit rough around the edges."

"A bit?" Lisa said. Her expression of contempt turned into one of bitter amusement. "I bet we could get a better-looking place on the Gaza Strip for less."

The front door opened with a creak. Stephen went in first. He scooped up a handful of letters that had collated on the doormat and placed them on a nearby radiator cover.

Harry followed. With a visible reluctance, Lisa was last to cross the threshold.

"I thought you said that the owner still lives here" Harry said, squeezing into the tight hallway. "That looks like at least a week's worth of post."

"She moved out recently" the estate agent said. "I believe she's living with her sister now."

Harry shot Lisa an excited smile. Although she acknowledged this, she did not smile back.

"That seems odd" Harry pressed. "She still owns the house but she's living with her sister? Why would she do that?"

"I don't really know much about her situation" the agent said. "It's a nice bright hallway, isn't it?"

"Do we need to take our shoes off?"

Lisa's eyes traced a trail of muddy footprints which snaked up and down the hallway toward the cramped looking kitchen at the back of the house.

"I don't think that's necessary" the agent said. He too eyed the mud that had been tracked through the house. "If you follow me this way, we'll head into the living room."

The agent went through a battered looking door and into a compact room at the front of the house.

"Bloody hell" Lisa said, "It looks like a bomb has gone off in here."

This was not an exaggeration. A large crack ran down from the top of the windowpane to the tattered wooden ledge at its base. Moth-eaten curtains framed torn yellow netting. Whole sheets of fading wallpaper had sluiced away from the walls exposing cracked plaster. A fireplace dominated the middle of the room. In it, a mound of old bricks sat where wood might've been had the fireplace been in a working condition.

There had been carpet at one time - this much was evident from the jagged grippers that ran the outskirts of the room - but this was now gone. In its place, exposed floorboard rotted away into nothing. In the far corner of the room, a hole had opened up giving way to the space below the house. From where Harry was standing, he could see dull copper piping underneath.

"Are all the rooms like this?" Lisa said.

"The living room is the one that needs the most work" Stephen said. "The listing did state that the property would need some structural repairs if it were to become habitable."

"How long ago did the owner leave?" Harry asked, unconcerned by the state of the room.

"Like I said, I really don't know much about her."

"Is there any way to find out? I was hoping that she would be here. I have a few questions that I wanted to ask."

"Harry..."

The agent carried on despite Lisa's warning.

"Mrs. Fisher has said that she doesn't want to be on the property while potential buyers look around. It's not uncommon."

"Can we look upstairs?" Lisa asked.

"Of course. Would you like to see the kitchen first?"

"Yes please" Harry said.

The kitchen was not big enough for all three people to occupy at once. Instead, Harry and Lisa stood in the room while the agent talked at them from the hallway. The space was pokey, consisting only of the essentials. An oven sat amongst tired cupboards, its hob coated in the grease of an untold number of meals. The tiles on the floor were intact but dirty. A cheap metal sink was located under a window which looked out onto an overgrown back garden and a derelict old shed.

"It's a good-sized lawn" Harry said. Lisa did not respond.

"It'll be great for get-togethers once the weather picks up a bit" the agent said. "There's plenty of room out there for a barbeque or some decking if you wanted to really make it a nice social space."

"We wouldn't be buying this place to live in it" Lisa said. An odd defensive tone had situated her voice.

"Are you buying to rent?"

"We'll be renting it in the long term" said Harry.

Lisa opened a cupboard. A gust of stale smelling air filled the room. She shut it quickly, wafting the air in front of her face.

"Hopefully not too long of a term" she said. "We already have a home. We're just hoping to try our hand at building a property portfolio."

"Oh, lovely" said Stephen. "We get quite a lot of that around here. Are you from out of the area?"

"Yes. Was the accent not a give away?"

The agent smiled politely, ignoring the harshness in Lisa's voice.

"Well, the houses need some work as you can see, but the prices are right for those who are willing to put in the hours."

The agent led the couple upstairs, showing them the two reasonable sized bedrooms and waving his hand over the tiny box room that overlooked the street.

Harry had smiled politely at the suggestion that this room would make a perfect nursery. Lisa busied herself looking around the bathroom.

The bathroom felt the most cramped out of all the rooms in the little house. The bath dominated an entire half of the room and a dark shower curtain that had been drawn closed until the agent had opened it, had sucked what little light there was out of the space. A single frosted window looked out onto the back garden. Harry struggled to open the window, finding its hinges were caked in a black substance that stuck to them like glue. When he did manage to open the window, the air that rushed into the room was no colder than the air inside.

"What are the neighbours like?"

"They seem nice enough. There's a young woman on the east side. On the west wall there's an old lady. I've spoken to her a good few times over the years."

"Yeah" Harry said. "I had heard that this place has changed owners quite a lot over the last few years."

"Three times since I've been doing this job. I've made quite a bit of commission off of this property, truth be told."

"Why do you think people buy it and then sell up so quickly?"

The agent stopped to wipe dust off a yellowing banister out in the landing. Harry got the impression that he was trying to find a way to sugar coat his response.

"I think people buy it and don't anticipate just how much work there is to do here. There are a few houses on the street like it. Some of them change owners again and again until the right person comes along with the right amount of know-how and then that's it. They either live there forever or they use the house to turn a tidy rental profit."

"Well, I really like it" Harry said. "I think it's got a lot of potential."

"Good" Stephen smiled, rubbing his hands together.

"I would feel better if I could speak to the owner though."

His smile vanished as quickly as it had arrived.

"Like I said, I'm afraid that's not going to be possible. She's made it clear that she will not be coming back onto the property."

"I'd give her the asking price if she would just speak to me."

"Harry!" Lisa snapped, annoyed that what should have been a joint decision was being discussed without her.

The agent faltered, his mind worrying behind eyes that

glinted at the prospect of another sale.

"I can give her a call. I'll see if she'll consider speaking to you on the phone."

"I want to meet her in person" Harry said.

Stephen scratched at his chin again.

"I really don't think that she'll want to do that."

"OK" Harry said with an air of finality. He closed the bathroom window, held out his hand for the estate agent to shake, and started toward the stairs.

He had made it down the first two steps before Stephen stopped him.

"I can't make any promises" he said, clearly panicked at the thought of losing a sale "but if you're serious about taking this place off her hands, I know that she's eager to get rid of it. Don't tell her that I told you that."

"I won't say a word."

"I'll make some calls and see if I can arrange a meeting. I'm making no promises though."

"I'm sure you'll try your best" Harry said, trying to ignore the sound of Lisa grinding her teeth beside him.

CHAPTER 02
0 SUBSCRIBERS

Lisa had seethed quietly for just enough time to make it out of the street before unleashing her anger onto Harry. He had sat quietly in the driver's seat, listening to her heated criticism, knowing that she was justified in her fury. He had been bullish, and he had been pushy, and worst of all he had disregarded her feelings.

Despite this, Harry found it difficult to feel remorse. He wanted that house, and he would do whatever it took to get it.

"We're not buying it" Lisa said. "It's a wreck. Barely even bricks and mortar."

"It's nothing that we hadn't anticipated."

The conversation had stopped there.

That night they'd slept in the same hotel bed, the anger that Lisa felt not quite fierce enough to force them apart, but they had each slept on their own side, being careful not to shift in the night and make any sort of physical connection, lest this be conceived as a backing down of their positions on the matter.

At breakfast they had sat separately - Lisa at the dressing table and Harry on the hotel bed. The ambient sound of the television in their room did nothing to mask the growing rumble of the quiet stalemate that they had arrived at.

It was only by the afternoon that Harry and Lisa had begun to carefully negotiate the first tentative steps of a conversation.

"We'd need all new floorboards in the living room" Lisa had said. "Even with the carpet over the top, those things are so crooked that the place will look a state."

"I know someone who sells them on the cheap" Harry

said.

"You can't fill the house with cheap boards. You'll end up-"

"The boards aren't cheap. The price is right. That's all I meant."

The drive to the cafe where they were to meet the house's current owner, Mrs. Fisher, took them through several rundown looking estates. Lisa had locked her car door as they had pulled up at a set of traffic lights. Two kids on a noisy moped had pulled up alongside them and had stared greedily into their car. Behind them, houses sat crumbling into disrepair. Green boards covered the spaces where some of their windows used to be.

"God. It's so rough around here" Lisa had said.

"Well, that's why the house prices are so low."

The light had changed to green, and the moped had sped away without incident, but Lisa had kept her door locked just the same. After arriving at the town centre, Harry had found a well-lit car park and they had exited to the sound of a burglar alarm ringing in the distance.

They held hands as they walked through the quiet High Street. A great many of the shops sat abandoned, graffitied shutters pulled closed over their windows. People slowly shuffled about with no real aim or direction. A cold wind whipped litter across the pavements.

Harry and Lisa arrived at the coffee shop and went inside. The interior was predictable. Mismatched furniture sat around easy to clean tables. Warm orange light glowed from exposed bulbs, illuminating teenage workers who hurried to-and-fro collecting empty mugs and rushing them back behind the counter to be washed.

In the corner of the room sat a lone woman who Harry recognised to be Joanne Fisher.

When they arrived at the table the woman did not get up

to meet them. Instead, she watched as Lisa took off her coat and sat down on the chair opposite her.

"Hello" Lisa offered politely.

"Lisa?"

"Yes. Are you Mrs. Fisher?"

"You can call me Jo."

Harry eyed the empty space on the table in front of the woman.

"Are you not a coffee drinker?" he asked her.

"I haven't brought any money."

"Oh" he said, slightly taken off guard. "That doesn't matter. What can I get you?"

"Tea" Jo said. "Milk. No sugar"

"I guess you're already sweet enough."

Jo Fisher did not respond.

Harry ordered drinks from the counter and watched as Lisa and Jo made difficult small talk at the table. Jo sat hunched forwards, her hands clasped tightly in front of her as if she were preparing to snatch up her belongings and leave at a moment's notice.

The teenage barista loaded up the tray with a cup of tea and two coffees and a couple of cookies that Harry had paid for. He carried the tray back to the table, placing it down carefully, taking great care not to spill anything.

"This is a nice little coffee shop."

Jo picked up her tea, blew across its surface and then set it back down in front of her.

"It's a Costa Coffee" she said. "It's the same as all the others."

"I suppose it is" Harry said. Mrs. Fisher's demeanour made him feel uncomfortable. He picked up his mug and drank from it tentatively.

"Were you waiting for us long?" Lisa asked.

"What am I doing here?"

Harry placed his mug down in front of him.

"I wanted to ask you a few questions about the house" he said.

"I told the estate agents everything that they needed to know" Jo said. "If you had questions, they should have answered them for you."

"They tried" Harry said, "but they don't know the place like you do."

He turned the tray and offered Jo a cookie. She didn't even notice it.

"Look. There's not a lot to know. The place is falling to bits, but that's why the price is so low. It needs a lot of work doing, and it's in a rough area. The electrics and the water work most of the time, the council tax is low, the bin men come on Fridays. There really isn't much else to say."

"I already know all of that stuff."

"So, I'll ask again. What am I doing here?"

Harry stole a look at Lisa who quickly looked away, staring out of the window onto the dreary looking High Street. She shook her head disappointedly, her breath airing loudly down her nose.

"I'm going to ask you something" Harry said, "and I want you to answer me honestly. Please don't just give me the answer that you think I'll want to hear."

"Go on then."

"Is your house haunted?"

Jo's expression flattened.

"What?"

"Is the house that you are selling haunted?"

"Is this some sort of joke? Of course it isn't haunted. There's no such thing as ghosts."

For a moment nobody said anything, and then, slowly but surely, cracks started to appear in Jo Fisher's composure.

"I asked you not to give me the answer that you think I

would want to hear."

Jo picked up her handbag and pushed her mug of tea across the table. She got to her feet and began to pull a tattered-looking jacket off the back of her chair.

"Where are you going?"

Jo Fisher fixed Harry with an infuriated gaze.

"Do you have any idea how long it took me to walk to the town centre? I came here because I thought you were genuinely interested in buying my house and when I get here, I find you just want to ask me stupid questions!"

"I don't think it is a stupid question" Harry said.

"Well, it sounded stupid to me" Jo said, zipping up her jacket.

She walked around the table and wove past a barista carrying a tray of empty mugs. Harry watched in panic as she pushed open the door and stepped out into the cold.

"That went well" Lisa said, sipping at her coffee.

Harry snatched up his own jacket and ran out into the street. He hurried to catch up with the woman who moved surprisingly quickly for a lady of her size. She rolled her eyes when he eventually caught up and placed his hand on her shoulder.

"I didn't mean to upset you."

"Well, you did" she said. "This was such a waste of time."

"Please come back inside. Just sit and finish your tea. I am genuinely interested in buying your house but have a few questions to ask first."

"About ghosts?"

"Yes" Harry said flatly, "about ghosts."

Jo stood and searched for any hint of malice in Harry's eyes. The first few drops of a freezing rain began to fall around her. She pulled her worn jacket tight around herself.

"Ten minutes" Jo said. "Or as long as it takes for this rain to stop. I don't fancy getting soaked on the walk home."

"We can drive you to your sister's house" Harry offered.

"No thank you" Jo said.

When they arrived back at the café, Lisa was still sitting at the table, eating one of the cookies that Harry had bought. She looked surprised to see them both return.

Harry took his seat and Jo followed, not bothering to take off her jacket this time.

"Do you want another drink?" Harry asked Lisa. She shook her head, covering her mouth as she chewed her cookie.

"I don't know" Jo said. "Whether the house is haunted. I don't know."

"Why not?"

"Because I don't believe that ghosts are real" she said, hunching over her tea. "But there was something strange about that house. I'll admit that much."

Excitement bubbled in Harry's guts. He tried to compress his smile.

"And how would this *something* manifest itself?"

"Manifest isn't really the right word. That implies there's something in there. I always thought of it as the house playing tricks." Jo stopped and looked over her shoulder, fearful that someone might be listening. "That doesn't mean there's a ghost in there" she half whispered.

Harry took his phone from his pocket and opened his Instagram app. He opened his saved videos, scrolling through a playlist he had entitled *Evidence*, and then pressed his thumb onto a small square tile. His phone screen came to life. He pressed the volume button on the side of the device just in time to catch the tail end of the video. In it, a woman was screaming.

Harry turned his phone around and slid it across the table toward Mrs. Fisher. Her face turned an ashen shade of grey. She only half glanced at the images on the screen.

"That bloody video" Jo said, lifting her mug with shaking

hands.

"You filmed this video, didn't you? In the house that you're selling?"

Jo slid the phone back across the table, nodding silently.

"And that's the reason that you live with your sister now? That's why you don't live there anymore?"

She nodded again. Her face continued to drain of colour.

"Do you mind if I have some of that cookie?" Jo asked. Harry pushed the tray toward her.

"My daughter filmed that" she said, speaking with her mouth full of crumbling biscuit. "I told her not to upload it anywhere, but you know what kids are like. Everything has to be shared with everyone these days. Nothing is private anymore."

"So, there is a ghost in your home?"

"I didn't say that. I said that the house played tricks. I never said there was a ghost."

"But this looks like pretty convincing evidence."

"Well," Jo said, stuffing the rest of the cookie into her mouth. "Looks can be deceiving, can't they?"

"But-"

Lisa squeezed Harry's leg firmly under the table. He bit his tongue, swallowing the questions that were forming on his lips.

Jo Fisher suddenly struggled to her feet.

"Will you excuse me a moment? I feel a bit funny. I just need some fresh air. Don't worry. I'm not going to do a runner again."

Mrs. Fisher headed to the door, exited the shop and then stood in the doorway, half sheltered from the rain, watching as clouds rolled over a slate grey sky.

At the table, Harry let the video play out.

In it, two girls danced for the camera, poorly synchronizing to a rhythmic dance beat. Laughter ebbed from behind the screen, and the whole scene shook as a voice that Harry recognised to be Mrs. Fisher's howled at the girl's antics. They danced around a poky living room, their hips swaying and hair swinging, until the lightbulb over their head swung wildly as if struck by some unseen force.

"Mum!?" one of the girls said, her dance coming to an abrupt stop. "What was-"

The bulb above the girls exploded, sending a shower of sparks and glass spilling to the floor. They screamed, and the camera lost its frame, falling to the ground as Mrs. Fisher made her escape. The scene reframed on the doorway as the phone came to rest. In the fleeting moments before the video stopped, a dark shape glided past the phone and out of the room.

The video reset and began to play all over again.

"It still looks like a person to me" Harry said, more to himself than to Lisa.

"Just remember the deal" she said, finishing her coffee. "Do not go a penny over the asking price. I'm serious."

Mrs. Fisher returned to the table and sat down. She looked windswept, and it was clear that she had not been able to totally shield herself from the rain, but the colour had returned to her skin and she looked a little better than she had when she had left the coffee shop.

"I... we're going to put an offer in on your home."

"Really?"

"Really" Harry said. "But it's going to be low."

"How low is low?"

"Seventy-five thousand."

"But the asking price is eighty-five."

Harry shrugged. Mrs. Fisher furrowed her brow.

"Eighty" she said.

"Our offer is non-negotiable."

"Seventy-nine."

"Our offer is non-negotiable. You're selling a house that can barely stand under its own power anymore. And it's haunted!"

"It's not haunted" Jo Fisher said. "Seventy-seven. *Please*."

Harry looked at Lisa for guidance. Her expression was soft. The desperation in the woman's voice had clearly tugged at Lisa's heartstrings. She nodded minutely.

"We could go to seventy-seven" Harry said.

Jo Fisher promptly broke down and cried.

Lisa, startled by the sudden display of emotion, snatched up her handbag and began rummaging for a packet of tissues. Finding none, she instead rushed to the counter, collected a handful of napkins and pushed them into Jo Fisher's hand.

"I'm sorry" Jo snivelled, "It's just that... I never thought that I would sell that place. I don't have the money to do the repairs it needs and... I thought it was just going to rot away to nothing. You don't know what this means to me."

"That's ok" Lisa said, not really sure what else to say.

"And then when that stupid video started doing the rounds, I thought that was it! I've been living with my sister for so long, and I just couldn't go back there... I just... couldn't."

The floodgates opened on Jo Fisher's emotions. Harry and Lisa sat awkwardly as her sobbing drew uncomfortable stares from the patrons of the coffee shop. A young barista, upon being assured that Jo was alright, showed visible signs of relief that he would not need to intervene in their conversation.

"I'm sorry" Jo sniffed. "Really, I am. Look at me. I'm a mess."

"That's alright" Harry said. "Do you want me to get you another napkin?"

Laughter now, watery but bright. Jo Fisher suddenly looked ten years younger. The wrinkles around her eyes flattened out, her back straightened.

"I'll call the estate agent this afternoon and put an official offer in. You're sure you'll take seventy-seven?"

"I'm sure" Jo said. "Unless you want to offer more."

"No" Harry said. "Seventy-seven is fine."

The couple shook hands with Jo as they all got up to leave. Outside, the rain had stopped and the sun had emerged as a dull silver coin in an otherwise grey sky. They thanked the young man behind the counter for their coffee and headed out of the door.

It was here that Jo Fisher's face screwed up, her smile giving way to a look of confusion.

"I'm not trying to put you off buying it, but can I ask why you would want to buy a house like mine, knowing what you know about it?"

Harry felt Lisa stiffen beside him. She had asked him this very same question countless times before.

"It's complicated" said Harry.

CHAPTER 03
0 SUBSCRIBERS

Lisa winced as the car shuddered over another pothole.

"Sorry" Harry said.

"It's fine" said Lisa, "It's just making me feel sick."

"These roads are really bad. It's hard to avoid them."

"I said its fine."

The moving van ahead of them trundled down increasingly narrow streets. Cars parked at jaunty angles flanked either side of the road, slowing their progress to a near snail's pace.

"How much longer is this going to take?"

"We're nearly there now" Harry said. "Don't you recognise where we are?"

Lisa looked out of her window at the rows upon rows of red bricked terraced houses.

"Everything in this town looks the same."

The van in front stopped at a junction. A police car cruised by.

"I need to get out of this car"

"Open a window" said Harry. "We'll be there in five minutes. You just need some fresh air"

"This was a bad idea" Lisa said. "This place is a dump."

Harry did his best not to let Lisa see his smile. He turned his head and looked out of his own window. The rusted chassis of a broken-down car sat rotting in a nearby garden.

"It's not that bad" he said, a chuckle breaking free from his weakening resolve.

Lisa swatted him with the back of her hand.

"Seriously," he said, "open your window. You'll feel better."

"No. It's too dangerous around here to be driving around with our windows open."

Harry was unable to hide his laughter this time.

"What do you think is going to happen? Do you think someone is going to lean in and snatch you out of the car?"

"Have you seen the people that live around here?"

They drove past a primary school getting ready to finish for the day. Lines of parents stood chatting, many of them wearing Pyjama bottoms under their long coats.

"Jesus..."

"Come on" Harry said, reaching over and squeezing his wife's knee. "Cheer up. This is supposed to be our big adventure! We're finally doing it! We're getting into the property game"

"I didn't think it would be like this." Lisa winced as the car juddered over another pothole.

"We were always going to have to start at the bottom" said Harry. "It won't always be like this."

"It had better not be. God, I feel so sick."

"Once we get this one done and start making some money off of it, we can look for another house a bit closer to home. It's just that right now we can't afford to buy anywhere else in the country. Teesside is really our only option."

The van slowed and pulled off to the side of the road. It idled for a moment before its engine died and its doors opened.

The men inside began to pile out. The two younger men hurried to the back of the van while the driver rolled a cigarette and put it between his cracked lips.

Harry pulled in behind the van and killed his own engine.

"Here we go" he said, unbuckling his seat belt.

"Fucking hell. Some journey that" the driver said, smoke billowing from between yellowed teeth.

"I did tell you it was quite a trek" Harry said. He hurried

along the cracked paving stones of the driveway and unlocked the battered front door. He pushed it open with a creak. The stale smell of dust wafted out of the hallway and into the street.

"Did you see how people park around here?" the driver said, watching his lackeys unpack the van. "You'd get your car keyed for parking like that down my end."

"Are you from round here?"

The driver shook his head, puffing another cloud of smoke into the afternoon air.

"Not round here mate. This is the rough part of town. No offence, like."

"None taken" Harry said.

"Ah!" The driver smiled as Lisa exited the car. "The lady of the manor"

The two workmen busied themselves pulling furniture down from the back of the van. Harry watched as they carefully negotiated a wardrobe onto a wet pavement.

"Do you need a hand?"

The driver flicked his cigarette away and went to join his men. "Nah. That's what you're paying us for isn't it? Where do you want these cupboards putting?"

"Just put them in one of the bedrooms. It doesn't matter which one."

The men carried the wardrobe toward the house. They argued back and forth as they tried to force it through the front door.

"This is worse than I remember" Harry said.

The house had somehow deteriorated further since the last time they had been here. The yellow cladding that had clung to the walls was beginning to give way, revealing grey brickwork underneath. The crack in the living room window was far more evident now, and the wooden framework around the glass seemed to have been seized by a sudden and aggressive rot.

The faint smell of marijuana hung loosely over the street, suggesting that it was growing in large quantities not far from here. A dog bark loudly from the house next door.

"You've got your work cut out for you in there" the driver said exiting the front door and returning to his van. "Do you do this sort of thing by trade? Fix up houses?"

"Not really"

"But you have a trade though?"

"I work in graphic design. At least, I did work in graphic design."

"Right."

"Listen, this might sound a bit weird, but would you mind if I got some shots around the house as you and the lads are loading the gear in?"

The driver straightened up, stretched his back and groaned. "Shots?"

"Camera shots" Harry said. "I was hoping that I could film you as you brought the stuff in."

The two lackeys exited the house and stopped, listening in on the conversation with quiet amusement.

"What for?"

"Well, part of our reason for buying this house was so that I could make some films about fixing it up. I thought that all of this would make a nice introduction to one of them."

The removal men looked at one another, testing the waters of each other's feelings on the matter.

"Where's the film gonna go?" one of the lackeys asked.

"I'll probably stick it on YouTube."

There was a pause as the driver waited for any objection from his men. When he did not get one, he broke out in a smile.

"Who would want to watch these two ugly mugs from the comfort of their own home? Me, I can understand. I'm film star material, but these two..."

"So, you don't mind then?"

"Of course we don't mind" the driver said over a puffed out chest. "Just make sure you get my good side though, yeah?"

"Great" Harry said. "I'll need to get you all to sign a couple of release forms when we're done so that-"

"Woah" the driver said. "Sign what? I'm not signing anything mate"

"It's nothing to worry about. It's a pretty standard document. It just means that-"

"Nah" said the driver, shaking his head vehemently. "I'm not signing anything."

With a nod from the driver, the three men went back to work carefully removing a television set from the back of the van.

"How about I just get a shot of you saying that you don't mind appearing on film then? That would work just as well."

"I tell you what mate, I don't think I thought it through before I said yes. A couple of the lads here work cash in hand. I don't really want them on camera doing a day's graft when they're still claiming from the dole office, you know? I could get in a lot of trouble."

"How about I just make sure not to get your faces in the shots?"

"How about you wait for us to leave, and then you can film the place all you want?"

With that, the conversation was over, and the three men seemed to work at a faster pace than they had before. When they were done, Harry handed them six hundred pounds in cash, and they went on their way.

Harry went inside of the house and he found Lisa standing in the hallway.

"Everything alright?" he asked.

"I'm not sure" she said. "I suppose that only time will tell."

They spent the next few hours going back and forth to the car, taking the clothes that they had piled into the boot and onto the back seat and running them up to the wardrobes that the workmen had put in the back bedroom. The couple worked quietly, each trying to get a feel for the house that they were going to call home for the foreseeable future.

When this job was done, they began on the boxes that had been piled up in their tiny kitchen, stopping only when they found their kettle which they filled with water and set to boil.

"Have you found the mugs yet?" Lisa asked.

Harry shook his head and opened another box.

They drank tea in the ruin of their new living room, sitting on the second-hand sofa that they had bought only a week before. They did not speak, and instead listened to the sounds of the neighbourhood around them. The dog next door continued to bark; its voice only slightly muffled by what seemed to be paper thin walls.

"That's going to get annoying" Harry said.

"It already is."

When they finished their tea, Harry clambered back through the mazework of boxes and furniture which littered the hallway and kitchen and put the mugs in the sink. He turned the tap to find that while it did work, the water that came out sputtered and spat and soaked the worktop surfaces.

They busied themselves organising the essentials. Harry collected his toolbox from the car, and they fixed the TV to the wall above the fireplace. They dug the modem out of its box and plugged it in, only to find that the internet did not work.

"I'll give them a call" Lisa said. "I want to get that connected as soon as possible."

She headed upstairs with her phone in her hand. The sudden space between them flooded with a sense of relief. It was only now that Harry realised what an odd mood Lisa had been in since they had arrived this afternoon. It wasn't quite a bad mood, but he got the feeling that there was something being unsaid. The sound of her voice floated softly down from upstairs, and the murmurs set him at ease. He would not push to find out what was wrong with his wife. She would tell him when she was ready, and he could probably work out most of it for himself. She had never been as excited about this endeavour as he had, even if she was as eager as he was to reap the potential rewards.

"Wednesday" Lisa said when she came back into the room. "They said that they can get us sorted a bit quicker given we already have a modem."

"That's good" Harry said. He stood at the window and looked out onto the road. Behind the stubborn rain drops that still peppered the glass, the houses across the street seemed to loom over their home.

"They pack them in tightly in this part of the world, don't they?"

"Hmm?"

"The houses. They seem so close together."

"I think this is what most council estates are like," said Lisa. "They built as many houses as they could in as small of a space as possible to keep the riff raff all together. God. Can you imagine living somewhere like this in the long term?"

"No" Harry said. "It's quite exciting though, don't you think? Sort of like an adventure. And I feel like slumming it will help us appreciate what we do have all the more."

To Harry's surprise, Lisa laughed. The brief space between them seemed to have gone some way toward improving her mood.

"We'd need a nicer place than this is if we were going to slum it. I daresay some cavemen lived in nicer surroundings than we do."

"You just wait" Harry said. "This place is going to put

Buckingham Palace to shame by the time I'm through with it."

"Ok Mister Fixit. I'll have to take your word for it."

By now the sun had fallen low in the sky and had glided silently behind the terrace that ran opposite the house. The sky had turned a deep shade of blue before the first tinges of a black vignette had settled across the horizon.

"We should get the curtains up" Lisa said. "I don't like the idea of lying in bed, totally exposed for anyone to see."

"And how are people going to see you through a top floor window?"

"I don't know" she said, quickly, "but I won't be able to sleep if we don't put the curtains up."

As if on cue, the lamp post in the middle of the street burst into life, sending ugly orange light spilling into the living room.

"OK" Harry said. "I'll dig out my drill. Do we know where the curtains are yet?"

"They have to be in one of the boxes"

"Well, obviously" Harry smiled, "but which one?"

"I'm not psychic. Go and have a look."

"I need to go and get my drill from the car. *You* look for them."

Playfully, Lisa pushed Harry on her way to the kitchen. He feigned falling over, his back pressing against the wall in a mock attempt to keep himself upright.

Lisa began tearing at the boxes, opening them and pushing their contents around clumsily as he searched for the missing curtains. Harry opened the front door and stepped out into the street. A car was sat idling opposite the house. Music thumped loudly from its open window. A blonde woman stood hunched over, shouting loudly at the driver.

Harry opened the boot of his car and scooped up the black case that housed his drill. He stole quick glances at the blonde woman who seemed to be in the middle of some sort of argument. Her voice was harsh and shrill, and it irritated Harry to no end.

Suddenly, she stood, kicked the door of the car with a slippered foot, and stormed down the driveway of the house next door.

The driver shouted something undistinguishable and then peeled away, his tyres screeching against the wet road. The lingering stench of scorched rubber remained his wake.

"Hello" said Harry as the woman passed him on the other side of his driveway fence.

"Alright?" She did not wait for him to answer. She opened her door to the sound of a barking dog and went inside, slamming it closed behind her.

Harry took his drill and went back into the house.

Lisa looked infuriated.

"I think I just met the next-door neighbour."

"I can't find the curtains anywhere."

"Well, they have to be here somewhere" said Harry. "Have you checked all of the boxes?"

"Of course I've checked all of the boxes" Lisa snapped. Do you think that I would say I couldn't find them without looking in all the boxes first?"

"I was only asking" Harry said. The stress of the day was beginning to settle heavily on his shoulders. "Let me have a look."

He joined his wife in the cramped kitchen, dropped to his knees, and began rooting through the boxes. He moved books and appliances around, dug past bed sheets and makeup cases, shower gels and the old DVDs that Lisa had begged him not to bring. He pushed aside light bulbs, plastic wallets full of legal documents, but no matter how hard he looked, he could not find the curtains.

"Does it feel like there's a box missing to you? I could have sworn there was more than this."

"I have no idea" said Harry. "How am I supposed to know

if there's a missing one? They all look the same."

Lisa sat back, rubbing dust across her sweaty forehead.

"Are we missing anything else that could have been in the box with them? Anything that's obviously not here?"

Harry thought, his mind struggling to inventory everything that he had just rummaged through.

"Did we bring utensils with us? Earlier on I ended up stirring the tea with my finger because I couldn't find any teaspoons."

"I definitely packed teaspoons" Lisa said with a dawning horror. "Did you see any knives or forks in any of the boxes? Or plates? Or towels? I think I put them in with the curtains and the cutlery."

Harry looked around at the boxes which now sat open throughout the ground floor of his home.

"I think we're missing a box" he said.

Lisa sighed deeply. She pushed the balls of her hands into her eye sockets.

"I bet there was still one in the van when they left. The removal guys were in such a hurry to get away after you asked about filming them."

"This isn't my fault."

"I didn't say that it was."

"OK" Harry said with a sigh of his own. "I'll give the moving guy a call."

Lisa got to her feet and flicked the kettle on again. She ran the kitchen tap and washed her dusty hands, drying them on the front of her sweater.

"What are we going to do for tea tonight?" she asked wearily. "I was really eager to see what my beautiful new oven could do, but without pans or utensils I'll have to wait."

Harry reached across the tiny kitchen and pulled his wife into a tight hug. She stood against his chest, her body firm and tense.

"You stink" she said to him.

"So do you."

"I think I saw a pizza shop around the corner earlier. We could do takeaway for tea."

"Sounds like a plan. I'll have a wander over there. I can call the moving guys on the way round."

Lisa tensed further, pulling away from Harry and eyeing him with a look of complete disbelief.

"You're going to walk round? In the dark?"

Harry tried to pull his wife back into his embrace. He elected simply to hold her at arm's length when she refused to be pulled back in.

"Honestly" he said, "it's a bit working class out there, but we're not living in the middle of Beirut. We'll have to get used to living our lives here sooner or later. It might as well be tonight."

"Fine" she said with a dismissive wave of her hand. "You've got your phone if you need me. Just try not to get it snatched before you get a chance to pay for the pizzas."

"Pepperoni?" he asked.

She nodded and poured steaming water into one of the mugs from the sink.

When Harry returned, he found Lisa sitting cross legged in the middle of the broken-down living room floor. Two dinner plates sat in front of her, and a candle burned brightly between them.

"Romantic" he said.

"I realised as I went to set the table that we don't *have* a table. This is how all our meals are going to be from now on."

"And the candle?" Harry said placing the pizza down carefully on the uneven floorboards.

"The lightbulb doesn't work."

"I'll get one ordered. Can we eat first?"

"Of course" Lisa said. She opened the box, letting a plume

of steam into the room. The food smelled wonderful, not least because it masked the smell of the old house that they had not yet become accustomed to.

"Did you manage to get in touch with the moving guy?"

"Yeah" Harry said, bracing himself for his wife's immediate outrage. "He said there was nothing left of ours in the van."

"What? How can that be? I definitely packed a box full of curtains before we left. You remember me doing it, don't you?"

"I don't know" Harry said, "but if you say you did, then I believe you."

"So what are we supposed to do then?" Lisa pulled a long string of cheese from her chin.

Harry shrugged. No answer he could give would placate the anger that Lisa now felt.

"This is ridiculous" she said. "Those things cost a fortune. I bet he didn't even bother to check the van when you phoned him."

"There's not a lot we can do."

"Aside from leave a scathing review all over his social media accounts" Lisa said. "I'm not going to let him get away with this."

"He's an arsehole" Harry said, and this seemed to be enough to end Lisa's venting.

He picked up the remote that was balancing precariously near the hole in their living room floor and flicked on the TV. Blue light filled the room, mingling with the orange from the lamppost outside to create an otherworldly feel. On the screen, a couple were touring Spanish villas while nit-picking over the décor choices the current owners had made.

"So, on a practical level, what are we going to do tonight? About the curtains I mean."

"I was thinking we could just cut up some of the boxes and

tape them across the windows."

Lisa stared absently at the TV. "I suppose we don't have a choice" she said.

When they were done eating, Harry took what was left of the pizza into the kitchen. He opened the fridge and was met by an instant and unpleasant musty smell. Reeling, he closed the fridge door and simply pushed the pizza box into the far corner of one of the worktop counters. He made a mental note to buy bleach in the morning so that he could clean out the fridge.

The two of them moved the contents of the boxes around freeing up three of them in total, and then they cut them up with a large kitchen knife.

They taped one of the boxes over the living room window, one over the kitchen window and finally one over the master bedroom window. They set about putting the duvet and sheets onto the bed, and when they were done, Lisa sat down and yawned.

"I'm shattered" she said rubbing dirty hands into her eyes. "Would you mind if I went to bed? I know it's early."

"Not at all" Harry said, bending down and pulling off his wife's socks. "You have work in the morning. You need to get some rest."

"God. Don't remind me" she said, pulling off her sweater and sliding underneath the covers. "Are you going to join me?"

Harry hesitated.

"I think I might try to organise downstairs a little bit more, just so I can hit the ground running tomorrow."

"OK" Lisa said. The first thin tendrils of sleep weaved through her. "I love you."

"I love you too" he said, and then closed the door.

Harry tiptoed down the creaking stairs. He picked up his keys and went out to his car. The street was quiet now, the general chaos of the day giving way to an easy calm that felt pleasant by comparison.

He opened one of the back doors to his car and took out a long black case which he slung over his shoulder and carried back to the house.

Closing the door behind him, he went into the living room and unzipped the case. In it was a compact tripod underneath a little camera. Harry took the tripod out of its case and attached the camera to the top.

The camera beeped cheerily in his hands when he switched it on. The possibility of an infinite number of shots raced through his mind.

Harry hit record and then panned the camera across the living room, capturing the hole in his floor and the rubble that made-up the interior of his fireplace. The decay of the room seemed amplified on the tiny screen that extended from the camera's side. A sense of intense satisfaction ran through him as he framed the cracks in the wall, finding beauty in the ruin of the home he had bought.

He stopped the camera and then turned the lens onto himself. In the darkness Harry reached out and pressed the little record button on the back of the device. It chirped quietly, signifying that it was once again recording.

With a sense of trepidation, Harry sat back and smiled for the camera.

"Hi everyone" he said. "Welcome to our haunted home."

CHAPTER 04
0 SUBSCRIBERS

Harry woke to find Lisa already awake, her eyes glinting in the darkness as she stared up at the ceiling.

"Everything alright?" he asked her, his voice intrusively loud in the quiet of the room.

"Can't sleep."

"Did the ghosts keep you awake?"

"No" she said, ever the unbeliever. "Nothing that exciting. First day nerves. That's all."

"You'll be fine." Harry turned onto his side and draped an arm across his wife's bare chest.

She pushed him away, swung her legs over the side of the bed and sat up, squinting into the cracks of light that broke through the makeshift blackout blinds they had stuck up the night before.

"That's easy for you to say. You get to stay home all day."

"I'll swap you" he said. "Breakfast?"

Harry went downstairs while his wife pulled on her pyjamas in the cold darkness of their bedroom. He boiled the kettle and poured two mugs of tea. He opened the pizza box and put two slices onto two plates, and then carried all of this up to the bedroom. He left a trail of spilled tea up the wooden staircase behind him.

Lisa was sat on the end of the bed, fixing her makeup using her phone camera in place of a mirror.

"Do you think you could try and sort this room out today?" she asked.

"I'll put it at the top of my to-do list."

"I just think that I'll feel much better when the bedroom works. This is a bloody nightmare."

"I said I'll sort it. Can I do anything to help you get ready?"

"Do we have any lamps that we could bring in here? I can't see a thing."

Harry moved to the window and ran his finger along the edge of the parcel tape they had used to secure the cardboard into place. He dug at it with his fingernail until it became loose enough to be pulled down entirely. The cardboard came away to reveal a miserable looking day. The sound of rain against the windowpane filled the room.

"You haven't torn that have you? We're going to have to stick it back up tonight."

"Will you just calm down a bit?" Harry said, recognising the early stages of one of his wife's rare but explosive meltdowns. "Firstly, we have plenty more boxes we can use if we need to, and secondly, I'm hoping to get actual curtains put up throughout the whole house this afternoon."

Lisa stopped what she was doing and stared at her husband. An expression, equal parts shock and amusement, sat tightly across her face.

"You're going to choose what curtains we have in the house?"

"I helped choose the last lot."

"You did not. You stood around sulking while I picked them out"

"But I was there when you bought them. They were grey. I'll just buy some more grey ones. They were fine last time."

"They were not grey" Lisa said. "They were pewter."

"Same difference" Harry said.

He checked his watch.

"What time did you say you had to be at work again?"

*****

The standard of living seemed to rise exponentially the further away from the house they drove. The potholes which snagged at the car gave way to smooth road. The houses that flanked either side of the street grew bigger and seemed to be more looked after, as if the people living in them really cared for their homes. Suddenly, Harry was hit by an unsuspecting pang of homesickness.

"Are you feeling alright?" he asked, pushing the feeling down into the depths of his stomach.

"I'm a bit nervous, but I'll be fine."

"Of course you will. Everyone gets nervous when you meet new people. It's only natural."

"I know" Lisa said, smoothing out the NHS scrubs she had hastily ironed on her bedroom floor. "Are you sure I look alright?"

"You look like a nurse. Just like you always have."

Suddenly, Lisa sat forward and sighed deeply into her hands.

"Oh, I really hope that they take to me. I have this weird feeling that I'm going to inherit a team full of arseholes. I could just tell from the way they didn't even bother to respond to my emails. Do you know of anyone else who would take the time to introduce themselves via email before moving into a new hospital? Wouldn't you at least acknowledge them if they did that?"

"I don't know" Harry said, trying his best to be diplomatic. "What did it say?"

"I can't even remember now. I think I just told them my name, and I left my number for them to call me if they needed anything from me. I just didn't want to come across as one of those new team leaders that shows up and wants to take over straight away. I wanted to seem a bit more human than that."

Harry merged lanes onto a busy dual carriageway which was quickly filling up with bumper-to-bumper gridlock.

"What were you hoping they would say in response?"

"I don't know. Nothing I suppose."

"Then what are you worrying about?"

Lisa laughed joylessly.

"Everything" she said. "I just want to get today over and

done with. I'll feel better once I've met them in person."

The car slowed to a juddering crawl. The engine whined angrily as Harry rode the accelerator in second gear, never quite gaining the speed to tip into third.

"I'm sure they'll love you just as much as I do."

Harry leaned over and patted his wife's leg. They pulled off the carriageway and onto a slip road that wove into the outskirts of a busy industrial town. She looked at him with a raised eyebrow, the way she always looked at him when she suspected that her husband was patronising her.

"Piss off" she said, knocking his hand away.

The rest of the journey seemed lighter, the atmosphere in the car less tense than it had been before.

When Harry pulled up to the drop off point, he leaned over and craned his neck, trying to see all the way to the top of the hospital that Lisa was going to work in.

"I'll see you here at four-forty-five."

"I'll be here"

"And don't forget, we need pewter, not grey curtains. And you need a seventy-two-inch drop."

"Seventy-two inches" he said. "See you tonight."

Harry watched as Lisa went into the building. He waved happily, despite the reservations that he had about his wife's first day.

The truth was that Lisa had every reason to be nervous. Harry loved his wife intensely, but he knew better than anyone just how difficult she was to be around at times. At her old job, Lisa had risen through the ranks quickly, starting at the very bottom and within two years, she had climbed the ladder into the middle echelons of the management structure. On her way there, she had made more than a few enemies, and had lost more than a handful of friends. Lisa was demanding, and she was blunt, much like she was at home, but while Harry had his love for her to soften even the hardest of her words, her co-workers could do nothing to cushion the brunt of her personality.

Harry tried to put this from his mind as he weaved through the rush hour traffic that led to the tired town centre in which he had met Mrs. Fisher.

Exiting his car, Harry walked past the empty husk of a bookshop. He felt a twist of guilt as he ignored a homeless man who was sitting outside of it. The musical jingle in his pocket as he had hurried past the man made his guilt burn brighter. He dipped quickly into a department store and looked for the homeware department.

Neon lights buzzed painfully bright, dazzling him as he entered the shop.

The place was a jumble of produce with no real sense of order to be felt by the unfamiliar shopper. Faded signs hung over the aisles, guiding customers to the different departments. Harry followed one that read "Home Furnishings" only to find that the shelves there contained nothing but stationary.

"Are you OK?" asked a woman who looked too old to work there.

"Not really" Harry said. "I'm looking for the homeware department. The sign-"

"Ah" the old woman said. "That thing hasn't been changed in years. Homeware has moved. It's on the second floor now."

"This place has a second floor?"

"It certainly does" said the woman. "Crafts, fabrics, tools and furnishings."

"Do you sell curtains?" Harry asked.

"We do. Follow me."

The old woman took a couple of slow and shaky steps toward the stairs at the back of the shop.

"It's OK" Harry said. "I can find them on my own."

"No, you can't love" she said. "Let me do my job. I'll take you there."

She continued on her way, her knees shaking with the effort of the steps. Harry followed along behind her, feeling like he might need to reach out and catch her at any moment.

His impatience grew as the old woman stopped halfway up the stairway to chat to one of her co-workers.

"Really, I'll be able to find them on my own."

"Just wait there" the woman said, half scorning. "You'll need me when you get up there. Trust me."

The old woman was right.

If the ground floor had been untidy, then the top floor was in a complete state of disarray. Most items had been shoved onto shelves with absolutely zero sense of order, sorted neither by colour, nor type, nor price, nor use. Bins full of pillows and throws were stacked to overflowing, those items on the top rendering those on the bottom completely inaccessible. Tubs of cutlery housed loose items made up of several mismatched sets.

The old woman walked past all of this and led Harry toward the corner of the shop that displayed the curtains. Some of them hung loosely from battered looking display rails, but most remained in their plastic wrapping, packed tightly into shelves with a familiar sense of disorder.

"Wow" Harry said. "How am I going to find anything here?"

"What type of curtains are you looking for love? Maybe I could help you find them."

"I doubt anybody could, it's like a dumping ground in here. I mean, who would organise their shop like this?"

The old woman smiled gently.

"*I* organised my shop like this" she said. "I do everything around here now it's just me running the place. My husband died last year. I suppose he was always the tidy one."

Harry felt his heart sink and his face begin to flush red.

"Jesus. I'm sorry. I didn't mean to offend you."

"And you didn't love. Now, what sort of curtains was it you were looking for?"

"I need a seventy-two-inch drop" he said sheepishly.

"Seventy-two. Any colour preference?"

"Grey."

"Grey."

"I need a curtain rail too. I don't suppose-"

"We'll get to that" the old woman said, waving a dismissive hand in Harry's face. She leaned into a shelf and began pulling at packets of curtains, squinting at the faded labels inside. She wrenched feebly at a packet jammed at the back of the shelf, pulling several other bundles out with them. They spilled onto the floor at her feet.

"These ones are grey. They have a seventy-two-inch drop."

The woman handed Harry the curtains and he eyed the label. *Platinum*. They were too light, far lighter than the ones Lisa had poured over when they had bought the first sets together.

"I don't suppose you have any a bit darker. Or better yet, any that are labelled as Pewter."

"Pewter…" The woman stopped, her eyes scanning across the shelves. "I can certainly have a look for you. Are you in any sort of hurry to get away?"

Without waiting for an answer, the woman began pulling more packets down from the shelves.

*****

Harry arrived back home to find a car blocking his driveway. He waited patiently for a while, pulling up tightly behind it and idling his engine. The woman from next door stepped out of her house and padded down the driveway in her slippers and dressing gown.

The car's windows wound down and she leaned in. Harry waited for the car to move, but the sound of shrill laughter told him that she was in the midst of a conversation that would not be over any time soon.

With a hint of embarrassment, Harry tooted his horn. The neighbour woman jumped, then pulled her head out of the passenger side window and glared through Harry's windshield.

"Go around" she said, her face ugly with anger.

"You're blocking my driveway."

"Go around" she shouted again, leaning back into the window and continuing on with her chat.

Anger flared inside him. Harry mashed his hand into the middle of his steering wheel, holding it there, allowing his horn to blare for longer this time. To his horror, the driver's side door opened and a tall fat man in a baseball cap stepped out with fury on his face and violence in his eyes.

The woman in the dressing gown walked up to Harry's car, motioning for him to wind down his passenger side window.

"What's your problem?" she trilled. "You've got loads of room to get round. Can't you see I'm talking?"

"That's my house! You're blocking my driveway."

Without saying a word, the woman returned to the car and shouted something to the driver. He flipped Harry his middle finger and got back into his car, the suspension dropping low under his significant weight. The engine roared as the driver overrevved the engine, and then it pulled forward just enough for Harry to squeeze onto his driveway.

He parked up and then pulled his key from the ignition. The car had reversed back over his driveway before Harry had even stepped out of his car.

Not wanting to cause any further confrontation, Harry tried not to look in the direction of his next-door neighbour. He got out, popped the boot open and gathered up the bags of curtains that he had bought from the old woman in the department store. Mismatched cutlery jingled lightly in the bottom of the bags.

The house was once again as cold inside as the street was outside. He closed the door behind him and twisted his key in the lock. The way the driver of the car had looked at him made Harry feel that he was not beyond simply walking into somebody else's home to register his displeasure. The sound of the car peeling out of the street a few moments later went some way to set Harry's nerves back at ease.

His phone pinged in his pocket. It was Lisa.

"Did you manage to get any curtains? I really don't want to sleep with cardboard over the windows again."

The question irritated Harry. Exactly what Lisa had expected when moving into a house as rundown as this was beyond him. Of course, they were not going to be living a life of luxury for the first few months – or ever for that matter, given their plans to get the house into a habitable space and not a soft furnishing further – but surely she must have known that until the basic structural repairs had been made, the home comforts would have to be foregone.

"I got them" he text back. "Pewter. Seventy-two-inch drop."

The time on Harry's phone read 11:53. The day was almost half gone. The drive back from Lisa's work had slowed him down. The roads had been choked by slow drivers who did not seem to possess a shred of urgency between them, and the old woman in the department store had eaten up a good chunk of the morning with her painstaking search across every shelf in the homeware department. In hindsight, Harry supposed that he should not have offered to help her tidy the mess that her search had made, but residual guilt from his refusal to acknowledge the homeless man had spurred Harry on to commit a good deed and helping the old woman had seemed as good of a deed as any.

Defeatedly, Harry picked up the pizza box and carried it through to the living room. After lunch, he would get started on the house, but for now an angry rumble in his stomach and the hellish morning that he had endured endeared him to eat leftovers in his derelict living room.

He leaned back, the sensation of cold peperoni on his tongue toying the line between pleasant and ghastly. Harry's hand found something cold and metal protruding from underneath his sofa.

His laptop.

The sight of his laptop stirred excitement in the flurry of Harry's chest. He had spent last night shooting what he hoped would be his first upload to his new channel, working well into the early hours of the morning, spurred on by the pleasure of unbridled creativity.

Taking another bite, Harry opened his laptop lid and found the folder in which he had dumped his footage early this morning. With another flutter of excitement, he opened his editing app and dragged his monologue shot onto the timeline.

The footage looked great. Harry had framed himself off to one side, allowing the camera to capture a deep crack that traversed his living room wall by way of a backdrop. The light from his TV fluttered intermittent blue across his face, giving an eerie look to Harry's master shot. Harry watched his piece to camera and smiled through a mouthful of pizza.

"Hi guys, my name's Harry, and I've just bought a haunted house."

As far as introductions went, Harry could not really conceive of one much better than this.

"A few years ago, I came across a video that I found frightening, but intriguing. I couldn't get it out of my mind. It started out innocent enough. It was two girls dancing to a backing track while their mum filmed them. It was run of the mill – mundane almost. In fact, I was about to scroll past this video when something happened that would ultimately lead me to hunt down this house and buy it so that I could answer a question I had been pondering for years. Do ghosts really exist?"

Goose bumps erupted across Harry's skin. It felt wonderful to finally be putting into motion the plans that he had brooded over for so long. The video on the screen was over dramatic, but it was the first step toward creative fulfilment, something which he had not felt for a long time.

Harry found the raw footage that Mrs Fisher had shot and dragged it onto his timeline. The onscreen Harry continued to talk, his words bristling with a dark allure and a sombre tone.

"You are about to see the video that changed my life. A word of warning though. What you are about to see may frighten you."

Harry slipped the Mrs Fisher video into place and watched as the footage rolled. The grainy quality of the film added to the tension, but Harry wasn't done yet.

He opened another folder filled with sound clips that he had curated from the internet. He scrolled through them, reading their names aloud past a mouth full of cheese.

"Dark ambient piano reverb"

"Mysterious drone - dry"

"Piano delay - minor key."

He selected one and dragged it underneath his video. The effect was immediate.

With the addition of the music, the true horror of Harry's words came to life. The footage of the event looked nightmarish.

He sat over his keyboard, working in the clips he had filmed the night before. He placed footage of the jagged carpet grippers that looked like rusted teeth jutting out from the living room floor onto his timeline. Harry placed an exterior of his house into his film, revelling in the satisfaction of his creation taking form.

When he was done, Harry watched his film from the start, sliding into place one last music bed to accompany his final piece to camera.

"What are we going to find here? Well, I'm not sure I can say. There's a good chance that this house will be just like any other - bricks and mortar and not a lot else. On the other hand, there is always a chance, as small as it may be, that this house I have bought, could be so much more."

The onscreen Harry smiled broadly, his ominous delivery slipping in the last few frames.

"Thanks for watching guys. If you've enjoyed this video, please don't forget to subscribe and tap that bell icon so that you can get regular updates. My name has been Harry. Thank you for joining me in *Our Haunted Home*"

Pressing the save button with an enormous sense of

satisfaction, Harry leaned back to find that the light outside of his living room window had turned a deep shade of blue. He checked his watch. It was half past three.

"Shit!"

Harry sprung forwards on feet that had gone numb. He stumbled his way into the hallway, his eyes scanning frantically for the bag of curtains he had bought earlier in the day. It was nowhere to be seen.

"Shiiiiiiiiiiiit!"

If Harry collected Lisa before he had installed the curtains he had promised her, he would be in for an evening of blazing rows and periods of intense, seething silence. Harry's wife had been reluctant to buy this house in the first place - much of her reluctance fuelled by a suspicion that Harry did not have the technical know how to make a space like this habitable. Falling at the first relatively low hurdle she had laid out for him would only confirm her misplaced fears. He needed to work, and he needed to work quickly.

As Harry tore into his hallway, a shifting sound came from the kitchen right before a sharp clatter of metal. Knives and forks spilled out onto the tiled floor, right over the curtains that had sat atop them in the bag. By some stroke of luck, the bag had fallen from its place on the worktop. He was too frantic to wonder how.

Harry raced into the kitchen and scooped a set of drapes up off the floor. He would tidy the mess later. If he could install the curtains before Lisa came home, he could find an excuse as to why there were knives and forks strewn all over his floor.

The stairs creaked in protest as he took them two at a time. He bounded over the landing and pushed open his bedroom door, tearing open plastic wrapping as he hurried toward the window.

The curtain rails were nowhere to be seen.

"Come *on*!"

Harry hurried down the stairs. He fumbled with the front

door key which hung loosely in the lock, and then ran down his driveway barefoot. Pulling open his car door, Harry grappled with the three curtain rails that had lain on the back seat. An old woman making her way down the driveway next door called a polite "Hello." Harry ignored her and ran back to his house.

In the bedroom Harry picked up a pencil and his spirit level and slammed them down onto his window ledge. He rushed through the spare bedrooms, finding his step ladder in the smallest one, cut off from his reach by a pile of boxes. They clattered loudly to the ground as he wrenched the stepladders out of the room.

Harry mounted the ladder and marked out the holes where the screws would need to be fixed to hold the curtain rail in place.

Snatching up the drill and wrenching the bit into its mouth, he pressed metal against wood and pulled the trigger.

Nothing happened. The battery was dead.

"Oh, you have got to be bloody kidding me! This is a fucking *nightmare*!"

Harry jumped from the ladder and tore open his drill case. He took out the charging mount and plugged it into a socket by his bedside drawers. A blue window lit up on the unit, telling Harry that the battery currently held a 0% charge.

"This is a fucking nightmare" he told himself again. Images of Lisa's snarling face were already filling his mind's eye. "This is a disaster. I-"

Down the hallway, Harry could hear a gentle knocking.

He stopped his ranting and tilted his head toward the sound. It happened again. Unmistakably coming from inside the house, the gentle tapping sound carried with it a pattern that felt convincingly sentient.

The hairs on Harry's arms prickled, standing stiffly on end.

Slowly, Harry reached out and knocked three short taps onto the wooden floor.

For a moment, nothing happened, and then, as if in

response, came three short taps.

Tap... tap... tap.

Harry launched into action, critically aware that he might miss this phenomenon if he took even a moment to question exactly what was happening. He pulled his phone from his pocket and opened up the camera. Switching to selfie-mode Harry whispered into the device.

"Guys, this is day one... well, day two really, but already I think we have something supernatural happening."

He reached out again and tapped out three more knocks onto the wooden floorboards. He spun his phone around and pointed it toward the door.

Out in the hallway, the knocking responded in kind.

"Oh my God!" Harry hissed into his phone. "Did you hear that? I hope that my phone is picking that up! This is incredible."

Elated, Harry got to his feet and moved to the door. He quietly cursed the creaking floorboards that groaned in protest under his weight.

At the top of the stairs, Harry issued a shaky "Hello?"

Nothing. Then three knocks. One... two-three...

"Is... is anybody there that's willing to communicate with me? Can you give me one knock for yes and two for no?"

Nothing. Then knock... knock-knock... knock.

Harry twisted his phone to film himself once again. On the screen, he was smiling from ear to ear.

"This is amazing" he whispered. "I don't think the message is clear enough to be considered a form of communication, but it's obvious that-"

A *boom* rattled downstairs with enough force for Harry to feel it through the floorboards. The phone leapt out of his hand in his state of panic. Harry managed to grab it out of the air before it clattered to the ground.

"Hello? If I've upset you in some way and-"

BOOM!

The sound was cavernous. It felt like whatever it was

carried enough energy to tear a hole right through the house. It was angry and fierce. It sounded-

BOOM! BOOMBOOM!

Too frightened to speak but driven by a will to capture the unbelievable events that were occurring in his home, Harry began descending the stairs. He took them two at a time, propelled by the adrenaline the coursed through his veins.

He ran, following the sound to a patch of wall in the hallway.

BOOOM!!!

It sounded as if someone were trapped just beyond the wall, beating their fists in protest at being sealed into the darkness.

"Jesus... Jesus Christ."

With a shaking hand, Harry reached out toward the wall.

"Hello? If you want to communicate, I think we should-"

Harry's phone captured the moment a crack formed under his hand, running from the tip of his middle finger to the heel of his wrist. He stepped back and pointed his camera at the wall as more cracks began to form, weaving in and out of one another like spider's webs in the plaster. The pounding continued.

"This is like nothing I have ever experienced. This kind of activity is almost never heard of so early on in-"

The thin jet of water that squeezed through the crack in the wall quickly gave way to a deluge of black sludge. Plaster began to burst from the wall, allowing water to spill out of the growing gaps in the house's structure. Behind the wall, a copper pipe bled like a slashed artery.

"Fuck!" Harry screamed, falling backwards away from the ruptured heating pipe. All around him, scalding hot water pumped out onto his hallway floor. Somewhere in the back of his mind, Harry was realising that he would not manage to put up Lisa's curtains any time soon.

CHAPTER 05
0 SUBSCRIBERS

Lisa was waiting at a bus stop by the time Harry arrived. He pulled in at the last minute much to the annoyance of the driver behind him, who blasted Harry with his horn. The blinking indicator illuminated an expression of pure fury on Lisa's face.

"Sorry" Harry said as his wife flopped down into the passenger seat beside him.

"I've been waiting for almost an hour."

"I know. I'm sorry."

"Do you have any idea what it's like down here once the sun goes down?"

"No."

"It's not exactly the sort of place I'd choose to be hanging around, put it that way. Where the hell have you been?"

"I was dealing with a burst water pipe."

Lisa snapped her head toward her husband, holding him in a red-hot gaze.

"You knew you had to get me at five! Why did you wait until the last minute to-"

"Did you hear what I just said?" Harry asked. "I've been dealing with a burst heating pipe. As in, our central heating line ruptured today."

"Yes" Lisa said, her voice shaking with indignance. "I heard you. And I asked you why you waited so long to start fixing it if you knew you needed to get me at five o'clock!"

Whipping the wheel hard to the left, Harry pulled onto the side of the road to the sound of more horns blaring at him. The driver of a passing Audi flipped his middle finger at Harry as he tore past.

"What are you doing?"

Harry pulled his phone from his pocket, unlocked his screen and found the video he had been shooting as his hallway wall had erupted under a stream of hot black water.

Lisa watched on, her anger morphing into quiet shock as she observed steaming water spill out onto her hallway floor.

"Oh my god" she said when the video had rolled to its conclusion. "I thought you meant that-"

"I know what you thought."

Harry pushed his phone back into his pocket and indicated before joining traffic again.

"I'm sorry" she said quietly. "I didn't realise that it would be that bad. I thought that you found a leak or... my God. Our hallway..."

"You should have seen the mess it caused" he said, his temper simmering to more manageable levels. "It went everywhere. I never realised that boiler water could smell like that."

They joined a row of cars waiting behind a red traffic light. In the darkness, Lisa watched Harry with soft eyes, the despair on his face now more evident than it had been before.

"So, is the house going to be a state when we get home?"

"You just watched one of the walls come down. What do you think?"

"I was only asking."

"Well, I was only telling you. Yes, it's a state. It's a fucking disaster if you must know."

The cars in front pulled away as the light shifted first to amber and then to green. Harry followed them, gripping the steering wheel with whitening knuckles, quietly wondering how many more stupid questions he could answer before he would really lose his temper.

"So, what happens now? Are you going to be able to fix it?"

"No" said Harry. "I could maybe fix the wall, but the pipe is going to need a plumber."

"Is it still pumping water into the house?"

"No. But I've had to turn off the water, and the electrics, and obviously the heating doesn't work."

"The electrics?"

"There's an outlet right under the leak."

Lisa ran her hands through her hair and leaned forward in her seat. Through his peripherals, Harry could make out the deep expression of worry on his wife's face.

"I've already got a plumber sorted" said Harry, anticipating the next line of questioning. "He's going to be with us at eleven tomorrow. Said he already had a job first thing otherwise he would have come sooner."

"OK" Lisa said from behind her hands. "I notice you haven't mentioned the cost yet-"

"About sixteen hundred quid"

For a while, they both sat in a stunned silence, Lisa trying to digest the information and Harry held in place by a heavy financial burden that he had not anticipated. As the car gently rumbled through the stop-start flow of the rush hour commute, a cold awareness swept over Lisa.

"Why were you filming rather than trying to stop it? If you knew the pipe was going to burst, why not do something other than just film?"

"What did you want me to do? Stand with a roll of paper towels ready to soak it up before it hit the ground? The water was boiling. I got burned just from the steam."

"That still doesn't explain why you were filming it" Lisa said in the darkness.

It was Harry's turn to be quiet now. The car lurched to another stop behind the one in front. Harry toyed with the idea of lying to his wife. In the end, the inevitable emergence of the truth was something he simply could not ignore. She would find out why he was filming one way or another, either from him now or when she found that he had uploaded the footage to his YouTube channel in a day or so's time.

"I thought it was knocking" he said sheepishly.

"Knocking?"

"You know. Like a tapping. It sounded like somebody was tapping on the wall."

"Harry... I'm not sure if I-"

"Like a ghost" Harry said. "I thought that it might be something supernatural, like a ghost tapping on the wall. I was trying to get footage for the channel."

Embarrassment twisted in Harry's gut.

"Oh, for goodness' sake"

"What?" Defensive. Vulnerable.

"You thought a ghost was tapping on our wall, rather than assuming it was something any ordinary person would, like old pipes or the house settling?"

"The house *settling*?"

"You know what I mean."

"Yes" Harry said. "If I'm being totally honest, I thought that I was capturing something really extraordinary, and that the footage would be good for the channel."

Lisa started to laugh. It was the sort of laughter that Harry had not heard in weeks, the kind of laughter that was commonplace before Harry had introduced the stress of the move and the renovation and the YouTube channel to their relationship.

"What?" he asked, the fringes of her laughter infecting his own voice. "I really thought I had something good for the channel. What's so funny about that?"

"Oh, you got something good for your channel" she laughed, swatting playfully at her husband as he negotiated the rush hour standstill. "I don't think anyone will deny you that!"

"Oh..." Harry said, trying unsuccessfully not to break down completely into an exhausted giddy state. "Shut up, would you?"

He turned the wheel, finally able to merge onto the slip road that would carry them home, squinting against the tears of laughter that had shrink-wrapped his eyes.

*****

Stepping back into the house was a far less jovial affair than driving to it had been. Lisa recoiled at the stench of spoiled water that met her in the hallway. The odour seemed to radiate from the mouldy space beneath the bare floorboards. Chunks of wet plaster which Harry had not yet tidied up lay strewn across the ground. The hole in the wall dominated the room, the exposed heating pipes hanging dull in the blackness beyond.

Unable to speak, Lisa broke into a flood of desperate tears.

"We'll fix it" Harry said, draping an arm around his crying wife. "It won't be like this for long."

They stood for a while in the mess of their hallway before Harry suggested that they get a change of scenery by finding somewhere to eat. Solemnly, Lisa nodded into her husband's chest, and they headed back out to the car before setting out to find food.

The bright lights of a chain pub had called to them as they drove on by, and they had headed in, finding a quiet spot in the corner where Lisa could cry, away from prying eyes.

"So, how was your first day?"

"Good."

"Really?"

Lisa stopped still; her pint suspended just below her chin.

"You sound surprised."

"I'm not surprised" Harry said, backtracking gingerly, "It's just that... you seemed anxious about going this morning. I didn't really know what to expect."

Harry picked up his beer and held it out in front of Lisa.

"To new beginnings."

"To new beginnings?"

"Why not?" Harry grinned. "You have a new job, we have a new house, I have my new project"

"Project?"

"The YouTube Channel. There are a lot of new beginnings

in our lives, and I think we should toast to them."

Lisa picked up her glass and clinked it suspiciously against Harry's.

"To new beginnings."

They eyed the food menu before ordering predictably, electing for chicken burgers all round. Lisa scrolled through her phone, enjoying the free Wi-Fi after a day of being disconnected. Harry was content to sit quietly and sip his drink, taking in his new local watering hole.

"Does it even feel like a new beginning? The job?"

"Again, with the new beginnings" Lisa smiled, her mood lightening the further down her pint she went. "How do you mean?"

"You're essentially doing the same job as you were at home, aren't you? Does it feel much different?"

Lisa did not take much time to think this over.

"Not really. Nursing is more or less the same regardless of where you do it. Obviously, the staff are different, so that's new."

"Are they nicer than at your old place?"

This reflection took a little longer than the last.

"I think so, yeah."

"That's good" Harry said, already wondering how long his wife would feel this way.

They ate their meals, chatting sporadically back and forth, enjoying one another's company in a way that they had not seemed to for some time. The conversation remained charged with the stress of the day, but it was flowing, and it was friendly, and it was better than Harry could remember it being in months.

"I got my first video edited" he said through a mouth full of chicken burger.

Lisa's eyebrows raised in mild surprise. She chewed quickly through her mouthful of food, swallowing before she was really ready to.

"How?"

"What do you mean how?" Harry smiled. "I shot it last night and edited it today. I have a design degree. I know my way around a video editor."

"No, I know that. I mean how have you made a video? Nothing has happened, has it?"

"Well, no. Nothing supernatural has happened yet, aside from the false alarm with the water pipe-"

"-which would make a great video" Lisa said, pointing her fork at Harry.

"True. But I've made an introductory video to the channel. I got some shots of the house, explained what we were doing here, that sort of thing. Not every video is going to be wall-to-wall paranormal activity."

"The guy you watch has spooky stuff in every video" Lisa said, pushing a fork full of chips into her mouth.

"King of the Haunt?"

"Is that what he's called?"

"That's what his channel is called. His actual name is Dean King."

Lisa smirked. There was something in her expression that Harry didn't like.

"Whatever he's called, he seems to show something creepy in all of his videos. You know I don't believe in this stuff, but I have to admit, his channel is pretty entertaining."

Harry nodded. A sudden surge of pressure washed over him as Lisa compared his as-of-yet none-existent channel to *King of the Haunt*. Dean King - the country's most successful paranormal content creator - had been the reason that Harry had dedicated his recent life to the hunt for ghosts. After stumbling across Dean's content late one evening, Harry had become obsessed. He had watched every one of the seven hundred videos that *King of the Haunt* had released over his five years at the top of the game, and had never failed to find inspiration in the way Dean told his stories.

"His channel is different though" Harry said, feeling like he was making excuses for himself. "*King of the Haunt* visits other people's houses and does a sort of showcase of them. My channel is a more focused one. It's just going to explore our house, at least to start with anyway."

Lisa thought this over as she chewed a mouthful of chicken. She still didn't look convinced.

"I can show you my video when we get home if you'd like?"

Lisa pushed the final two chips from her plate into her mouth.

"Why not?" she said. "We've got no electricity until morning. It's not like we can sit and watch TV all night like we used to."

"Yeah" Harry said. "We'll need to find other ways to occupy our time..."

"You can piss off" Lisa said, reading the undertones of Harry's words. "We have no shower either. You'll be lucky if I let you sleep in the same bed as me smelling like that, let alone anything else!"

They drove home with full bellies and lighter hearts. The darkness that surrounded the car felt somehow comforting, and the happy songs on the radio brought a sense of normality that had been missing from their lives over the last few days.

As they neared the house, the atmosphere in the car grew noticeably thicker. Lisa hunched forward in her seat, apprehensive about the destruction waiting for her behind their front door.

She cried when she saw the devastation in her hallway for the second time. Harry pulled her into his arms and held her as she sobbed into his chest.

"I'll sort it. Don't worry"

When she was done crying, Lisa looked up at her husband with tired eyes.

"I think I'm going to go to bed. You don't mind, do you? There's no sense sitting up in the dark."

The silence caught between them.

"Are you not going to watch my video?"

"Can I do it before work tomorrow? I'm not really in the mood anymore. I just want to sleep."

"It's only ten minutes long" Harry said. "I was hoping to upload it tomorrow. I would really appreciate you putting some eyes on it and so I know if there's anything that needs changing before I do."

"*Putting some eyes on it?*" Lisa's stifled a yawn. She wiped at her still watering eyes. "Come on then" she said finally, "Lead the way."

Harry led his wife into the living room and sat her on the sofa. He opened his laptop and placed it onto her lap, shifting nervously from one foot to the other.

"I'm not precious about it, but if there's anything that doesn't feel right, or anything you think doesn't quite work-"

"Play the video Harry."

With a nervous flutter, Harry pressed the spacebar, and the laptop screen came to life. He stood and watched his wife watching his work until she asked him not to, and then he headed out into the hallway and pretended not to listen.

He picked at plaster that had fused onto the floorboards, listening for the closing words of his video and the soft sound of his laptop lid closing once the film was over. For a moment, neither of them said anything.

"It's finished."

Harry walked back into the living room to find Lisa looking quietly impressed.

"Well?"

"Well, what?"

"Well, what did you think of the video? What do you mean *well, what?*"

She ran her hands across the smooth lid of Harry's computer. Her wedding ring glinted in the orange light of the lamp post outside.

"I thought it was good."

Harry waited.

"But..."

"No buts" she said. "I thought it was good. Better than I expected it to be actually."

"Really?"

"Really."

"The sound was alright? Because I thought that in the last part-"

"The sound was good. The pacing felt right. It made me want to watch more. Its easily as good as the stuff that other guy makes."

"You think its comparable to *King of the Haunt*?"

"Yeah. It's good."

Relief washed over Harry. He took his laptop from his wife, put it to one side, leaned forward and kissed her softly on her forehead. She relaxed into his touch and pulled his face into hers.

"Ok... if I was being really picky, there was maybe one thing that you could improve."

"Oh?"

"I don't know who was presenting that, but Christ he was ugly. If you could find a replacement, I think you'll get more views."

Harry plunged at Lisa's waist, digging his fingers into the spot he knew was her most ticklish. She kicked her legs and thrashed her arms and did her best not to scream.

"No! Please! I've not long eaten!"

Harry let his wife go. He took her by the hands and pulled her to her feet.

"Thanks for watching it. And for the feedback, and for agreeing to do this whole thing with me in the first place."

"What whole thing?"

"The move, the transfer to your new job. The YouTube channel. All of it. There aren't many women out there who would do all this for their husbands."

"I won't argue with that."

"I want you to know that I appreciate it."

They kissed in the wreck of their dusty smelling front

room, and then, stifling another yawn, Lisa asked "Can I please go to bed now?"

Harry stepped to one side, motioning dramatically to the living room door.

"You are excused" he said. He slapped her playfully on the behind as she went by.

As Harry watched his wife ascend the stairs, the urge to open his laptop and begin work on his second video came on strong. Eager to seize on his creative impulses before they were overtaken by a heavy drowsiness, Harry headed into the kitchen and tried to make coffee before remembering that the electricity was still out. He began to chuckle at his own mistake but stopped abruptly when Lisa's furious voice rattled upstairs.

"Oh, for God's sake!"

Harry ran up the stairs two-by-two.

"Is everything alright!?"

"Are you fucking serious!?" he thought he heard her ask.

"What's the matter?"

"I asked if you were serious!?"

"About what? What's going on?"

"I asked you to do two things today. Sort the bedroom and put up the curtains, and you've done neither of them! In fact, I'd say the bedroom is in a worse state than when I left it this morning!"

"Is it?"

Even in the near perfect dark of the room, Harry could see his wife's face turning puce.

"What do you mean *is it?* Look at it! I can't get into bed because there are bloody ladders blocking my way!"

"Yeah" Harry said, reeling at Lisa's sudden ascension into all out fury. "Ladders I was using to put the curtains up."

"But they *aren't* up. They're strewn all over the bed."

Harry was lost for words.

"I'm sorry. Have you not seen the state of the hallway? I was too busy dealing with about forty gallons of scalding water spilling out of the walls to finish the job."

"But when did that happen? You told me that the pipe burst just before you had to come to get me from work, and that was why you were late collecting me. Is that not what happened?"

"That is what happened" Harry said, struggling to keep his voice at a reasonable level.

"Then what the hell have you been doing all morning?"

"I dropped you off at work-"

"Yeah..."

"And then I had to go to the shop to buy the curtains in the first place-"

"Ok..."

"And the woman in the shop was the slowest old lady that I have ever encountered in my life-"

"Right..."

"Then, I had to drive back home, and there was some idiot parked across our driveway-"

"Mmm hmm..."

"So, I had to get him to move before I could even get in the place-"

"Ok... go on..."

"So, it was a nightmare morning."

"It sounds like it" Lisa said. "Why aren't the curtains up?"

Bitter laughter caught in Harry's throat.

"Did you hear what just I said? How was I supposed to find the time to-"

"You had time to edit the video you've just shown me."

Time seemed to stop in the murk of the bedroom.

"Oh" Harry said, a cold realisation whistling through him. "Here we go. I see what this is about."

"No" Lisa said, struggling to shove the ladder aside as she moved to her side of the bed. "Do not try to make me out to be the bad guy here. I asked you to do two jobs and you put them off in favour of making videos all day, and as a result, I'm now sleeping next to a ladder in a room with no curtains other than the ones piled up on the bed."

"I'll move the ladder" Harry said.

"It's not about the ladder!" Lisa screamed as her patience finally ran out. "It's about you pulling your weight and actually doing the things I ask you to do when I ask you to do them! I am now the sole breadwinner of a home I did not want to move into in the first place, and so when I ask you to do something to make my time here a little bit more comfortable, I would hope that you have the common decency just to do it."

"You knew that part of the reason we moved here was so that I could do this investigation-"

"Oh" Lisa laughed in mock surprise, "It's an *investigation* now, is it?"

"Yes" Harry said, "You knew that part of the reason we moved here is so that I could conduct this investigation and shoot some videos to go alongside it in hopes of making a little extra money."

"We bought this house in the hopes of making a little extra money!" Lisa said, tears starting to roll down her face. "You cannot prioritise making videos about some non-existent ghost over getting this house ready to go on the market. I am not going to support your half-baked plan for years while I go out to work every day."

"Half baked?" Harry said, not quite believing what he was hearing. "You think my passion is half baked?"

"There you go again! Trying to make me out to be the bad guy."

A dog started to bark on the other side of the shared wall. A woman's angry voice shouted something that sounded remarkably like *will you keep the bloody noise down?*

"You've just said it yourself. There aren't many other women out there who would have put up with moving to a shithole like this. I left my family, my life, my friends, everything behind so that I could follow you out here."

"Friends!?" Harry spoke before he could stop himself. "What friends? You don't have any friends because you treat everybody like this!"

The room fell into a shocked silence, punctuated only by the heavy breathing of Lisa and the barking of the dog next door.

"Get the fuck out of this room" Lisa seethed. "You aren't sleeping in here tonight."

"We only brought one bed. Where am I supposed to sleep?"

"You can sleep in the middle of traffic for all I care. Get out of this room."

Harry stood for a moment. His mind grasped at ways he might make this right, but ultimately he found it was like grasping at smoke. Lisa shrieked at him to get out again. He made his way out of the bedroom and across the hallway to the sound of his wife weeping in their bed.

CHAPTER 06
0 SUBSCRIBERS

Breakfast was eaten in separate rooms. Harry ate in the living room, sitting on the sofa he had slept on the night before. Lisa ate her breakfast in the bedroom as she applied make up using the reflection of herself in the black screen of her dead phone.

"I might have a power bank somewhere" Harry said as he called into the bedroom to collect his clothes for the day.

"I'll charge it at work."

The first tentative reconciliations began as they sat in the car, once again suffering the painful crawl of rush hour traffic.

"What time is the plumber coming today?"

"Eleven" said Harry.

"Has he rung to confirm?"

"I don't know. My phone is dead. I'll have to find that power bank when I get home."

The rest of the journey was scored only by the overly bright chatter of breakfast show hosts, until a particularly annoying ad prompted Lisa to reach over and turn the radio off. The silence that followed had been almost unbearable, but Harry felt a nagging suspicion that his discomfort had been part of her plan all along.

"I finish at five" Lisa said as she stepped out of the car.

"I'll be here."

"Don't be late."

"I'll be here."

She closed the door, not bothering to kiss her husband goodbye. Harry slipped the car into first gear and was about to pull away when Lisa knocked sharply on the passenger side window.

"Yeah?"

She opened the door and leaned back into the car.

"I expect the curtains to be up and the bedroom to be cleared by the time I get home tonight."

With that, she shut the door and headed toward the building.

"Piss off" Harry growled as he pulled onto the road.

A huge van was parked across his drive when Harry arrived home. The words MASTERMAN PLUMBING were emblazoned across the side in orange writing, and a gruff looking man was sat smoking in the driver's seat. Harry checked his watch. It was barely nine-fifteen. The plumber was almost two hours early.

Harry got out of his still-running car and approached the side of the van. The driver was sat scrolling through his phone, its screen displaying a video of a woman in a bikini dancing suggestively on a beach.

He knocked gently on the window.

"Yeah?" the driver grunted through the glass.

"You're blocking my drive" Harry shouted.

"Eh?"

"This is my house. You're parked over my drive. I need to park my car."

After leaning forward and squinting into one of his wing mirrors, the driver wound down his window and glowered at Harry. The smoke that plumed out of the van was thick enough to make Harry cough.

"You what?" the driver said, shouting over his radio.

"I said, I want to get my car on the drive, but I can't while you're blocking it. Would you mind pulling forward a bit so I can park up?"

"Your house?"

"Yes."

"Ah right. Where've you been?"

"Dropping my wife off at work. Look, my engine's still running. Could you just pull forward so that-"

"There's no need to shout mate" the driver said, winding his window up.

The van lurched forward. Harry stepped back for fear his feet were about to be run over.

"I wasn't shouting…"

Harry hopped back into his car and pulled onto the drive. When he got out, the plumber was pulling his van back into the space across Harry's driveway. Harry waited as he climbed out of the van and ambled across the broken paving slabs.

"I didn't expect you to be this early."

"We said nine. You're the one that's late."

"I'm sure we said eleven."

"We didn't" the driver said as he flicked his cigarette into the tangle of thorns in Harry's front yard. "Check yer email if you don't believe us."

"I can't" said Harry. "My phone's dead. I haven't been able to charge it since you told me to turn off all the electrics in the house."

"What have you done that for?"

A deep frustration twisted at Harry again. The constant questions were beginning to get under his skin.

"Because you told me to. When we spoke on the phone yesterday. You told me to turn-"

"I never spoke to you on the phone yesterday."

"What?"

Harry began to wonder how many other plumbers there were in this town, and if it was too late to cancel this one.

"You are with Masterman Plumbers, aren't you?"

"Yeah."

"I called you yesterday after the pipe burst. You said I should shut off the electricity because the leak was over a power outlet."

"Didn't speak to me mate" the driver said. "Probably spoke to Liam. Liam Masterman. I'm John Masterman."

"Right."

"Liam's me nephew."

"I got that."

"He handles all the phones and that. Says I don't have the interpersonal skills for that."

"You don't say" said Harry.

The conversation ground to a halt. John Masterman stood and stared at Harry with a slack jawed expression and eyes that were alarmingly milky for a man of his relatively young age. It was clear to Harry that this was going to be a difficult morning.

Eager to hurry things along, Harry opened the front door to his new house.

"Come in."

The plumber walked through a brown puddle on his way up to the house.

"Don't worry about taking your shoes off..."

Masterman stepped into the house, leaving the front door wide open behind him. A rush of cold air followed him into the hallway.

"That's where the damage is" Harry said, motioning to the hole in the wall.

"Fuckin' ell. You're not a trained plumber too are yer? How did yer work that out!?"

Harry clenched his teeth. John Masterman stood and stared at the hole in the wall as a biting gust of wind blew through the hallway. Harry twisted his hands into his pockets.

"I'll shut the door."

"Don't" the plumber said. "I need some tools from the van."

The man in Harry's hallway stood and stared at the hole in the wall for what must have been three more minutes before silently leaving the house and heading out to his van.

"Jesus Christ..."

Harry went into the kitchen and flicked the kettle on, only to remember that the power was switched off when the boil light did not light up.

The sound of John Masterman's heavy footsteps rattled up the driveway.

"Bloody hell" he said, traipsing muddy water across the floorboards. "It stinks in here."

"The water that came out of that pipe was pretty dirty" Harry said, taken aback by how blunt the plumber was.

"Nah. It's nowt like that. It's mould or something." He tilted his nose into the hole in the wall and sniffed with the intensity of a pig searching for truffles. "It stinks. You've done well to trick someone into buying this place. It's a fucking shithole."

Harry reeled; his confusion clearly evident across his face.

"There's a *sold* sign in the garden. Who've you sold it to?"

"I... we've just bought it. We moved in on Sunday."

For the briefest of moments Harry thought the plumber was about to apologise. Instead, he burst into loud, mocking laughter.

"*You* bought it!?"

"Yeah."

More laughter. Cruel and unpleasant.

"Two days in the new gaff and you've already bust a heating pipe!?"

"It's not been ideal."

Masterman slapped Harry on the shoulder with enough force to knock him sideways. He fought to catch his breath in between clumsy guffaws. Spittle flecked onto Harry's face.

"How much did you pay for this then?"

The gall of this man.

"That's really none of your business" Harry said, finding himself becoming more polite the ruder John Masterman was.

"Well whatever it was, ye've paid too much. Ye'd be better off tearing the whole place down and starting again."

"Do you have any idea why this has happened?"

The plumber dropped to his knees and opened a toolbox. He took out a torch and squinted into the darkness beyond the hole in the wall. He breathed in loudly through the gaps in his crooked teeth as he inspected the damage.

"Hard to say."

Harry waited for more. It didn't come.

"No idea at all? You couldn't even guess, just so that I can try to stop this from happening again?"

Masterman put down his torch and took up a heavy looking mallet instead. He reared back and swung it hard into the broken edge of the wall, sending plaster exploding into the cavity.

"What are you doing!?" Harry yelled.

"I can't get in there to replace the pipe."

Masterman reared back and swung again. More plaster fell into the wall. An ugly crack snaked up toward the ceiling.

"How much bigger does it need to be!?"

"Big enough for me to get in. It's gonna be a proper big job this, mate. This pipe is fucked. Go and stick the kettle on, would yer?"

Harry winced as the plumber struck the wall with three more quick blows.

"The electrics are off. You... your nephew told me to turn them off. That plug socket there was soaking last night."

Masterman continued hammering away at the wall as if he hadn't even heard Harry speak. The hole now was at least twice as big as it had been when he arrived. He leaned into the gap and ran his finger over the reverse of the white power outlet in the wall.

"Feels dry enough to me. Stick the lecky back on and get a brew going. I need to go back to the van."

The plumber grunted to his feet and headed back out the front door, once again leaving it wide open. Cold air chilled the house all over again.

Harry picked up the plumber's torch and shone it into the wall.

Masterman had not been exaggerating when he had described the pipe as *fucked*. Jagged copper teeth ran along the two foot of pipe where it had blown apart from the inside, blooming outwards like the petals of a copper flower. Water dripped intermittently from the pipe's maw, giving it the look of a set of jaws, drooling at the prospect of devouring their next meal.

"Get off my gear" came a voice from the doorway. Startled, Harry fumbled the torch into the hole in the wall. He swiped for it while it hung in the air, his hands coming dangerously close to the jagged edge of the tattered pipe. In what felt like the very last second, Harry caught the torch, saving it from falling into the nether of his home.

The plumber's face was pulled into a tight scowl. In his hands he held a huge looking machine, yellow around its framework with a spinning blade turning loosely at its end.

"Was a time I would have battered you for touching my tools yer know."

"Excuse me?" Harry said, the overly polite aggression seeping back.

"You don't go through another man's tools. It's like going through his underwear drawer. You just don't do it."

"I didn't realise."

"Nah" Masterman said. "You don't look like the sort that would."

Harry's fingers clenched into tight fists.

"What?"

"I said, you don't look like the sort who knows not to go through other people's stuff."

"The sort?"

"Yeah, you know the sort. You're the kind of lad who moves in from out of the area, buying up cheap houses so you can do em up and rent em out. You know people round here can't get the deposit together for a mortgage, so instead they have to come to landlords who charge em twice the price for rent. Happens a lot round here."

"Just who the hell do you think you're speaking to-"

Another shower of plaster exploded into the hallway as John Masterman swung his mallet back into the wall.

Harry leaned into the space under his stairs, reached into the fuse box and turned the power to the house back on. From here he went into the kitchen and flicked the kettle on, not because the plumber had asked him to, but because he knew if he didn't his mouth was going to dig him a hole that he feared he would not be able to climb out of.

John Masterman was easily five stone heavier than Harry, and his body had become toughened from a lifetime of manual labour. If their clash of personalities were to become physical, Harry knew that there would be no contest. John Masterman was his physical superior in every conceivable way.

He stood in the kitchen and watched the plumber hammer a hole into the wall that was easily big enough for Harry to step through.

"Right. I'm done."

"Done making the hole?"

The plumber was back on his knees, putting his torch and his mallet back into his toolbox.

"Done for the day."

"But you haven't fixed the pipe!"

"Can't. It's a two-man job. I'd call my nephew but he's already out on a job. I didn't think the damage would be this bad, truth be told."

Inside of his veins, Harry's blood began to boil.

"So, you've made the hole in the wall worse, and now you're about to leave me with no heating in the middle of winter until..."

"Saturday"

"Until Saturday!?"

"I can't do it on my own" Masterman said, offering an excuse in place of an apology. "It's a two-man job. It'd be dangerous for me to try and do it on my own."

"You have got to be kidding me!" Harry said, his patience finally wearing away to nothing. "What the hell were you thinking making the hole bigger if you knew you weren't going to be able to fix it today?"

"Never put off till tomorrow something you can do today. You can say what you want about me, if there's a job that I can do here and now, I'll do it. I'm a grafter me mate."

Philosophy lessons from a man in overalls. Harry's vision turned a deep shade of crimson.

"You're a fucking cowboy!"

Calmly, John Masterman stood up from his tools, the full magnitude of his size now registering with Harry. Harry backed into the kitchen, reaching out behind himself for anything he could use as a weapon if push turned into shove.

"I'll tell yer what" the plumber said in a flat whisper. "I can see that yer desperate to get the job done, or you wouldn't have been daft enough to say something so hurtful to my face, would ye?"

Harry said nothing. His hand felt for the knife he was sure he had seen on the kitchen worktop behind him.

"If yer really desperately need the job doing today, you could always help me to get it done."

"Alright..."

John Masterman took another heavy step toward Harry.

"There is one thing though. I'll have to ask you for an extra hundred quid."

"What for?"

Masterman reached out with a hand that was bigger than Harry's face. He squeezed Harry's shoulder with an incredible grip.

"I need to use some specialised tools."

"OK..."

"Great" the plumber said, squaring two hard taps against the side of Harry's face.

He backed out of the kitchen and opened his toolbox once again, taking out his torch and holding it out towards Harry.

"Come on then" Masterman said. "I've got other jobs ter get to after this."

Harry approached with visible caution and took the torch out of Masterman's hand. The plumber nodded toward the hole in the wall. Harry interpreted this as his sign to illuminate the darkness.

"See that pipe there?"

"Yeah."

"We're gonna have to cut it out, and you're gonna have to hold it steady while I do."

Harry watched in silent terror as the plumber turned and retrieved the huge yellow machinery from its place at his feet. He held it up, inspecting the loose saw which swung lazily back and forth.

"What is that?"

"Angle grinder."

"Isn't that a bit... big?"

"Why do you think the hole's so big?"

"It looks dangerous"

"It *is* fucking dangerous" Masterman said. "Look, if you want the job doing now then this is what I'm gonna have to use. If you want to wait until I can get hold of something smaller, then you can always wait for me to-"

"Let's get it done" Harry said. By now he would have been happy enough to gnaw through the pipe with his teeth if it meant he could get this idiot out of his house any quicker. "What do you need me to do?"

"First, I need you to put the electrics back on so that I can plug this bastard in."

"They're already on" Harry said.

"Alright. Then I need you to follow my instructions very fucking carefully. Big job, this."

Masterman bent down and plugged the angle grinder into the plug socket directly below the hole. He squeezed its trigger and revved the machine a couple of times. The sound it made was deafening in the tight confines of Harry's hallway.

"Stick the light on and get that torch in your mouth. You're gonna need both hands here."

"Are you sure this is safe?"

"For who?"

"For me."

"Do you want this job doin or not? Fuckin ell. There's no

wonder your missis doesn't think you can fix this place up."

"What did you-"

"Get hold of that pipe there. Hold it tight. It could fly off and hit me in the face if you don't. Is that what you're after?"

"No" Harry lied, silently relishing the idea that the man in his hallway might come to an unpleasant end.

"Then get your hands in there and get em round that pipe."

With a wave of sickening anxiety, Harry reached into the hole and gripped the metal tenderly with both hands. The jagged edge began eating into his flesh the moment he applied the smallest amount of pressure.

"This is gonna be loud. Try not to look right at it, there's gonna be metal shavings flying everywhere. And hold on tight. I don't want that comin nowhere near my face."

"I'm not sure that-"

Before Harry could finish what he was about to say, the plumber leaned in with his angle grinder and fired up the blade. He pressed the spinning edge to the side of the pipe, sending sparks flying into the darkness and onto Harry's hands. Harry yelped in shock. Instinctively he tried to draw his hands away from the blade.

"Don't let go!" Masterman yelled over the scream of the grinder.

Harry doubled down, clenching the pipe tightly with both hands. Tiny metal teeth began to eat their way into the flesh of his fingers. Harry clenched his jaw to prevent himself from screaming.

"Come on you bastard!" the plumber screamed, leaning into his grinder. Harry tried to position himself away from Masterman's armpit but found that he could not. The sour aroma of sweat hit Harry square in the face, overloading his senses and adding nausea to his sense of fear.

"Come on!"

"I don't know how much longer I can hold onto this!" Harry yelled; his voice lost to the whine of the saw.

"Just fucking hold it would you? No wonder she doesn't

love you no more!"

Harry closed his eyes against the shower of sparks that arced out of the wall and bounced off of his face.

"Its lads like you that are the reason houses fall into states like this in the first place. Fucking college educated pricks! No sense of what the world is like out here!"

"What?"

"You move into places like this, and you rely on the sweat of others to build your fortunes, and it makes me fucking sick."

"Stop" Harry shouted. "I can't hold on anymore."

"I've been in this house before" Masterman continued, his words losing what little diction they had as his rage intensified. "People move in and they think they can fix it, but it's always going to be the same. Nobody can fix up this place!"

"Please" Harry shouted, barely listening to a word the plumber was saying. Thick trails of blood were now running down Harry's wrists, spilling out of the chewed-up flesh of his fingers that the jagged pipe bore on its way towards his bone.

"The problem is that this place is rotten to the core! The people that live here end up rotten! You'll be rotten, and that thing growing in your wife's guts will be rotten too!"

Harry let go of the pipe, no longer able to hold onto it as the vibrations dug the jagged metal into his flesh. At the same moment, the grinder ate through the outer edge of the pipe, loosening it enough to send a section of it flying out of the hole. The dislodged piece of pipe hit John Masterman square in the neck.

The grinder stopped spinning. Masterman fell backwards colliding with the opposite wall, his hands instinctively clamping around the opening wound in his throat. Thick red blood began to gush through his fingers.

Harry watched as the man's milky eyes stared terrified at him, searching for help that Harry did not know how to give. The plumber made choking sounds as his life began to pump over his overalls, saturating them in only a matter of seconds.

Harry's mouth opened and shut silently.

"Jesus" he managed, his words coming out in a thick gag.

Masterman dropped to the ground. He rolled onto his back and held a blood-soaked hand towards Harry. Harry could see the inner workings of Masterman's neck as they pumped ropes of hot blood out onto his hallway floor.

"Fuck. What do I do?"

He needed to stop the bleeding, and he needed to do so fast. Harry surmised that Masterman was only minutes, if not seconds from death given the rate at which his blood was pooling on the floor.

Stepping over Masterman's haemorrhaging body, Harry turned the corner and launched himself up the stairs two at a time. Nausea racked his body but he did not allow himself to slow. If a man died in his house, he would never be able to rent it out, and it would take years to sell the place on given it would likely become the talk of the town. He would be ruined if he couldn't at least preserve John Masterman's life long enough for an ambulance to arrive and take him away.

Harry snatched up the packet of curtains that he had left on the bed. He tore at the packaging with his teeth as he sprinted back down the stairs.

Turning into the hallway Harry braced himself for the worst. If Masterman had not been able to stem his bleeding, there would be a good chance that he would have passed out and bled openly onto the wooden floor. Blood pumping at that rate would mean certain death, and if-

Harry stopped.

Reality seemed to fold in on itself.

For a terrifying moment, Harry thought that he must be in a dream.

Masterman was gone.

He looked around, searching, as illogical as it was, to see whether Masterman had managed to crawl out of sight.

He was simply not there.

The grinder that he had been using was gone. The toolbox

he had brought in from his van was gone. When Harry rushed to the front door to see if somehow - despite every sense of reason that he could muster, John Masterman had gotten to his feet and cleaned his blood from the floor before exiting without saying a word - he found that the van was gone too.

Harry's head vibrated with the Illogical nature of what he was experiencing. His stomach lurched with the promise of vomit. The sight of the blood had been stomach-churning, and the smell of it had been even worse, but the fact that it had apparently never been there to begin with was the most stomach-churning thing of all.

Harry stood and stared at the space where the van had been for what felt like an age. When he was done, he went back into his hallway, closed the door, and began to cry.

CHAPTER 07
0 SUBSCRIBERS

For a while Harry did nothing of note, resolving just to stand in his hallway too frightened and too confused to move. He let himself cry, not quashing the purging of emotions that poured out of him. When he was done, he took himself into the kitchen and flicked on the kettle ready to make the coffee he had attempted to make the thing that he had thought was John Masterman.

Harry drank it while it was still too hot to drink. His mind raced as he swallowed the black liquid. He thought so hard that he could not feel the skin on his tongue puckering under the coffee's intense temperature.

Who had been stood in his hallway?

The hole in the wall had returned to the size it had been before the Masterman thing had begun hammering at it. The plaster that had cascaded onto the floor was gone. The blood...

My God Harry thought. *The blood...*

...The blood was gone now too. For this, Harry was grateful.

The first sparks of coherence began to fire in his mind. Harry drank two more mouthfuls of scolding coffee and then left the kitchen, surprised to find that he was scared to walk through his own hallway. Each footstep felt like it was carrying him towards something waiting behind a closed door, readying itself to jump out at him when he least expected it. Harry stopped outside the living room door. From the relative safety of the hallway, he ordered a shaky and uncertain "hello?."

Nothing. He was completely alone.

Harry made his way up the stairs as slowly as he had crossed his hallway. After digging through one of the boxes labelled *electronics*, he pulled out his phone charger and took it back downstairs.

Collecting his coffee mug, Harry went back into the living room and put his back against the far wall. He could see the full room from here. He could see anything that might try to get in.

Harry plugged his phone in and sat silently. The screen glowed white as the device came to life. He picked it up, careful not to dislodge the power cable and typed out a text to Lisa without stopping to think.

"You'll never believe what just happened" he typed. "Tell you about it tonight."

Harry hit send with his shaking hands.

Had that really just happened?

Harry forced the thought from his mind. He was not ready to fully embrace the morning's events.

His phone pinged.

"God. What now? Another pipe hasn't broken, has it? Please tell me the plumber hasn't cancelled on us."

The plumber...

Opening his e-mail app, Harry scrolled until he found the one from Masterman Plumbing.

"Eleven" Harry said to himself. "I knew he was due at eleven."

Harry checked his watch and found that it was exactly thirty minutes until eleven AM. Just enough time for him to install the curtains that were threatening to tear his marriage apart.

By the time Harry stepped back off the stepladder after hanging the curtains, he was beginning to lose hope that the plumber was going to arrive at all. Eleven AM had been and gone, and now noon was within spitting distance.

He was preparing to leave the house when a large orange and white van pulled up outside.

The sight of it caused Harry's insides to clench.

The van that had parked across his driveway was an exact

duplicate to the one the Masterman-thing had climbed out of a few hours before.

Tears welled in the corners of Harry's eyes. He wiped them away, swallowing the lump that had formed in his throat and took himself downstairs.

Harry opened the door just as the van's driver was exiting his vehicle. He eyed Harry with a look of embarrassment as he collected a toolbox from the back of the van. He hurried up the driveway with an aura of deep remorse and an outstretched hand for Harry to shake.

"I am so sorry" the plumber said, shaking Harry's hand warmly. "This is so unprofessional of me. I don't think I've ever been so late to a job in my life."

"Don't worry about it" Harry said, watching the replica of John Masterman's van that sat across his driveway.

"Have you been waiting in especially?" the plumber asked before adding "I'm Liam by the way"

"Harry. And no. I've had a pretty busy morning around the house."

"Good" Liam Masterman said, his shoulders relaxing a little. "Shall we go and take a look at what we're dealing with then?"

"Come on in" Harry said.

Harry closed the door behind Liam when he entered the house. As much as he tried not to, Harry could not help but look closely for any sign that Liam Masterman might not be what he seemed. At this distance he looked solid enough. He was friendly and the hand that he had shaken felt warm and firm, and yet Harry still could not let his guard down just yet. Looks could be deceiving. He had learned that the hard way.

"Oh, wow" Liam Masterman said. "This is a bit of a disaster, isn't it?"

"The whole thing just erupted" Harry said. "One minute it was fine, the next minute it started banging, then water was pouring all over the floor and half of the wall had come down."

Liam scrunched his face in confusion.

"Banging?"

"Like a pounding sound coming from the inside."

"Strange" Liam Masterman said, running his hand gently over the coarse surface of the ruptured pipe. "When these things go, they tend to just pop once and that's your lot. I've never seen one blow through a wall like this. In some ways I suppose you're lucky that it did."

"Lucky?" It was clear that Harry's definition of *lucky* varied massively with the plumber's.

"Well, not lucky. But what I mean is if the wall hadn't broken like this there's every chance you wouldn't have realised you had a problem for a few days. Your foundations could have been under six feet of boiling water. At the very least, you knew there was an issue right away."

"You can say that again" Harry said.

Liam Masterman withdrew his hand from the hole and sniffed at the air. Puzzlement etched across his eyebrows.

"Is that... coffee that I can smell?"

Harry looked towards the kitchen.

"I've just brewed the kettle. Do you want one?"

Masterman shook his head quickly. The smile on his lips betrayed the concern in his eyes.

"No. Thanks. Do you have the electrics on?"

"Oh. Yeah."

"Did I not tell you to turn them off yesterday? When we spoke on the phone? It looks like the leak might have bled into this power outlet."

"Ah." Harry's suspicion flared. Had the thing that had pretended to be John Masterman tried intentionally to electrocute Harry? "I can turn it off again if you think that's best."

"I do." Liam took an obvious step away from the plug socket. When he was at a safer distance he placed his toolbox down and began to unpack.

Harry found the fuse box under the stairs and killed the

power. The humming of the fridge ceased. Eerie silence fell over the house once again.

"How are you going to use your tools without the power on?" Harry asked.

"I don't need to plug anything in. It's not a particularly big job."

"Oh. I thought you would need to cut out the old pipe."

Liam Masterman picked up a small looking tube and tossed it to Harry. He caught it and rotated it in his hands, observing a sharp steel blade that had been worked into the middle of the tube.

"Pipe cutter" Masterman said. "No power needed."

"Wow" said Harry. "I thought you would need one of those things. You know the ones with the big spinning blade at the end?"

"An angle grinder?" Liam took the pipe cutter back out of Harry's hands.

"Yeah"

"No mate, I wouldn't use an angle grinder to do a small job like this. It would be quicker, but it wouldn't be very safe. Those things are really dangerous if you misuse them."

Somehow, this did not surprise Harry. His ears were still ringing from the one that had been held next to his head as he had gripped the pipe earlier in the day.

"In fact," Liam said wistfully, "I actually had an uncle who was killed using an angle grinder."

"John?"

Liam stopped what he was doing, sat his tools down and locked Harry with a suspicious gaze.

"That's right. You knew him?"

"Did he work with you?"

"I worked for him" Liam said. "That's his van outside. I took over the company when he... I'm sorry. Did you say you knew him?"

Harry's heart began to pound in his chest. His mind raced for an answer but found only ones that were entirely unbelievable to anyone who had not experienced what he had experienced.

"I think I met him a couple of times" Harry lied. "He did a couple of jobs for me a few years back. When did he die?"

"A couple of years ago" Liam said. He picked up his tools and resumed his tinkering. "Probably about three. Did you get along OK?"

"I wouldn't say that."

"Nah. Me neither. He was family, but he was hard to work with."

"Could I ask you a favour?" said Harry.

"Depends on what it is." By now Liam was not even bothering to hide his growing impatience with Harry's constant questions.

"Would you mind holding the fort while I nipped out for half an hour? I'm assuming that you'll be a little while getting this done?"

"No problem at all mate" Liam said.

"Great. I just need to go and buy-"

"Not a problem at all" Liam said, leaning into the hole with his pipe cutter in hand. "You take all the time you need."

Harry left the house feeling sure he had upset the plumber by bringing up his dead uncle. He had wanted to probe further, to pry information about what John Masterman had looked like but felt that he knew what the answer would be. John was a stocky man, with a tatty beard and milky eyes. Harry had encountered something which had been imitating the dead man in his hallway, and all asking Liam about him would have achieved would have been a bigger chance of Liam packing his tools up and leaving the job half finished.

Harry drove to the tired looking town centre. This time he dropped a pound coin into the cup of the homeless man who asked him for change. The man nodded his thanks as Harry made his way into the department store.

"Hello again" the old lady said with a smile, recognising Harry as he walked up to the counter where she was busy fidgeting with the till. Suddenly, her face dropped. "Is everything OK with the curtains? Wrong shade of grey?"

"They're fine. I'm actually after some electronics. I thought it would be easier to ask you about them than to look for them myself."

"You thought correctly" the old lady said. She closed the till and walked around the counter. "Anything in particular?"

"Security cameras. Indoor ones ideally."

"Oh. Trouble?

"Sort of" said Harry, and then he said no more.

The old woman rubbed at the back of her neck, then looked around her shop with the same lost expression that Harry had when he had first entered.

"If you don't have any I can-"

"No, I have some. I just don't remember exactly where I've put them. Are you in much of a hurry to get home?"

"A little break from the renovations might actually do me some good" said Harry.

By the time Harry returned, Liam Masterman was waiting in the front seat of his van. Harry flashed his lights and then tooted his horn, hoping that the plumber would not be offended by his request to get the van moved from the front of his driveway.

"All done" Liam said, meeting Harry as he stepped out of his car.

"That was quick."

"You've been gone nearly an hour and a half" Liam said with a touch of impatience in his voice.

"An hour and a half?" Harry checked his watch and was surprised to find that Liam was correct.

"Don't worry about it. I'll wait here while you go see what I've done."

"Are you not coming in with me?"

"I'll wait here if it's all the same to you."

Harry went into the hallway and leaned into the wall. The new section of pipe gleamed brightly in the darkness.

"Looks great" Harry said stepping back out onto his driveway.

"Good. We all right to square up?"

Something was the matter. Where before Liam had been welcoming and pleasant, now his words felt clipped and tight, beyond a simple annoyance that Harry had kept him waiting.

"Of course" Harry said. "If you give me your details, I'll transfer the cash right away."

"Great."

Liam handed Harry a tatty scrap of paper through his driver's side window. As Harry typed Liam's details into his banking app, he got the impression that Liam was making an effort not to look at the house.

"The money should be with you any moment" Harry said, putting his phone back into his pocket.

"OK."

Liam reached forward and twisted his keys in the ignition. In the hard light of day his skin now looked two shades paler than it had when Harry had left him.

"Listen, I'm sorry again that it took so long for me to get what I needed. I really didn't think that you'd get the job done so quickly."

"It's fine. Nothing to worry about."

There was something being unsaid. Harry could feel it.

"And I'm sorry I brought up your uncle. I didn't mean to upset you."

"I'm not upset" Liam said, his eyes still staring out of the windshield and into the distance. "I have to go. I have other jobs to do."

Harry stepped back from the van, still not satisfied that he had found what had upset Liam Masterman.

"You know" Harry said, "this probably won't be the last time something like this happens. I'm going to need some plumbing work doing when I get the new bathroom put in. I'll give you a ring when the time comes."

Liam looked as if he was searching for something beyond

the horizon. Finally, his head swivelled, and he held Harry with a thousand-yard stare. His eyes were watery and red. They were the eyes of a man who had seen something that he could not unsee.

"Don't call me again" Liam said. "I don't want anything to do with that place."

A car horn blared causing both Harry and Liam to jump. Harry looked back to see the blonde woman from next door gesturing wildly from the driver's seat of a cramped looking hatchback.

The van engine roared. Harry leapt back as the vehicle pulled quickly away, almost knocking him over in the process.

A moment later the woman from next door almost hit Harry on the way to her own driveway.

"You were blocking the whole road" she said as she piled out of her car.

"Don't you dare" Harry said walking back to the house and slamming the door behind him.

Harry collected up some paper towels and wiped furiously at the power socket below the hole in the wall. When he was absolutely certain that he had gotten it as dry as possible, Harry flicked the electricity back on via the fuse box.

The hallway, the living room, and the landing light all burst into life. It seemed as if Liam Masterman had tried to turn on all the lights in the house, despite his knowledge that they would not come on.

Harry collected up his drill from the bedroom and then went to the car to retrieve the security cameras he had bought from the old woman at the department store. He unpacked them onto the kitchen worktops and tore open their packaging with a kitchen knife.

He walked around the house, looking in the corners of each of the rooms so as to find which angles would give him the best coverage. The hallway facing toward the front door was the most obvious choice. The far corner looking into the living room seemed another obvious place to install one. Harry decided against installing a camera in his bedroom, already hearing Lisa's protests in his head that he would use them to spy on her as she got changed. Instead, he elected to install the third and final camera at the top of the stairs.

The wide-angle lens here would give coverage leading into the bedrooms and of both the top and the bottom of the stairs. This way, if anything like what happened today were to ever happen again, he would make sure he had evidence for what had occurred.

The version of John Masterman that had invaded his home had been as real as the man who had just peeled away from the house in some unexplained state of horror. If Harry had managed to capture that on camera, he could prove to the world that ghosts did indeed exist. Footage of the thing catching a copper pipe in the neck and then bleeding to death on Harry's floor would have made the news, especially as it had seemingly disappeared into thin air when Harry had gone to get help. Harry would have been able to prove to Lisa that this was not just some fantasy that had dogged his every waking moment since seeing the Fisher family video. This would have proved to her that this was real.

And it would have made him rich.

The YouTube revenue alone on a video like that would have paid for this house and the furniture within it. It would probably have paid for the next property that he and Lisa would invest in. He would appear as a feature on *King of the Haunt*, raising the profile of the house, establishing it as the haunting hotspot of the UK, and then he would sell the house. He could charge double, maybe triple the price he had paid to some ghost hunter, or some TV channel wanting to make a quick profit from the reality TV shows they would be able to shoot here.

And that would only be the start of it. From here he'd hit the talk shows, the morning breakfast magazine shows, sitting opposite smiling hosts who would talk in hushed tones. He'd write a book. He'd work as a consultant on the movie adaptation that he would inevitably sell the rights to about this house.

Capturing footage of the event he had witnessed this morning would change his life. No more debt. No more stress for his wife as she struggled to negotiate her new working environment. He would change everything for everyone around him, but first he would have to capture something as irrefutable as this morning's events had been.

The cameras would mean no more missed opportunities. From now on nothing would happen in this house without Harry filming it.

He fetched his step ladder and climbed up into the corner of the hallway.

He revved his drill and began to work the bit into the flaking plaster.

This was it now. This was how he would make his fortune. This would be how he would prove everyone wrong.

CHAPTER 08
0 SUBSCRIBERS

"She's such a control freak, and so rude" Lisa said, her face illuminated red by the brake lights of the car in front. "It's like *please* and *thank you* are words she's never heard before. She sent me an e-mail today that started with *you must*, rather than *would you mind*. That's not how a normal person asks for something."

"Mm-hm" Harry said, only half listening to his ranting wife.

"She's one of these people who makes a big point out of the fact that she doesn't drink."

"How on earth did that come up in conversation?"

"It didn't" Lisa said. "Well, it sort of did. She asked what everyone was doing this weekend, and one of the girls said that her and her boyfriend were off out for a couple of drinks, and she made this big song and dance about how she likes to keep control of her faculties and how she doesn't see why anyone should have to drink to have a good time. Don't you think that's pretentious?"

"I…"

"I think it's rude" Lisa said, not waiting for Harry's response. "She was basically saying that Becky has to have a drink to enjoy time with her boyfriend."

"Was she though?" said Harry, before he had a chance to stop himself.

"Yes. She was. If you had heard the way she said it…"

"Are you sure that you maybe haven't gotten off on the wrong foot with her?" Harry said. "You've only really known her for a day. Shouldn't you give her a bit more time before you decide you don't like her? If you fall out, she could probably make things quite difficult for you if she wanted to. She is your line manager after all."

"You don't need to remind me that she's my boss" Lisa said, clearly not ready to let this go just yet. "She does that enough for me."

"She tells you that she's your boss?"

"No. She tells *everybody* that she's my boss. She walked me around the office today and introduced me as *Lisa, the girl who'll be working directly under me*."

"It sounds to me like she just wants you to fit in. It's polite to introduce you to everyone, isn't it?"

Lisa glowered at Harry from under knitted eyebrows.

"Are you taking her side?"

"How can I take her side? I've never even met her."

"Well, it sounds like you're taking her side."

"I'm just saying that I think you should give her a second chance. Don't do it if you don't want to. I'm not sure what you want me to say."

"I didn't really want you to say anything" said Lisa. "I just wanted to vent, and I wanted you to nod along."

"Fine" Harry said, nodding over enthusiastically.

Lisa shifted in her seat, muttering to herself under her breath about the woman at work. A residual of anger flared suddenly.

"Are the curtains up?" she asked.

"Yes."

"In all of the rooms?"

"In all of the rooms."

"And the electricity is back on?"

"Yes"

"So the shower works again?"

"As far as I know. I haven't been able to go in it yet. We still don't have any towels."

"Bloody movers" Lisa hissed. "I can't go another day without showering. I'm starting to smell as bad as I look. Can we call past a supermarket on the way home and get some?"

Harry's heart sank.

"I haven't stopped all day."

Lisa cast a wide-eyed look at her husband. He refused to acknowledge it as he worked his way through the rush hour traffic.

"I'm sorry" she said. "Has it been hard staying home all day while your wife works to put food on the table?"

"That's not fair."

"Look" Lisa said with an air of finality. "I'm not going another day without showering. You might be content to stink, but I'm not. Either call off at a supermarket on the way home or I'm going to get right back in the car and go myself when we get back."

Without saying a word, Harry pulled off the slip road and merged once again with a long line of slow-moving vehicles that trudged along the dual carriageway. Lisa continued to mutter to herself as they chugged along, not speaking directly to Harry, but very much speaking about him.

Harry parked up near to the door. They walked across the car park, not holding hands as they went, getting slowly more wet from the drizzle that had settled in for the evening.

The inside of the supermarket was familiar enough to Lisa to guide them to the homeware section without having to ask anyone for help. Upon finding the towels she began leisurely perusing them, taking them between her thumb and forefingers and talking to herself about the colour.

"Oh" she said, the act of shopping already having a calming effect on her mood, "what did you want to tell me about?"

"What?"

"You sent me a text today saying that you had something to tell me."

Harry had all but forgotten the message he had sent his wife. The adrenaline that had coursed through his system as he had sent the text had a similar effect to texting when drunk.

"It was nothing."

"Are you sulking? Just tell me. Do you like this colour by the way?"

"Yellow towels?"

"You think this is yellow? It's labelled as lemon."

Harry shook his head. He could argue all he liked. If these were the towels that Lisa wanted then they would be the ones that they would be buying.

"So, come on. What was it you wanted to tell me? You told me I wouldn't believe it."

"Really. It was nothing."

"Was it something to do with the house?"

"It was just that the plumber had finished the job. That was all."

Earlier in the day Harry had decided that telling Lisa the truth would not be a good idea. He knew that there would be no way he could recount the tale without fear saturating his voice. If Lisa suspected that he was frightened, then she would be frightened, and she would likely want to leave the house. Lisa was a sceptic, and while Harry was the exact opposite, he had always maintained that ghosts were nothing to fear. If she got a hint of the fact that he was frightened of the house, Lisa would nag him until he agreed to leave.

"Are you sure that's all it was?" Lisa asked suspiciously.

"That's all it was. I promise."

Lisa placed a roll of green towels back onto the shelf and then took her husband by the wrist.

"Why are you lying to me?"

"I'm not."

"You just did it again. That was a lie, when you told me you weren't lying."

"It wasn't."

"Harry…"

A turbulent anger swirled just below Lisa's composure. Harry tensed. Lisa was not above giving him a public dressing down, and if he didn't play his next card exactly right, that's exactly what he was going to get.

"Fine" he said, "But don't say I didn't try to protect you from this."

"Protect me? My God, Harry. What's going on? For Christ's sake tell me!"

"I saw something in our house today."

"Something like what?"

"Like a person. A dead person. A ghost."

It was tiny at first, almost so small that it didn't exist, but then Lisa's smile widened, and her lips parted, and she began to laugh.

"You think you saw a ghost?"

"I *did* see a ghost"

"What kind of a ghost?"

"I don't know. Like a normal one. It was a man."

"What kind of a man? Where? What exactly did you see?"

"I was upstairs putting the curtains up, and when I came down the stairs to make a cup of coffee, he was just standing there in the hallway. Then he disappeared."

Lisa did not hold back. She laughed heartily at what she did not believe. For a moment Harry feared that she had seen through his lie and that she was laughing at how poorly he had told it, but then the mocking tone returned to her voice as she looked him in the eyes and said, "No you didn't."

"Fine" Harry said. "Don't believe me."

"Aaw, don't be like that. I didn't mean to upset you, but you do realise that sounds absolutely insane, don't you? You expect me to believe that you saw a man in our house who was there one minute and then disappeared the next?"

"I expect my wife to believe me when I tell her that I saw something that quite frankly was a little unnerving."

"Oh, I do believe you saw something" Lisa said, placing a patronising hand onto Harry's shoulder. "I'd like to think that you haven't completely lost your mind. It's just that I don't necessarily believe that what you saw is what you think you saw."

"OK" Harry said, stepping out from under her hand.

"It was probably just a trick of the light"
"Mm-hm"
"Or a shadow."
"It wasn't a shadow."

Lisa reached out and tried to take Harry's face in her hands. He pulled away from her as she tried unsuccessfully to touch him again.

"You're not upset, are you?"

"Just drop it would you? And can we hurry this up? I'm starving. Let's get something quick for tea. The oven is working again."

"Great" said Lisa, clearly not appreciating the upset she had just caused. She picked out a set of black towels with the words *His* and *Hers* emblazoned in silver lettering. "What do you think of these?" She asked, placing the towels in the basket without waiting for Harry's response.

*****

It took all of two minutes for Lisa to notice the camera in the top corner of her derelict hallway.

"What the hell is that?"

"What does it look like?" Harry said, trying to play down the expensive purchase he had made earlier in the day. "Do you want a naan with your curry?"

"Why have you installed a camera in our house?"

Lisa stepped into the space below the camera and waved frantically as if someone on the other side might be watching.

"I thought it might set your mind at ease" Harry lied, startling even himself with how quickly and easily it came. "You said it yourself, it's not a nice area. I thought a little extra security might make you feel more comfortable."

"Most people don't install them inside of their homes though. Security cameras tend to go on the outside, don't they?"

Harry's mind grasped at the next thread of the tale he was weaving.

"You *could* put them on the outside but that just advertises to everyone that you've got something worth stealing, doesn't it?"

Lisa said nothing. Instead, she waved at the camera again, ogling the reflection that waved back at her in the camera's deep black lens.

"I don't like it. It feels like I'm in some sort of zoo. I think we should take it down."

"You mean you think I should take it down."

"Alright then. Yes. I think you should take it down. It's creepy."

"How is it creepy? Who will see the footage other than us? You think it's creepy that we can see ourselves?"

Lisa stepped backwards, still not taking her eyes off of the camera lens.

"What about when we rent the place out?"

"We're miles away from being ready to do that."

"But when we're not. What then? You think our tenants are going to want you watching them at all hours of the day?"

"I'll take them down when we leave. I just think that while we're here we should have an extra set of eyes watching the place, seeing what's going on. That's all."

Harry watched as realisation turned Lisa's face to thunder. She turned away from the camera and searched him for the unmistakable mask of his lies. She found it nestled tightly between the lips he pursed when he was not telling the truth. It was as if he clamped his mouth tightly shut to stop the truth from getting out.

"Oh, I see what this is" she said, prodding an accusatory finger into her husband's chest. "This is all part of the ghost thing, isn't it?"

"No. There's a weak spot in the wall now where the pipe burst. Imagine how much easier it would be to claim on the insurance if we had footage showing the damage was nothing to do with us."

"We do have footage" Lisa said. "You filmed the whole thing on your phone."

"Yeah" reeled Harry, feeling the noose of his fabrications winding around his neck. "But what if I'd been out when it happened? What evidence would we have then?"

"Where are you going to go? You don't have a job. You don't know anybody around here."

"I don't know. Anywhere. Taking you to work maybe."

Lisa went back to the corner and stood on her tip toes, trying to get a better angle on the camera that loomed over her.

"This looks expensive."

"It wasn't that much."

"How much?"

"It was on offer" Harry said.

"How much?"

"The woman in the shop said that-"

"How much did the camera cost, Harry?"

He scrambled looking for anywhere to go, but Harry found himself firmly backed into the corner, both physically and metaphorically.

"A hundred and ninety-nine."

"You spent two hundred pounds on a camera to watch our hallway for ghosts?"

The dog next door began to bark at the sound of Lisa's elevated voice. The muffled sound of its owner shouting at the animal came not long after.

"I got it to keep us safe" Harry said.

Lisa threw her hands in the air in a monumental shrug.

"I'm sorry" she said, "but what the hell is this? This is the second time you've lied to me in an evening."

"I'm not lying."

"You lied to me in the shop when I asked you what the text was about and you're lying to me now."

"I'm not."

Harry's lips pursed again, holding back the truth, keeping it pressed tightly under his tongue. For a brief moment there was violence in Lisa's eyes. Harry was surprised when without a word headed up the stairs.

"Lisa! I-"

"Make the food" she shouted over the sound of the dog barking next door.

"Wait" Harry called after her. "I need to tell you something!"

"Are you fucking kidding me?"

Lisa's voice was electric in its outrage. Harry braced himself for the inevitable fallout of her discovery of the camera at the top of the stairs, and yet he still found himself backing into the kitchen as she thundered back into the hallway.

"You bought two of them!?"

"They were on offer."

"Are there any more?"

Harry said nothing.

"Please tell me there aren't any more."

Slowly but surely Harry's gaze drifted over towards the living room door. Lisa's jaw stiffened. She backed up to the door holding Harry's gaze the whole time until at the last moment she turned and went into the dark hollow of the living room.

With a widening horror, Harry watched as his wife exploded into the hallway and charged at him. She grabbed wildly at his collar, swinging an open palmed hand at his face, trying desperately to make some sort painful of contact with the man she had married. She wanted to hurt him for being so selfish in a time when she was giving so much. She wanted him to feel a little bit of the hurt that he was making her feel by dragging her here on the pretense that he would fix up this house and use it to make a better life for the pair of them.

Harry caught hands and shoved them away.

"You spent six hundred pounds on security cameras for the inside of the house!?"

Lisa swung at her man again. The edge of her fingers caught him across the delicate skin of his throat. Tiny pebbles of blood erupted from the red track marks they left behind.

"It's my money too! I saved up just as much as you did!"

"How can you spend this sort of money without at least asking me first?"

The sound of the barking intensified next door. This time the angry woman's voice was not directed toward the dog but was instead directed at Harry and Lisa.

Lisa threw her hand at Harry's face again. This time her fist was balled rather than open. He pushed her back hard enough to knock her from her feet. Lisa stumbled backwards, hitting the tiled floor of the kitchen with a meaty slap. Her hands instinctively went to her stomach.

The angry voice of the woman next door brayed against their shared wall. The sound of pounding fists against plaster added to the cacophony.

"What are you doing?" Harry said, reaching out to help his wife back to her feet.

She pushed him away, her hands once again cradling her belly in a quasi-protective stance.

The voice of the John Masterman thing entered Harry's mind from somewhere deep in his memory. The words suddenly took on meaning.

That thing growing in your wife's gut's will be rotten too...

"You're pregnant?"

Lisa nodded solemnly from her place on the floor.

"Since when?"

"I don't know" she said as Harry hurried to get her to her feet. She kept one protective hand looped gently around her belly.

"Could be a couple of weeks. Maybe a couple of months. With everything that's been going on I haven't really been keeping track of my cycle."

Harry stepped back from Lisa, eyeing her as if she were infected with some sort of parasite.

"Have you seen a doctor?"

"No."

"Have you done a test?"

The woman next door pounded on the wall again.

"Of course I have"

"And when were you going to tell me?"

More pounding on the wall.

"*Will you shut up?*" Harry shouted toward the wall. The woman's muffled response came back, aggressive and reinforced by the barking of her dog.

"I really think that you should see a doctor."

"Harry. Will you just give me some room? I'm still trying to work this out for myself. I don't need you telling me what to do with my body."

"I'm not trying to tell you what to do with your body. I'm trying to look out for my baby."

Lisa's hand jerked away from her stomach.

"Oh Jesus. It is my baby, isn't it?"

"Of course it is. How can you even say something like that?"

"You just looked shocked when I said that."

For a moment it looked like Lisa became unsteady on her feet. Harry reached out to take hold of her, but she pulled away from him.

"I just... I haven't really thought of it as one of those before now."

"As what? A baby?"

She nodded her head.

"Calling it that makes it sound too... I'm not sure what the word is."

More barking. More shouting from next door.

"If she doesn't stop that I'm going to go around there and-"

"Can we agree not to call it that for a while? Just while we decide what we're going to do with it."

"What's that supposed to mean?" Harry asked. "You're not

thinking of getting rid of it are you?"

Lisa said nothing. She didn't need to say anything. The shameful look in her eyes told Harry everything he needed to know.

"Don't I get a say in this? We've talked about having a... about having one in the past"

"No. *You've* talked about it" Lisa said. She stroked her belly again. Harry wondered whether this was indeed the protective motion he had first interpreted it as, or whether Lisa was trying to somehow soothe a growing ache in her belly.

The woman next door pounded on the wall again and shouted something aggressive at the top of her lungs.

A boiling rage took over Harry, fueled largely by his wife's lack of consideration. Pushing past her he stormed across the hallway and tore open the front door. He stomped across the driveway barefooted, his socks turning brown in the filthy puddles of water that congregated on his driveway. He turned and marched across the patch of grass at the front of his neighbour's house. There he pounded on the front door with a tight fist.

"Stop banging on the wall!" Harry yelled, kicking the door as he shouted. The dog inside tipped into fever pitch, barking with the ferocity of an undomesticated wolf.

The handle turned and the woman next door tore open the door. She held the dog's collar in her hand. The animal reared up on its hind legs in a wild attempt to get to Harry. He took a step back. The dog was far bigger than he had anticipated it would be.

"Can you stop shouting through the walls?" He kept one eye on the dog as he spoke. "And can you try and keep that *thing* quiet?"

"*Me* be quiet?" the woman yelled. "All I've heard for the past few days is you two screaming at each other. I've got a seven-year-old in here. You need to keep the noise down."

"You let that thing near a child?" Harry said pointing at the dog that was now going berserk against her restraint. "Do you have any idea how dangerous that is?"

Truth be told, Harry did not have any idea how dangerous it was, but his frustration at this woman and the one he had left behind was so great that he was happy to simply ruffle her feathers with whatever hand he could get to her.

"Simba's a proper sweetheart! You don't know what you're talking about."

"Just keep the noise down, ey?" Harry turned and hurried across her lawn, secretly happy to be getting away from the dog.

The woman next door leaned out of her house and continued to berate him as he went.

"How come right, everyone who moves into that house spends all their time screaming and banging on the walls at all hours of the night? You'd better not be like the last lot mate. It was bad enough with the ones before them. Just once I want some neighbours who aren't screaming bloody murder the whole time they're home."

Harry stopped in his tracks. The sudden urge to ask the woman some questions about her previous neighbours outshone the anger he felt towards her.

Much to his disappointment she slammed the front door before he could ask her a single question. Her dog flew into a whole new level of hysterics. For a while Harry stood and looked at her home, before spending a few moments observing his. He wasn't sure exactly how it was the case, but he noted that his own home looked significantly less welcoming than the one with the giant dog inside of it.

THE ENGAGEMENT PARTY

Lisa tugged uncomfortably at the fabric that clung tightly to her swollen belly. She shifted in her seat, pulling at her dress and lifting one leg as if trying to wriggle away from a stomach-ache.
"You alright?" Harry mouthed from his seat next to her.
"It's got hiccups again" she said. "Bloody typical."
A spotlight swung overhead and shone bright pink light directly onto their table for the briefest of moments. It was just long enough for Lisa to have to raise a hand to her face and turn her head away. She rolled her eyes as the DJ shouted something indistinguishable into his microphone, his voice getting lost in the opening chords of a Black Eyed Peas *song.*
"I don't think that rubbish is helping either. Does anyone else think it's too loud in here?"
The woman next to Lisa set down her drink. Rose wine sloshed over the edge of her glass and soaked into the white linen tablecloth. She stared down at Lisa's pregnant belly.
"Is this your first?" she asked.
"Yeah" Lisa said.
The woman winced, her expression juxtaposing her rhythmic chair dancing.

"You know what they say about firstborns who get the hiccups..."
Rolling her eyes again, Lisa shook her head.
"Believe it or not, I don't."
The woman picked up her drink and glugged loudly. Harry picked up his own drink and sipped the head off of his pint, glad that he could use alcohol to make this experience at least a little more tolerable.
"Hiccups means that one's gonna be a terrible sleeper" the woman said. "My first born had terrible hiccups and honestly, he didn't sleep through until he was four. Can you even imagine what four years of no sleep feels like?"
"It can't be any worse than sitting through this party" Lisa said just loud enough for Harry to hear.
"What?" the woman asked.
"I said, I can't imagine that it's easy."
The woman next to Lisa threw her head back and laughed. More wine sloshed over the side of her glass, this time settling onto the tight dress that was wrapped around her thighs.
"Easy? It was a bloody nightmare. The worst part was that once he started to sleep through, he started to wet the bed not long after, you know, because he was in such a deep sleep? You two have got all that to come you know, especially if he's hiccupping like that already."
"He?" Harry asked, leaning over the table and shouldering his own share of the small talk burden. "How do you know it's going to be a boy?"
"Firstborns always are" the woman said. Harry looked to Lisa who shook her head, desperately pleading with Harry not to get into it with this woman. Harry however, simply could not resist.
"I don't think that's true" he said.
"Of course it is."
"But it can't be true" Harry said. "There's no way that every firstborn baby is male. The odds surely have to be fifty-fifty, or thereabouts."
The woman looked first at Harry, then at Lisa with eyes that were no longer looking in the same direction. For a moment she looked angry, and Harry braced himself for her rebuttal, but then she simply turned her thumb toward him, a wide grin breaking out in Lisa's direction and said "Is he for real?"
Lisa began to laugh. It was more to smooth out the conversation than the

result of any sort of genuine amusement. She reached out and squeezed Harry's leg under the table. He got the message loud and clear. Leave it, she said without saying a word.

"*Let's hope the little one doesn't take after his dad in the brains department*" *the woman said. Harry got up from his seat and waited impatiently for Lisa to finish fake laughing.*

"*I'm getting another beer*" *he said.* "*Do you want another coke?*"

"*I'd better not*" *she said.* "*Any more caffeine and I'll be up all night.*"

"*You might as well get practising now*" *the woman next to Lisa said.* "*The thing is, most people don't appreciate just how little sleep you're gonna get. I thought my first born was bad, but when my second born came along...*"

Harry pulled away from the table before he could be lured into another argument with the idiot sitting next to his wife. He worked his way across the busy dance floor, feeling the familiar discomfort that he felt in all grand social occasions, especially the ones where he was the plus one.

He joined the line of people waiting at the bar and undid his top button under his tie. All around him people were shouting to one another under an ever-shifting set of disco lights. The smell of the ransacked buffet table stood a deep hunger in Harry's belly that he promised he would satisfy with a takeaway pizza the moment he and Lisa got home. For now though, he would fill his belly with beer and hope that this would suffice in staving off his discomfort.

"*So*" *came a voice from behind Harry,* "*how do you know Mel and Grant then?*"

"*Who?*" *Harry asked. He turned to find an old and mostly bald man standing slightly too close to him.*

"*Mel and Grant*" *the old man said.* "*It's their engagement party.*"

"*I don't know them. My wife works with one of them. I forget which one.*"

The old man smiled a tired smile and nodded empathetically.

"*Ah. You've been dragged along like I have then?*"

"*I'm afraid so*" *Harry said.*

"*Which ones your wife?*"

Slightly taken off guard by what felt are like an intrusive question, Harry squinted through the dwindling dance floor and pointed to Lisa who was currently sat staring into space while the woman next to her talked at the side of her head.

"The pregnant one. The one that looks like she's about to burst."

"Ah" the old man said. To Harry's surprise he gripped his hand and shook it firmly. "Congratulations."

"Thanks."

"Your first?"

"That's right."

The old man clapped Harry hard on the back.

"That's great. Girl or boy?"

"We don't know yet."

"Blimey. You're brave!"

"That's what they keep telling us" Harry said. He laughed, feeling comfortable for the first time this evening. There was something irresistibly warm about the old man's demeanour. He had a grandfatherly quality to him. He was familiar and friendly, but he had a mischievous twinkle in his eye.

Harry reached the front of the line and ordered his drink. The old man ordered his and then, just as Harry was about to ask him if he wanted to join them at their table he said "Well, good luck with the baby, son" and took his leave.

Harry worked his way back across the dance floor and set his drink down. Lisa looked exhausted. She continued to tug at her dress with an almost habitual motion. The fabric had become pinched and wrinkled.

"I think you're mad you know" the woman next to Lisa said.

"Excuse me?"

The woman leaned across Lisa. Harry gasped audibly as her elbow hovered precariously over Lisa's belly.

"Lisa's just been telling me about your house. Why on earth would you ever buy anything in that part of town? It's a bloody dump."

Harry became instantly annoyed at the prospect of having to defend his financial decisions against this imbecile.

"We didn't buy it so that we could live there. We're doing it up so that we can rent it out. As soon as it's done, we'll be heading back home."

A coy smile spread across the woman's face.

"How long have we been working together now?"

"Nine months" said Lisa, barely even listening anymore.

"It takes time to get a house in working order." Harry said, feeling himself already starting to lose his cool. "You didn't see the state of the place when we bought it."

"I did" she said. "Lisa showed me the photographs, which is exactly why I think you must be mad. Do you even have any DIY background?"

Frustration churned in Harry stomach. Here was another person quick to dump on his dreams.

"Yeah" he lied. "We do this sort of thing all the time. In fact, this is the third house we flipped. There's nothing to it."

The woman suddenly looked like a terrible odour had crossed in front of her nose.

"Lisa said that this was your first one."

"Did she?"

"I did" Lisa said, too physically uncomfortable to get into this. "Harry's lying."

"It was more of a joke really" he said.

"I don't see how that's funny."

"I'm sorry," Harry said through gritted teeth, "who exactly are you again and why do I need to justify my choices to you?"

"Harry..." Lisa moaned.

"Debbie" the smug woman said. She picked up her glass tipped the rest of its contents into her mouth.

"Oh, so you're Debbie" Harry said. "I've heard a lot about you."

The mood at the table shifted. Lisa stiffened in her seat. Debbie did the same, the light of her arrogance going out in an instant.

"Really?" she said uncertainly. "All good I hope?"

"Well..."

"Excuse me" Lisa said. She pushed her chair back and got unsteadily to her feet. "I think I'd better go to the bathroom."

"Everything alright?" Harry said.

"Fine" she muttered as she waddled past.

Harry watched his wife work her way across the dancefloor. Guests parted way for her as she passed by, looking at her with a mix of sympathy and condescension that had become the norm since she had fallen pregnant.

"Was it all good then? What Lisa had been saying about me?"

"Honestly Debbie, she hasn't said a bad word yet."

The woman eyed Harry, trying unsuccessfully to decipher the over enthusiastic grin that Harry wore. If this woman was truly anything like Lisa had described her as - rude, obnoxious, but incredibly insecure -then the ambiguity Harry was presenting would tear her apart from the inside.

"I think I'm going to go and get another drink" she said, getting up from the table.

"Sounds good" he said, not letting his smile fade yet.

As soon as Debbie was out of view, Harry's face settled into an expression of smug satisfaction. The way Debbie's face had dropped the instant Harry had even hinted that Lisa may not like her would live on in his memory for a long time. It would provide a spiteful little pick me up whenever he felt he needed it.

Sod it, *Harry thought to himself, lifting his pint and drinking victoriously from the foam. In two weeks' time his child would arrive, and Lisa would slip comfortably into her maternity leave, leaving a whole year for Debbie to mull her behaviour over in her mind. Lisa wouldn't have to deal with her or anyone else she worked with for that matter. They could just get on with their lives and put the final few touches to the house.*

The vibration of his phone against his leg brought a heavy reality crashing down on Harry's head. His anxiety doubled when he pulled it out of his pocket and saw Lisa's name on the notification bar. He was almost certain that he was going to open a text message full of fury at the way he had put his wife into such an awkward position with the woman at the table.

"I need help" it read. "Come quick."

Anxiety turned to panic, sobering Harry in an instant.

"Where are you?" he text back.

"Women's room."

"I can't go in there."

Silence. Then "Just come. Now."

Harry hurried past the DJ booth with its rotating light cannons and made his way to the toilets. He waited as a couple of women talking outside of the lady's room finished their conversation and moved on before going into the alien feeling bathroom.

"Lisa?" he hissed.

"I'm in here."

The sound of a cubicle door unlocking drew Harry towards his wife. He went in to find her sitting on the toilet, her dress hitched up around her waist and her soaked underpants around her ankles.

"Have you pissed yourself?" Harry asked.

"My bloody waters have broken." she snapped. "Why would I have pissed myself?"

"Oh my God" Harry said. "Are you sure?"

"Of course I'm sure. Look at the state of me. My dress is soaked. This is so embarrassing."

"Hey" Harry said, recognising the early stages of panic in his wife's voice. "It was going to happen sooner or later. What do you have to be embarrassed about?"

Tears began to flow from Lisa's eyes. She buried her face into her hands. "My dress is soaked. Everybody I work with is out there. How am I going to get out of here without everybody seeing?"

"Did you bring a coat with you?"

"No."

"We'll wrap my jacket around you then. Nobody will see."

"But it'll be really obvious that something's up. I feel like everybody is going to be watching me as I-"

Her words trailed off as she doubled forward, clutching at her swollen belly.

"Are you OK? Is that one of those... things?"

"A contraction" Lisa said through gritted teeth.

"OK. Just breathe through it."

The sound from the dancefloor swelled as the bathroom door swung open. Two women entered, chatting back and forth in slurred cadences, clearly worse for wear from the evening's revelries.

Lisa groaned as a contraction gripped her from the inside. The women's conversation faltered, replaced by a concerned silence and then a gentle knock on the cubicle door.

"Is everything alright in there?"

Lisa said nothing. Harry held his breath, nervously wishing that the women would just go away.

Lisa sat back on the toilet, her arms still folded tightly around her belly. "I'm... fine" she said unconvincingly.

The pause outside of the cubicle door was punctuated by loud drunken whispers.

"Are you sure? You don't sound alright."

Lisa breathed deeply as the contraction began to release its hold on her insides. Her brow was sweating enough for her fringe to stick to her head.

"Everything's fine" Lisa said. "I just need some privacy."

Again came the pause and the drunken whispers.

There was a shifting outside of the cubicle and then the sound of another cubical door closing. Harry let his breath go as Lisa sat panting on the toilet in front of him. To his horror, the top half of a woman's head peered over the cubicle wall.

"Have you got a fella in there?"

There was accusation in the woman's voice, her eyes clearly leading her to a conclusion that was entirely off the mark.

"It's not what it looks like" Lisa moaned. She doubled over herself as her insides twisted again.

"There's a lad in there with her" one of the voices said.

"Everything's fine" Harry said, feeling every bit the liar that the women were making him out for. "She just feels a bit unwell. I'm her husband."

Another head poked over the lip of the cubical wall and stared down at Harry.

"What have you done to her?" she asked. She pointed her phone over the lip and began to film the chaos unfolding in their cubicle.

"Stop" Harry pushed his hand up against the camera on the back of the girl's phone. "Can you just leave us to it, please?"

"Go and get someone Sophie" one of the voices said. "He's up to something!"

"I'm not" Harry said. He looked to his wife, desperate for some sort of support. Lisa sighed defeatedly.

"My waters have broken" she called out into the bathroom. "I'm going into labour."

A moment later, Harry was hurrying his wife out of the bathroom with his jacket wrapped tightly around her. Lisa glowed red as they crossed the dance floor and headed down the stairs that led to the exit of the venue. She smiled politely at the best wishes that people offered her as they hobbled by. She offered an apology as she passed the bride to be.

They slid into a taxi and Harry asked the driver to get them to the nearest hospital. In the back seat of the cab, Lisa continued to seethe.

"You promised me..." she hissed through deep and shaking breaths, "that I would not have to raise my child in that house. You said that the baby would never have to see the inside of that... place."

Harry shushed his wife and brushed hair from her sweaty forehead. He rubbed her back and spoke softly into her ear.

"Don't worry about that now. This is a happy occasion. We're about to have a baby!"

CHAPTER 09
46 SUBSCRIBERS

"Where did you go last night?"

Lisa's words dragged Harry out of a deep and desperately needed sleep. He made a sound that was not quite a word, but which was definitely a question.

"I said where did you go last night?"

He opened his eyes to find her sitting on the edge of the bed, facing away from him and barely moving at all.

"What time is it?"

"Seven-thirty" she said. "I woke up about half ten last night and you were gone."

"I went to the pub. The one in the town. They have free Wi-Fi there, so I uploaded the first episode of the show to YouTube."

Lisa nodded almost imperceptivity, apparently satisfied with her husband's answer. She leaned forward from the bed and picked up her dressing gown from the floor. She stood up, put it on and opened the curtains.

Grey morning light flooded into the room, hitting Harry hard in the face.

"Couldn't you sleep?" Lisa's voice was cold. Residual anger from the night before still held fast.

"Are you surprised? I had a lot on my mind. I wasn't exactly given much opportunity to get it off my chest either. Can we at least talk about-"

"No" said Lisa.

She headed into the bathroom. Harry rolled onto his side, not yet ready to face the day. The room was stiflingly warm. The central heating seemed to be overcompensating for the weeks in which it had been switched off.

Lisa shouted something from the bathroom.

"What?"

She didn't respond.

Grumbling, Harry pulled his legs out from the twisted covers and swung them off the edge of the bed.

"What did you say?" he asked as he entered the bathroom, already becoming agitated only minutes after waking.

Lisa spat a mouthful of toothpaste into the sink.

"I asked you if you had a pen and something to write on."

"Not on me."

"Well, can you go and get a pen and paper please?"

"What for?"

"I want you to write down a list of things you're going to do today. You have to get organised. I know what you're like. If you don't set yourself goals, you'll just drift around all day and half finish jobs. And probably not the ones that we need doing either."

In the harsh light of the bedroom, Harry pressed the heels of his hands into his eyes. He wanted to be angry, but he knew that Lisa was right. The last few days had been a prime example of his inability to focus. An itinerary might be just the thing that he needed in order to make progress.

He left the bathroom, returning a couple of minutes later with a stubby looking pencil and the receipt for the cameras he had bought the day before.

"I'm ready."

"Fix the hole in the wall."

Harry leaned the receipt up against the wall and wrote FIX WALL in block capitals.

"OK. What else?"

"Nothing" Lisa said. "That's it."

Harry eyed his wife with a mix of suspicion and confusion.

"That's it? You don't want me to do anything else today?"

"Not today" Lisa said, putting her toothbrush back into her mouth. "Fixing the wall is a big job."

Harry folded the receipt and backed slowly out of the bathroom, still waiting for further instructions. His mood lightened when they did not come.

Heading into the kitchen, Harry suddenly found himself a lot more content to begin preparing the cup of tea he made his wife each morning. Harry wondered whether this was all part of some bigger plan. Perhaps she was going easy on him today in place of the apology, or in place of the conversation he felt he deserved about the fate of his unborn child.

"Harry…" came a call from upstairs.

"Here we go" he breathed to himself, before heading to the foot of the stairs and calling back.

"Yeah?"

"There is one more thing that I forgot to mention."

"What is it?"

"The internet guy is coming today. It's Wednesday. Can you make sure you're in when he gets here?"

"Yeah" he said, becoming bewildered all over again. "I can do that."

"Great."

The drive to work that morning was pleasant enough. They did not talk about anything of any real importance, and the weight of Lisa's pregnancy hung heavy and obvious over the journey, but they were civil with one another, and that's more than Harry had expected them to be.

Lisa kissed him lightly on the cheek as she left the car, and while it felt devoid of any real emotion, the gesture itself was enough to give Harry hope for their future together.

As he pulled the car out onto the main road, Harry's phone pinged.

"Sorry you found out that way. We'll talk about it soon. Not now though."

Good enough he thought as he negotiated the busy morning traffic.

The engineer from the internet company arrived exactly when he said he would. When he was done, Harry drove to the nearest hardware store he could find that stocked plaster and chipboard and everything else he would need to repair the hole in the wall.

He got home, then loaded up his YouTube app ready to watch a How To on fixing walls. What he saw on his phone screen however, stopped Harry dead in his tracks.

The tiny notification panel at the top of his screen glowed a tantalisingly bright red showing each of the notifications that had come pouring into his channel since he had uploaded the first episode of *Our Haunted Home* the night before.

Conscience told him to leave them well alone and to find a video explaining how he could fix the wall instead, but a heady cocktail of curiosity and excitement intoxicated Harry, and suddenly he found he was powerless to resist.

Harry clicked the icon. His eyes grew wide.

The video he had uploaded the night before had racked up nearly seven hundred views.

Harry clicked through, following the digital breadcrumbs and found that more than a handful of comments had been left on his work. The vast majority were positive, openly displaying intrigue as to what *Our Haunted Home* would bring to the table. Within this, there was a smattering of doubt as to how haunted Harry's house was, but right now he did not care. The main thing was that people were watching and engaging with his work, and that was enough to push his mood through the ceiling.

Possibilities began to swirl in his mind. If Harry could just take an hour before working on the wall, he could probably get the second episode edited and uploaded. The footage of the wall bursting would set the tone perfectly. It was funny and if nothing else would provide another talking point for the small community that was growing in the comment section of the first episode. If he worked particularly hard, Harry might even have been able to give the bursting wall a paranormal spin. Liam Masterman had told him that a burst like this was very uncommon. Who would be to say that it wasn't caused in part by unseen forces intent on making Harry's time at number 7 as difficult as possible?

"No" he told himself. His voice sounded loud in the empty front room. "Do the work first, then edit. Make good choices."

Pushing his excitement to one side, Harry took a last look at his follower count, which was astonishingly almost at fifty already, and then he began searching for videos on how to install a new panel wall.

The work was going to be far harder than he had anticipated.

With a growing sense of unease, Harry watched and then re-watched several videos in which at least two people grappled with a tricky combination of chipboard and messy looking plaster.

"Jesus" Harry sighed as he neared the end of the third video. "This is going to be a nightmare."

Harry trudged out to his car, opened his boot and retrieved the materials he had bought from the hardware store on his way back from dropping Lisa off at work. The urge to text her came on suddenly. Harry's mind reeled with the excitement of the relative early success his YouTube channel had achieved. Unable to tell anyone else about it, Harry felt compelled to send his wife a message, not so much as an *I told you so*, but more of an isn't this great? type of message.

Good sense prevailed once again. The bridge between them was precarious at best right now. There would be no need to navigate it with such heavy steps just yet. He would test the waters of her mood when she got home that night and if it was safe enough, Harry would slip the good news into their conversation later in the evening.

Harry pushed open his front door and then closed it with the heel of his shoe. The final bag of plaster in his hands felt significantly heavier than the previous three he had brought in. He dropped it to the ground in front of him and leaned up against the door. It clicked loudly as the latch slipped into place.

With an air of trepidation Harry locked the front door and then got to work.

The job was difficult and in more than a few places it had seemed impossible. The act of fixing the gaping hole required Harry to do more damage to the wall, and as he dug a saw blade into the crumbling plaster to cut away the frayed edges that the water pipe had wrought, he couldn't help but think of the thing that had pretended to be his plumber as it had brought its mallet into the wall in wide, meaty thwacks.

That memory now seemed bathed in a shimmering artifice.

Harry continued to work, forcing the unpleasant images from his mind. With a new, bigger, but tidier hole made in the wall, Harry placed two pieces of support into the hole and screwed the hardwood into place. It was an arduous task and the screws he drilled into his existing wall brought further anxiety with them, given how ugly they appeared in the wall. Standing back and wincing at the job he had done so far, Harry began the painstaking job of applying thick gloopy plaster over the hardwood.

Four letter words spilled from his mouth as Harry tried and then tried again to secure a flat finish to the new plaster he had applied. No matter how hard he tried, Harry's plastering trowel seem to want to leave thick ridges in the finish. When Harry found himself on the brink of giving up and searching for a professional plasterer to come and finish the job (*If I could get someone today* he told himself, *I might just tell Lisa that I'd done it all myself*), he stepped back, took stock of what he had done, and punched the words "How to plaster professional looking walls" into his YouTube app.

His notification icon had lit up all over again. This time Harry did not even battle with the decision to check it. Six new subscribers and almost eighty more views had registered on his first episode. The excitement of this pushed Harry to want to finish the job. The sooner he was done completing the one task on his to-do List, the sooner Harry would be able to get working on his second episode.

Following instruction, Harry smeared plaster over the newly fixed hardwood and then smoothed it into place. When he was done, he stepped back and observed the wall.

An overwhelming sense of pride in his work turned into a boisterous self-appreciative cheer. Sod the neighbours. She could complain about the noise all she wanted. This victory was too good not to shout about.

Predictably the dog next door began to bark.

Harry picked up his phone with hands that were now caked in quick drying plaster and fired out a text to his wife

"The wall is DONE" it said. He typed a second text message. "It looks great!"

"Wow" came the almost instantaneous reply. "Good job. Thanks for doing that for me."

"No problem. I love you."

He stood and waited for Lisa's response, marvelling with an almost teenage giddiness at his craftsmanship on the wall.

Harry's phone pinged. Lisa's response felt jarring relative to Harry's soaring accomplishment.

"Can you make sure the hallway is tidy when I get home? Could you maybe put your tools into the shed?"

"Oh" Harry said out loud. "OK then."

Battling against a heavy deflating feeling, Harry collected

up his tools and took them to the double doors that lead out onto his back garden.

Sodden ground sucked at his trainers as he crossed the waterlogged grass that led to the shed.

Having never stepped foot into the back garden before, Harry only now realised what a terrible state the shed was in. Rotten wood stood forced together by rusted nails. The small glass window - which seemed lopsided now Harry really looked at it - was a mess of cobwebs and dust and what appeared to be a pretty aggressive fungus that had spread steadily from the corners in toward the centre.

An ancient, rusted padlock sat camouflaged on the door. Rust had rendered it almost the exact same shade of brown as the rotten wood that surrounded it. Harry reached out and pulled the lock. It didn't budge. He pushed against the door and the soft wood bent inwards, catching on itself and emitting a sweet decaying smell.

After a minute of jostling, Harry resigned himself to the fact that he would need to break the lock.

Heading back into the house, Harry picked up his drill and brought it out into the garden. He ran his finger on the underside of the lock and found the keyhole hidden under a layer of rust. Harry pressed the tip of his drill bit against the opening. Gently, he revved the drill. The bit ground against the metal, shaving off rust and revealing glimmering steel underneath, but the tighter Harry squeezed the drill, the clearer the image of the jagged pipe flying out of the wall and embedding itself into John Masterman's neck became in his mind's eye.

I'm going to lose a finger thought Harry. *This is not a good idea.*

Harry stepped back and observed the crumbling structure of the shed. In its current state it would likely not survive the winter, let alone the time he expected the renovations on his new house to take. Breaking the door would be nothing more than the first step in the inevitable destruction of the shed, and so he reasoned it would be better to do it now and have a clear hallway than to have an intact shed that he could not use.

Harry would break the door.

Placing his drill onto the wet grass, Harry braced his shoulder against the soft rotten door. Carefully he leaned into it. Again, the wood ground against itself emitting that sweet decaying smell. The bulk of the door bend inwards, the far edge straining against the lock, but still it held.

Annoyed now, Harry backed up and crashed into the door. It groaned loudly under his weight. The lock rattled in protest of Harry's attempted intrusion, and yet still it would not budge.

"Alright" Harry said, determination breaking out across his face.

Looking over his shoulder to make sure nobody was watching him, Harry retreated out into the middle of his sodden lawn.

He took a deep breath and then hurtled forwards on a surge of adrenaline. His feet ground into the wet mud as he raced towards the door. Picking up speed he lowered his shoulder, squaring off just in time to collide with the door.

Rotten wood and rusted screws exploded into the interior of the shed. Harry's feet caught on the door frame and suddenly he became weightless. He flew forward on outstretched arms and hit the floor with a sickening thud.

Stars exploded across Harry's vision. A ringing invaded his ears. For a moment he was so disorientated that he could not quite tell if he was lying on his back or on his stomach. The tinkling sound of nails and screws dropping out of the shed walls resonated all around him like metallic raindrops, and still the ringing sounded in his ears.

Something squirmed underneath Harry as he lay on his front. The ringing in his ears gained enough clarity to take on a definitive source. In a state of pure confusion, Harry felt something hot and wet spreading under his stomach.

"Shit" he uttered against the ringing before realising that it wasn't ringing at all.

With sudden gut-wrenching recognition, the sound in Harry's ears became the panicked squeaking of dozens of rats. Animals squirmed out from under his belly, dragging themselves to safety on crushed limbs and broken backs.

He pushed himself up onto his hands and knees to find a compact nest of infant rats, each about the size and colour of a human thumb, each one screeching with the agony of what had just happened. Thick red gore coated Harry stomach and chest where he had crushed many of their number.

A huge brown mother rat clamped its teeth around Harry's wrist. Yelping in surprise, he drew back, lofting the rat into the air. Harry swung his hand and sent the beast careening across the shed and clattering into the wood of the far corner.

Simultaneously, Harry and the rat struggled to their feet. They locked eyes with one another, each trying to predict the other's next move.

The stench of the vermin was like nothing Harry had ever smelled before. Ammonia from their reeking urine invaded his nostrils, urging bile into his oesophagus.

The mother rat charged, maternal ferocity propelling it toward its almost certain death. Without even thinking, Harry lifted his foot and brought it stamping down on to the mother rat.

The animal's back gave a deep crunch as it was crushed against the rotten flooring. Despite her fatal injuries, the mother rat continued to snap at Harry from her infused place on the floor.

With a heavy feeling of guilt, Harry raised his foot again and finished the job, pressing his toes to the back of the rat's head and rocking forward on his feet.

Vermin scrambled for safety all around him, flooding from

the shed as quickly as their jagged little feet would allow them to. Soon, all that remained were the tiny pink rats in the tight ball of grass and hair that made up their nest.

The ammonia smell hit Harry again. His tee-shirt clung tightly to his chest by the blood of the crushed rats. The hot mess of the mother had begun to seep through his shoes and onto his feet. Harry retched.

As the baby rats continued to call for their now dead mother, a problem presented itself for which Harry could find no good solution. The tiny rats curled in the centre of his shed were now doomed to die a torturous death, either starving, or freezing, or being eaten by one of the returning rats to the colony Harry had just disturbed.

Despite a deep disgust at their mere existence, Harry could not find it within himself to simply leave them to die.

Part of Harry wanted to burn down the shed. He reasoned that doing so would kill two metaphorical birds with one scorching metaphorical stone. The shed was in a worse state than he had anticipated as he had stared at it through his kitchen window when he had first viewed the house. It would need replacing in order to store anything of any real value, so burning it would save him the job of taking it apart by hand.

But the fire would spread, likely burning down the fence, the house, his relationship with Lisa, his hopes and dreams…

Harry thought about giving the rats the same fate that their mother had found; lining up his boot and stomping them to death one by one. It would be an almost instantaneous death, but it would be messy. The sound their mother's body had made as he had put pressure onto the back of her head replayed somewhere in Harry's mind. He found this was all the persuasion he needed not to follow through with this idea.

He could poison them, or he could pour a kettle over them, but each eventuality conjured images of their tiny bodies writhing in agony as they slowly waited to die.

An idea suddenly formed in Harry's mind with terrible clarity. What if he were to put them in a bag, put the bag in the freezer and let nature take its course? They would freeze to death out here anywhere, but in this surprisingly mild winter their deaths could be days away. The dark confines of the freezer could do in hours what nature could only do in days. It was not a pretty option, but it was the best one that Harry had.

With a solemn dignity Harry turned to leave the shed and collect up a bin bag from his kitchen. He stopped still in the doorway, his eyes expanding with disbelief, his mouth dropping open with shock.

There, behind the white veil of the kitchen net curtains was an old woman. Harry's jaw dropped open and in that instant he forgot all about the rat gore that was congealing onto his skin. An apparition, as clear as day, was moving through his home.

Harry pushed a hand still slick with rat blood into his pocket and pulled out his phone. His thumbs worked over the screen. The device misbehaved as the goopy liquids that clung to his thumbs spread across the touch screen. He wiped his hand on his dirty jeans, never taking his eyes from the figure of the old woman in the kitchen. Finally, he managed to open up the camera app on his phone.

Harry framed the kitchen window in the centre of his screen. The phone could not pick up the same level of detail that he could see with his naked eye, but the woman's figure was clear on his screen nonetheless.

He pressed record and began speaking with shaking breath.

"Hey Guys, I'm in my shed, and I've just looked at my house, and correct me if I'm wrong but that looks like the figure of an old woman in my kitchen."

The figure moved. A large hunch in her back became evident as she turned sideways and moved back into the depths of the house.

Harry took a careful step out onto his garden, startling a particularly large rat that was dragging itself along on its broken hind legs.

Harry ignored it as he moved towards the house, padding carefully so as not to make any noise.

"I literally just turned around and there she was in my kitchen. My wife is at work, and we are the only people with access to our home. Nobody else is in the house."

Harry hurried past the crippled rat and slowly opened the back door of his home. The house seemed cold - much colder than it usually would have been. An eerie quiet rang throughout the place.

The sound of movement came in from the hallway. Putting his face close to his phone Harry whispered his narration to his future followers.

"I don't know if the camera is picking this up, but I can hear it moving out there. I think this could really be it. I think we might have a ghost!"

Harry's excitement intensified. He had expected it to take months before he truly started to capture paranormal activity on his camera, and yet here he was, just days into his investigation, doing more in two episodes than *King Of The Haunt* had managed in its five-year lifespan.

Harry tiptoed to the living room door and poked both his head and his phone around the corner.

The figure of the old woman was as clear as day. She stood in his kitchen, perfectly unaware of being observed. She was solid and haggard. Her skin was pocked and wrinkled. Her hair sprung out of her head in an array of wild angles. The distant smell of overly floral perfume invaded Harry's nose.

"Oh my God" Harry breathed. His voice was so quiet it was almost non-existent. "She looks so real."

The figure of the old woman turned, and its eyes locked

onto the camera poking around the corner. Shooting upwards they found Harry's face and then with an expression of complete and utter horror she opened her mouth and screamed.

Terror arced through Harry's body and his phone fell from his hand. Clattering to the floorboards, it slid across the hallway and toward the old woman which only seemed to frighten her more.

"Eeee my God!" the old lady screamed.

"What the... Who the hell are you?"

Anger flooded Harry's voice as he realised that this was no ghost. The figure was simply an old woman made of flesh and bone who had for some reason entered his house.

"I'm sorry love. God, are you alright!?"

"What are you doing in my house?"

"Is that your blood!?" the old woman wailed, her flesh turning pale, her stance becoming worryingly unsteady.

Harry looked down at the mess of rat blood that clung to his shirt.

"It's not mine" he said, his guard letting up as he reflected on how he must look to the old woman. "It's... a bit of a long story to be honest."

THE WARD

A passing nurse stopped and marvelled at Harry.

"It really suits you" she said quietly.

"What does?"

"Fatherhood" she said, looking doe eyed at the new-born sleeping in his arms. "You look very content there."

Harry looked down at his son as best he could. The infant in his arms shifted, making a soft cooing sound that Harry feared might build into a full-blown cry. In the end the baby simply exhaled made slow suckling movements with his puckered lips.

Harry and the nurse both laughed as quietly as they could.

"This is what life is for you now" the nurse said. "You'll spend hours doing that. Just sitting and staring at him. They are amazing little things, aren't they?"

"They certainly are" Harry said.

"What's he called?" the nurse asked

"Dylan" Harry smiled. "This is baby Dylan."

The nurse held her cupped hands over her heart as if to stop it from bursting. "Lovely" she said.

A voice, brash and loud and contrasting greatly with their whispered conversation called from elsewhere in the ward. The nurse took one last adoring glance at Dylan and then left, leaving Harry to hold his son and enjoy this moment of calm. He was all too aware that soon Dylan would wake again and would be eager to test out his voice, throwing him and Lisa into a frenzied state of trying to work out what it was he needed. But for now, all was calm, and Harry was happier than he had ever been in his life.

"How on earth have you done that?" whispered a voice.

Harry looked up from his son's face to find Lisa gingerly lowering herself back onto the bed, smiling wearily at the two men in her life.

"I think he did it himself" Harry said. "I suppose you can only cry so much before you need to recharge the batteries ready for the next round. I reckon he'll be out for a while now."

"Don't jinx it" Lisa said. She groaned as she leaned forward to pull her shoes on to her feet.

"Everything alright?"

"Yeah" Lisa said unconvincingly. "The stitches are holding up but they sting a lot. I'm going to have to come back next week to get them seen to."

Harry winced at the thought.

"It's all worth it though" Lisa said, noticing her husband's pained expression. "He's pretty perfect."

"Pretty perfect?" Harry asked. "Name one way that he could be improved upon."

Dylan shifted again in his father's arms. Both parents braced themselves in palpable fear at the thought of him waking again. The baby moaned, then whimpered and then the sound of hot liquid evacuating his body punctuated their silence.

Unable to stop herself, Lisa broke into delirious laughter. The sound of it prized Dylan's eyes open and he began to wail at the top of his lungs. "All right" Harry said against the din. "I suppose perfect *is a pretty strong word..."*

CHAPTER 10
89 SUBSCRIBERS

Stepping into the house next door was like stepping into a time warp. Had it not been for the clear signs of habitation - like the smell of microwave cooking and the pile of letters that sat uncollected in the hallway - it would have been easy to imagine this home as a museum piece demonstrating what life was like a generation ago.

"Ignore the mess" Nettie said as Harry bent down to pick up the old woman's mail.

"Mess?" Harry said. "You saw the state of my hallway. Your house is lovely. This feels like a proper home."

Nettie smiled politely as she moved through the hallway and into her compact little kitchen. Harry followed, running his hand through his still-wet hair from the shower he had rushed while Nettie had waited downstairs. Harry had tried to assure her that the blood was not his, but she had insisted on seeing him when he was all cleaned up. He got the sense that this was in part because she was lonely and that he was likely the only person she had spoken to in days.

As Harry Walked through her home, an overbearing sense of familiarity disorientated him. The house had the exact same layout as the one he had just bought, only everything was mirrored, flipped on its head and laid out the other way.

"Well, I've lived here a long time" the old woman said. "I've had the opportunity to get it just how I like it. It's a bit dated, I know, but it's comfortable, and that's all that really matters. That being said, with the amount of people who have moved in and out of your house, I would have thought that one of them would have managed to get the place looking a little more..."

Nettie struggled to find the right word, her face twisting into a pained little grimace.

"Finished" she settled on finally, before adding "No offence, love."

"None taken" Harry smiled, gazing out of the small window at the back of the kitchen that overlooked Nettie's garden. It was badly overgrown. Twisting weeds had taken over most of the lawn. A snarled bramble bush was constricting her shed as it grew up from around its base. "So, my place has had a fair few owners over the years then?"

"Sorry?"

"I said" Harry said, louder, compensating for the old woman's apparent poor hearing, "that my place must have had quite a few owners over the years."

"More than a few. For some reason people don't seem to last two minutes before moving on from there. Are you going to be around long?"

"I'm afraid not" Harry said, suddenly feeling an unexpected stab of guilt. "The plan is to fix the place up and then get it on the market for someone to let."

"Renters." Nettie said, filling the kettle from the kitchen sink. "When I was younger people didn't rent their houses. Everybody worked until they could afford a mortgage and then they bought their homes. It's only in the last twenty or so years that everybody started to rent. It's a shame really."

"When did you first move here?" Harry asked over the rumble of the kettle.

Nettie laughed warmly.

"I've always been here, love."

"You were born here?"

Nettie laughed at the younger man's surprise. She collected a pair of mugs and placed a tea bag in each of them. She bent forward and opened a cupboard. When she stood, Nettie groaned loudly with the effort of standing up straight again. She placed an opened packet of digestives next to the tea mugs.

"I was" Nettie said. "In one of the bedrooms upstairs if you must know. Hard to think that was nearly eighty-three years ago now."

Harry wanted to tell Nettie that she didn't look old enough to have lived in the house for eighty-three years, but he was worried that she would see through his lie. Truth be told, she looked every day of the eighty-three years she had spent on this earth. Her skin hung loose and wrinkled over eyes that seemed to have lost their sparkle some time ago. Her hands, the ones she now used to pour boiling water into waiting mugs, were gnarled and twisted by the arthritis that had claimed her joints.

The few teeth that remained in her head had taken on a crooked alignment and had greyed with what looked like a long-held smoking habit. Despite her outwardly rough appearance, Nettie exuberated an authority that set Harry on edge. Speaking to her felt like speaking to an old teacher, one that you had forgotten existed until meeting her again years later.

"Do you take sugar in your tea, love?"

"No thanks."

"Ah" Nettie said. "Too sour to be sweetened I see. Is it just you next door?"

Harry watched as Nettie struggled to pick up both mugs with her shaking hands. A sense of duty compelled him to try and take the mugs from her.

"I'll take those"

"You will not" she scorned. "You can bring the biscuits though."

Harry collected the digestives and followed Nettie to a living room that was bursting at the seams with ceramic ornaments and decorative china plates. A small television set played quietly to itself in the corner of the room. Subtitles danced underneath what looked like a daytime soap opera. Green carpeting blended sickeningly with green and cream striped wallpaper. A dull orange sofa called Harry into its throws.

Tea sloshed over the side of Harry's mug as Nettie set it down on a small table at the side of the sofa.

"Shit" she hissed.

"I'll grab a tea towel" Harry said, nipping out of the room and grabbing one from the kitchen before Nettie could insist on getting it herself.

When he came back into the room, Harry observed Nettie's struggle to get into her armchair. When she finally sat down, a deep and rattling sigh escaped from between her sparse teeth.

"It's not easy you know, getting old. Everything's five times harder than it should be. I used to be able to carry eight mugs in one go when I was your age. Now I can barely manage two."

"Why would you ever need to carry eight cuppas at once? Did you work in a cafe?"

"Big family" Nettie said, fussing over the biscuit packet. There was me, my mum and dad, four sisters and one brother."

"Bloody hell" said Harry. "Were your parents Catholic?"

"No. Nothing like that. We just didn't have a TV. They had to keep themselves entertained somehow."

They both laughed and then in unison, picked up their tea mugs and sipped at tea that was still slightly too hot to drink.

"So, is it then? Just you next door?"

"No" Harry said. He set his mug down carefully onto a crocheted coaster. "My wife has come up with me."

"Come up?"

"Up north. We live down south."

"No children?"

"Not yet. No."

"But you want them?"

"I do" Harry said. "I'm not so sure about Lisa."

With a final pull, Nettie untwisted the end of the biscuit packet and took out a crumbling digestive from the top.

"She'll come around. It's what we're made for. The best thing any of us can do is raised little ones. They give life purpose."

"You must have some of your own then" Harry said. He scanned the room but could not see a single photograph of anyone who might have been Nettie's children or grandchildren. Suddenly his question seemed very prying.

"Two boys" Nettie said with a tired smile. "They're all grown up now mind. Fifty-five and sixty-two. Not children anymore. I don't really see them as much as I'd like to, but they're busy. They've got their own lives now. It would be nice if one of them could have given me a grandchild though."

Uncomfortable silence fell over the conversation. Harry suddenly felt very much like he was intruding in the old woman's home. He picked hope his mug and drank. The slurping sound he made seemed too loud in the quiet front room.

"I am sorry again" Nettie said, watching Harry through milky eyes. "I wouldn't normally just walk into someone's home unannounced."

"I'm sorry that I surprised you like that. I can't imagine what I must have looked like."

This was a lie. Harry knew exactly what he looked like as he had caught sight of himself in the bathroom mirror as he had undressed. He looked like a man who had just murdered someone. It was a wonder he had not frightened Nettie to death.

The old woman waved a dismissive hand at this, but a

troubled look remained firm on her face.

"It's just... I could have sworn that I heard knocking on the wall."

"I've been doing a bit of DIY" said Harry. "A lot of DIY actually. A pipe burst and I've been fixing that. I was putting some curtains up on the walls, some other stuff too."

"The cameras?"

"You noticed?"

"You do right" Nettie said. "You can't be too careful around here anymore. It's not just the mortgage situation that has changed. The people that this area attracts, they're not like they used to be. Present company excluded."

Harry smiled politely, but something still tugged at his mind.

"You said the front door was open too?"

"I wouldn't have wandered in if it wasn't. It was the strangest thing."

"You're telling me. I could have sworn I locked it when I got home. I always leave my keys in the lock too. It's a bit of a habit of mine."

"No, I don't mean that it wa strange that the door was open. I mean the knocking. It was so odd."

"How so?"

"Well...." The flow of the conversation suddenly stopped. Nettie sat and thought as if she were choosing her next words very carefully. "I know you said you've been doing some DIY, but it didn't sound like that. It sounded more obvious. Like somebody was knocking to get my attention."

"Really?" Harry suddenly wished he had his phone with him. This sort of thing would make great content for his channel.

"Only, the thing is... well, you might have noticed, but I'm hard of hearing. In fact, I'm completely deaf in this ear."

Nettie brought a crooked finger to the side of her head and

tapped at the lobe of one of her drooping ears. Harry squinted at it, not sure what visual evidence he was looking for that the old woman had lost her hearing but nodding politely just the same.

"Is there anything else you can tell me about this knocking?"

Nettie's face scrunched with the effort of remembering.

"It's hard to say really. Sort of like if you were to knock on a door. I suppose that's the odd part about it really. I don't really hear when anyone knocks on my door these days, so for me to hear the knocking on the wall, it must have been coming through at some volume."

"That is strange" Harry said, trying to ignore the goose bumps that ran up and down his arms.

"Mmm." Nettie took a bite of one of her biscuits and crunched it loudly.

"Where were you when you heard it?"

"I was in the kitchen" Nettie said. Crumbs spilled from her mouth and settled onto her jumper.

"The kitchen isn't a shared wall though."

"I know. It wasn't as if it was coming from one point in the wall though, so that hardly seems to matter. It was like it was coming from everywhere all at once. In fact...." An odd, choked laughter escaped from Nettie's throat. "No, actually, it sounds too daft."

"What is it?"

"It was nothing. Probably just a senior moment, as my dad used to call them."

"You can tell me."

"Well... it was sort of like the sound was coming from inside of my head."

The wind suddenly died in Harry sails. Nettie was probably right. While most of her outward appearance looked every day of her eighty-three years on this earth, her eyes were easily ten years older than the rest of her body. Harry had noticed them clouding over several times during the course of their conversation. He would not have been surprised to find that Nettie was in the early stages of dementia.

He picked up his teacup and did his best to look concerned at the old woman's confession.

"So, that got my attention in the first place. The voice was the strangest thing about it all though."

"You heard a voice?"

"Yes. And this one was definitely coming from your house. Not from inside my head, like the knocking might have been."

"What sort of voice? Like my voice?"

Nettie shook her head.

"A woman's voice. That's why I asked if you lived alone."

"Oh my God" Harry said, now not even bothering to hide the goose bumps that burst out across his body. "Did it say anything to you? Where exactly was it coming from? Could you show me on the wall?"

Harry took a breath. Suddenly, the confusion was returning to Nettie's face, and it was clear that Harry's bombardment of questions was beginning to overwhelm her.

"Sorry" he said quickly, his voice smoothing out. "That was a lot of questions. Did it sound like it was coming from upstairs or downstairs?"

"Downstairs." With great effort the old woman twisted in her seat and extended a crooked finger toward the middle of the wall behind her. "From there."

Harry got out of his chair and traced his hand along the flat of the wall.

"Here?"

"No. Lower down. Toward the floor."

"Here?"

"That's right."

Dropping to his knees Harry pressed his hand to the wall

and revelled at the cool surface under his skin. He pictured his home beyond it. The sound had been coming from the foot of the stairs, at about the spot where the Masterman-thing had bled out only the day before.

"And you said it was a woman's voice? Definitely not a man's?"

"Definitely" said Nettie.

"Did it say anything?"

Nettie leaned forward and picked up her cup of tea with hands that were shaking with more than just old age. She held it in her palms and sipped minutely from the rim of the cup. Suddenly she looked very small, smaller than she had done when Harry had found her skulking around his hallway.

"It..."

"Yeah?"

"It was sort of...moaning. Like it was hurting."

Harry's heart began to pound in his chest.

"But did it say anything?"

"It asked for help. It called my name."

Harry searched the woman's face for signs that she might be confused. A senior moment might have her in its grips, wrenching reality away from her timeworn mind. Nettie however, looked clear. She looked frightened.

"You're sure it called your name?"

"That's why I got up and came around your house." She sipped again from her teacup as if taking nips from a hip flask for a rally of Dutch courage. "It's hard work when you're old. Moving around is so difficult. I wouldn't have gone to the effort of getting up and putting my shoes on and coming round if I didn't think it was an emergency. When I found the front door wide open, I thought something must be really wrong. I could still hear it a little bit when I got in there."

"But you said you were hard of hearing" Harry said.

"I am" said Nettie. "That's what made it so strange.

Normally I can barely hear anything. I lip read most of the time."

It was only now that Harry realised the old woman had been staring intently at his mouth this whole time.

"It was the strangest thing" she said again. "It was as if…"

A familiar frustration ruffled Harry's feathers. He did not press the old woman however, he let her words find her all on their own.

"It felt like I was hearing an echo. From the past."

"What do you mean by that?"

"Well, the voice… God. It sounds so silly to even be saying this out loud."

"You have to" Harry said, starting to worry that the old woman was about to close up on him. She looked at Harry with exhausted eyes. It was as if recounting the story was draining her energy.

"The voice. I've heard it before."

"Coming through the walls?"

"Well, yes, but it belonged to a lady who lived next door when I first heard it. The one from today couldn't possibly have belonged to her. She's been dead for so long."

It was everything Harry could do to not stand up and punch the air. He could feel the tendrils of the story he was chasing start to intertwine, coming together as a solid whole, rather than the frayed threads of disconnected happenings that they had seemed to be up until this point.

"Evelyn, they called her. Eva for short. God, I haven't thought about her in a while."

"Did she die in my house?"

A sigh escaped from Nettie. Harry got the impression that this was a story she had told many times before. The old woman pulled her thin rimmed glasses off of her face and rubbed a dry hand across her ever-watering eyes. When she put her glasses back on, Nettie fixed Harry with sad gaze.

"She did love. But that was years ago, so it's really nothing to be-"

"How long ago?"

Nettie stopped in her tracks.

"You know, it's rude to interrupt. It's even ruder to be looking so excited about a story like this."

"I'm sorry" Harry said, quietly reminding himself that not everybody held such an affinity towards tales of the macabre like he did.

"There was a time when people bought one home and then that was it for life. I did it. My mother did it too. My mother bought this house. She didn't leave it until she was carried out of it once her time was over."

"Did your mother die before you were married? Or did you and your husband live here with your mam and..."

Harry trailed off. Nettie had fixed him with another fiery stare.

"Sorry. I won't interrupt again."

"Make sure you don't. Mother left this place to me in her will, and I was pleased to have it. You don't need to know any finer details than those for this story. Eva moved in when we were really young, or at least when *I* was really young. Some of my brothers and sisters had grown up and had started to leave home by then, getting married, having children, all the sort of things that life expects of us when we become adults."

There was a pause in the conversation as Nettie sipped her tea. Harry felt this was a safe time to ask his questions.

"Are you the youngest?"

"I'm the baby of the family" she smiled. "Hard to imagine now to look at me, isn't it?"

Harry laughed gently in place of an actual answer for fear he might cause offence.

"She lived next door with her husband. A man called Ronnie. He wasn't around for long, you see. He'd work all day, then be out all night. The only time we knew he was even living next door was when we could hear them shouting at each other beyond the walls."

"What sort of things would they argue about?"

Nettie put a finger to her lips and shushed.

"Everything and nothing. Most of the time it sounded like he just wanted to argue because it upset her. I don't think he ever really liked Eva."

Much to Harry surprise, he found himself raising one of his hands. Nettie looked at him with a mixture of amusement and annoyance.

"Yes?"

"So why did they get married in the first place?"

"The same reason everybody got married in those days. Because they either wanted to have children, or because they had one on the way and didn't want to have it out of wedlock."

"And Eva was-"

"The latter" Nettie said. "She didn't have that baby though."

"Did she die when she was pregnant?"

Nettie shook her head. "She miscarried right after the wedding. And that wasn't the only one either. She had three more miscarriages that I can remember. The first two were purely down to bad luck, but the third one... he beat that baby out of her. Or that's what the rumour on the street was, anyway."

"Did you believe the rumours?"

Nettie stared at the muted television set in the corner of the room.

"I heard him do it" she said. "It might be hard to believe given you can probably hear me clattering and banging around from next door-"

"-I've never heard-"

"-but these walls have been soundproofed since before you

were born. My father paid a man to come along and add an extra couple of inches of plaster onto the walls to keep the sound out from next door. The whole room is about a foot smaller in real terms than it was when I was born."

The old woman breathed deeply. Her watery eyes threatened to spill over and cascade down her cheeks.

"The things I was hearing were really starting to upset me. They argued all the time. I would hear him threaten her, and then follow through on his threats. I would hear that woman screaming as he laid into her every night when he got home, full of drink and fury and God only knows what else."

"That must have been horrible."

"It wasn't as horrible for me as it was for her, but it still had an effect on me, I can tell you that."

"Was there nothing you could do? Could you not call the police?".

"About a husband beating his wife? In the sixties? Do you have any idea how common that was back then?"

Harry suddenly felt foolish for even opening his mouth.

"It's not like we didn't try to do anything about it." Nettie suddenly sounded defensive, as if Harry's question had actually been an accusation. "I remember my father going round one night and confronting him about it. Mother, my sister, my brother and I, we all stayed hidden behind the living room curtains and watched as dad went round and knocked on their door. He stood and spoke to him on the doorstep for a few minutes, and when he came back, he had this look on his face that I've never seen on anyone's face since. It was like he just spent days staring at the sun and then suddenly someone had just turned all the lights out. It was like his eyes couldn't find anything to latch onto."

"What did Ronnie say to your father?"

Nettie shook her head, her eyes ever fixed on the muted television set.

"I don't know what Ronnie said to my father, but I'll never forget what dad said to me."

What felt like an age passed as Harry waited for the old woman to continue. Tension built in the room as old memories washed over Nettie, turning her skin pale and hunching her forward in her seat. In the end, Harry found he could wait no longer.

"What did he say?"

Nettie's eyes tore away from the TV set, startled, as if she had forgotten Harry was even in the room.

"He said *as God is my witness he's going to kill that girl*. And he was right."

The old woman wiped at the stray tears that broke rank and charted down her face. She marked herself with the sign of the cross. Harry had the sudden urge to do the same.

"That night I lied in my bed and listened to my parents speaking in their own. Dad was warning my mother not to go round there no matter what she heard. Mum told him that if she heard anything else she was going to go and put a stop to it. The next day dad had a plasterer come by and thicken the walls. He was so frightened that we'd all have to hear it when it happened."

"And did you?"

The question was so blunt that it seemed to bring both people crashing back into the room. Harry felt himself flushing red. Asking that question felt like a huge invasion of something private. It was like watching the old woman undress.

"We did."

"And the voice you heard today... the cry for help..."

"Was exactly what we heard the night he threw her down the stairs and then locked the door. It didn't matter how thick dad made the walls, we all heard the argument, and we all heard as she fell down the stairs, and we all heard while she laid at the bottom and called for help and died."

Suddenly, and without warning, Nettie began to heave. Harry leapt to his feet, looking for anything that he might use to catch the wave of vomit he could hear rising in the old woman's throat.

"It's fine" Nettie said, waving with one hand and putting a balled-up tissue to her mouth with the other. "I just haven't thought about this for so long and-"

The old woman heaved again. Harry raced into the kitchen, pulled a dusty looking glass out of a cupboard, filled it with water and then rushed it through to Nettie. By this time, she had regained control of her bodily functions and was using her tissue to dab at her watering eyes.

"Are you alright?"

"I told you I was fine. Like I said I haven't thought about this for such a long time, but hearing that voice today... it brought it all back. It was like hearing it for the first time all over again."

Harry sat himself back onto his chair. He did not dare sink into it as he had before. Instead, he perched on the edge in case he needed to spring forward and help Nettie before she spoiled her pristine carpet.

"You're sure?"

"I'm fine."

"It's just that I have a couple more questions, but I don't want to ask them if it's going to upset you."

Nettie's eyebrows pinched together.

"We're talking about the time I heard my neighbour get murdered. How much more upset do you think I'm going to be?"

The old woman had a point.

"If you heard her fall down the stairs-"

"We heard her get *pushed* down the stairs" corrected Nettie.

"-if you heard her get pushed down the stairs while you

were all in the house, how is it that she died? Could you not call anyone for help? I know you couldn't call the police, but an ambulance could surely have helped."

"We were too afraid to do anything" the old woman said. It was clear from Nettie's expression that Harry simply did not understand the reality of the situation all those years ago. "Dad was frightened of Ronnie. Always had been since the night they spoke on his doorstep. For a while we just sat and tried not to listen to her. We didn't know she was so badly hurt. Like I said, it wasn't rare to hear him hurt her like that. It's just that this time she called for *us*, which she hadn't done before. Eventually we persuaded dad to go and look through the letter box, but by then it was too late. She had... Well, I think you can probably work out what had happened to-"

The old woman heaved again, this time projecting a stream of regurgitated tea and biscuit down her jumper and onto her trousers. Harry jumped to his feet and, unable to think of any real way to help, held Nettie's hand while she gasped for breath against her clenching stomach.

"Oh God" she huffed finally. A rattling cough raked up from her lungs. "I am sorry love. You shouldn't have to see that."

"No, I'm sorry" Harry said, his second-hand embarrassment giving way to a debilitating wave of sympathy for the old woman. "I shouldn't have pushed you for information like that. I didn't mean to make you ill."

Nettie waved her handkerchief at Harry before beginning the impossible task of cleaning herself up with it. Harry helped her up from her chair and followed the old woman to her bathroom, only leaving her side when she had absolutely assured him that she was more than capable of undressing and getting into the shower by herself. Harry did his best not to look relieved by this.

He left Netties home, locking the door behind himself and

posting her key back through the letterbox as he had promised he would. He made his way back to his own home where he immediately pulled his laptop out from its place under the sofa.

He booted the computer up and found his camera feed via his Wi-Fi connection. He loaded the footage from today and began scrolling through the feed, watching himself go about his day at double speed, leaving the house, fixing the wall and then heading out to the shed. Harry rewound the tape and re-watched the three second clip where the front door seemed to swing open of its own accord.

He leaned into the screen, looking for any sign but this could be the result of human interference. This was a rough area. Would it be too farfetched to find that a local kid had indeed been trying to break in, only to be scared off by the camera installed in his hallway?

The door handle in the footage did not budge. The keys hung impotently in the lock, and yet the latch inside the door must have moved in order for it to swing open like it had.

Harry pressed his finger to the trackpad and found the moment he had returned home from the hardware store. He watched himself enter the house with sacks of plaster in his hands, going in and out until he had emptied the contents of his boot into the hallway of his home.

The Harry on the screen kicked the door shut. Not only had he kicked the door, but he had leaned against it after he had set the last of plaster down in his hallway. Harry watched in amazement as the digital version of himself turned around and twisted the front door key in the lock.

It was locked. There was no way that the front door could simply swing open on its own. And yet, as Harry tracked forward several hours, he watched this exact event happen on his computer screen.

Getting up from his place on the living room floor, Harry

walked through his hallway and grabbed his door handle. He pulled it and was unsurprised to find that it would not budge. The door was not faulty. This was clearly more evidence that his house was haunted.

Excitement built as Harry scrolled through the footage, desperate now to find the final piece of proof that he would need to truly send his YouTube channel stratospheric once he could cut together his camera feeds into a convincing enough package.

Harry found the moment that Nettie had walked into his home. He began slowly scrolling backwards through the footage from there. He hammered the volume button on his computer until it was at max. Harry winced at the digital distortion that plagued the sound of the video.

He leaned in and listened to the hiss of the camera feed as the footage played backwards.

Nothing.

And then suddenly everything.

With a shaking hand, Harry pulled the footage back, picked up his laptop and pressed the machine tightly to his ear. In amongst the hiss and the distortion and the whirring of the computer's internal fan, Harry heard a woman's voice as clear as day.

"Help! Please help me!" it called, as if from some great distance away. A minute later, the hunched figure of Nettie walked into Harry's hallway.

COMING HOME

Harry placed a hand onto the small of his wife's back. He guided her carefully across the hospital car park and toward their waiting car. The baby carrier in his arms was far heavier than he let on. He swallowed the grunts and groans that bubbled in his throat as he struggled against the carrier's awkward weight. Inside it, Dylan slept softly, his loose cheeks bouncing along to the motion of his father's footsteps.

Lisa winced loudly. Her pace slowed.

"Everything OK?" Harry asked.

"Stitches" she said through clenched teeth.

"Let's get you home and get your feet up" Harry said.

Lisa hobbled forward, wriggling out from under Harry's supportive hand and instead taking it in her own. She held him in a vice grip. His hand ached, the pain amplified by the bruising Lisa had left across his fingers during her labour.

Harry opened the back door of his car. He fixed the baby carrier onto the back seat. Once he was certain that Dylan was clamped into place, Harry leaned forward and kissed him softly on the head.

"Can you take this from me?" Lisa said. Her overnight bag slipped out from between her tired fingers.

"Yep." Harry took it from her and put it into the boot of his car, then he hurried back round to the passenger side to open Lisa's door.

"I'm not an invalid" she said. "I can get my own door."

"I know you can" Harry said. He took his wife's hand and held her weight as she lowered herself into her seat. A tight whimper of pain sounded as she touched down. Harry leaned forward to kiss her on the head just as he had done with his son. She snapped her head back, moving out of her husband's reach and eyeing him with an overt irritation.

"I'm really sweaty" she said.

"No problem."

Harry got into the driver's seat, turned the mirror to check on his son, and then twisted it into position.

"Ready?"

Lisa's face was tilted down at her phone screen. Instagram tiles floated absently by under her thumb.

"Why wouldn't I be?"

"Then let's go."

Harry pulled out of the car park, finding that driving with his son in the back seat felt oddly like driving across ice. His perception of the road ahead seemed to stretch further than it did before. He anticipated turns earlier than he normally would, and he found himself paranoid of the other cars on the road.

Lisa locked her phone screen and placed it into her handbag

"No more hospital food" Harry smiled. He habitually reached out and squeezed his wife's thigh. She winced under his touch, and he snatched his hand away.

"Sorry love."

"Don't call me that."

"Sorry."

Lisa shifted uncomfortably in her chair.

"Chicken pasta tonight. I've put honey in it, and paprika. It's in the slow cooker. It should be ready whenever you are."

"I'm not hungry."

"Of course you aren't" Harry chuckled, carefully switching lanes so as to avoid a van up ahead that was swerving gently across the road. "It's not even lunchtime yet. Trust me, you'll be thankful I made it come teatime. It smells delicious."

Lisa sighed. She turned away from her husband and looked out of the window. A quiet sob escaped her body. Harry instinctively reached out to place a hand on her thigh but snatched it away again. Instead, he placed it awkwardly onto her shoulder.

"Lisa? What's the matter?"

She turned to face him, and Harry was alarmed to see that her face was now red and puffy, such was the intensity of her depression.

"Jesus" he said. "What is it?"

"You told me that I would never have to take him into that house" she said. "You said that we would be out of there before he was born. Now look at us. Look where we're going. Am I supposed to pretend that this is alright, that everything is fine?"

"What do you mean?" Harry gripped the wheel tightly in his hands, painfully aware that his attention was being diverted away from the road. "What about this isn't alright? We're bringing our son home from the hospital. This should be one of the happiest moments of our lives."

"Exactly, but it isn't because that place is not our home. It never has been, and it was never supposed to be!"

Lisa put her face into her hands and sobbed loudly against her palms. Harry twisted in his seat, stealing a glance at the baby carrier that was clipped into the back seat. Dylan was sleeping soundly, undisturbed by his mother's crying.

"I really wanted to be able to take him home. To our *home. The* real *one. We could go there now. There's nothing stopping us from doing that. I'm on maternity leave and the house renovations can wait, can't they? Let's just turn the car around and go."*

"We can't" Harry said. "The channel-"

"Fuck the channel" Lisa snapped loud enough for Dylan to stir behind them. "This is real life, not some make believe YouTube nonsense. Dylan doesn't even have a bedroom in that house. I want to go home Harry. You promised me that we could."

Harry said nothing. He held the wheel, focusing on the road ahead and continued his journey through Teesside on his way back to number 7 Ragworth Lane.

Lisa cried the rest of the journey home. Her sobbing became hysterical as they pulled into the street adjacent to the one that they lived in.

As they pulled onto their driveway Harry turned to speak to his wife only to realise that she was already trying to step out of the car. He reached for her, but she tore away, groaning in pain as she heaved herself out of her seat.

"Lisa..." She ignored him, then opened the back seat and pulled the carrier out of the car.

"I'll get that."

"I can do it myself."

"Lisa…"

"Harry, can you just leave me be for a little while, please?"

"No, wait. I have a surprise for you!"

Lisa looked at the crumbling walls of her house. "Another surprise? How could you possibly top all this?"

"Please, just listen to me for a moment."

"You never listen to a word I say. Why should I listen to you?"

Lisa slammed the door of the car and set off towards the house. Fresh anger flared up inside of Harry.

"Don't be petty" he said, his patience finally running all the way thin.

He caught up with his wife and pulled the carrier from her hands. He set it down in front of the door, next to a shallow puddle that had formed on their driveway and fumbled the keys into the front door lock.

Lisa followed as Harry stepped into the house. He reached back outside and picked up the carrier. The smell of the slow cooker was sickly in the air.

"I'm going to bed" she said suddenly, kicking off her shoes and taking the first couple of pained steps toward her staircase.

"Will you please just wait? I have something I want to show you."

"I told you I wasn't hungry."

"It's not the food" Harry said. "Let me show you. It's a welcome home gift. For both of you."

Lisa's progress faltered. She looked at her husband with the eyes of a woman finally ground down. Harry smiled regardless.

"Come with me" he said.

Harry waited at the top of the stairs for Lisa to arrive. He shifted excitedly from one foot to the next. Lisa tried to remain dour but Harry's excitement was irritatingly infectious. She hid a potential smile with a stifled yawn.

"This way" Harry said. "Actually, close your eyes."

"Harry, I really don't-"

"Please. I've worked hard on this."

With a reluctant sigh, Lisa shut her eyes. Harry placed the baby carrier by his feet. He took his wife by the hands and led her to the closed door of their spare bedroom.

"Alright" he said, positioning her right in front of the door. "Go on in."

Without fanfare, Lisa opened the door. Shock eradicated any ill feeling that she had been holding onto. She gulped openly at the room before her, not quite believing what she was seeing.

"Do you like it?" Harry asked.

"My... my God."

The room in front of Lisa had been completely transformed. Where before the spare bedroom had been nothing more than a dumping ground for unsorted boxes and Harry's extraneous renovation supplies, now it was a beautiful nursery, complete with everything Lisa would need to raise her young son in this house.

Tears begun to roll down her cheeks as she tried to take in the work that Harry had done.

"It's beautiful" she managed.

The walls of the room had been painted a gentle blue; the shade so light that it was almost white. Despite the rain that had lashed down for the last few days, sunlight was spilling in through the window, illuminating the room and giving it an ethereal glow that made Lisa feel like she was looking onto a dreamscape. In the centre of the room sat a cot, its wooden sides expertly carved to look like the stems of sunflowers. Harry had engraved a smiling face into the head of each flower, and they smiled down contently at the space in which Dylan would lay. On the walls were pictures of rabbits and ducks sitting in neat white frames. A carpet had been laid and as Lisa stepped onto it she marvelled at how plush it felt under her feet, especially when contrasted with the hard wooden flooring of the hallway she had stepped in from.

"This is amazing" Lisa said in a watery voice.

Her eyes traced a row of shelves packed with children's books to a rocking chair that seemed expertly placed in what would be the sunniest part of the room.

"My mother had a rocking chair just like that one" she gasped.

"I know" Harry said. "You told me that she did."

"This is too much" Lisa said, a fresh wave of emotion threatening to push her over the edge. "You shouldn't have done this."

"Oh. Then I probably shouldn't have done this either then, should I?"

Lisa was stunned to find Harry holding a small box in the palm of his hand. She took it gently and prized open the lid.

Inside sat a ring. White gold with a white stone sat clutched in its centre.

"It's an eternity ring" Harry said, recognising the confusion on Lisa's face. "I couldn't really afford a nice engagement ring all those years ago, so this is my way of making up for it."

The floodgates of Lisa's tears finally gave way. She threw her arms around her husband in an attempt to hide how overwhelmed by all this she had become. Her shaking sobs betrayed her intent.

"You like it?" Harry asked.

"I love it" she said. "And I love you."

"And I love you too" Harry said. "I know this isn't what you wanted but-"

"It's better. It's better than anything I had ever wanted. This room is perfect, and my ring. Harry, I don't know what to say."

Harry pulled back and beheld his wife. He wiped the tears from her eyes, and then he brushed the hair from her face. Strangely, Lisa now looked younger, like the woman he had met over a decade ago.

"Just say that you'll forgive me for not having the house finished by now."

Lisa laughed, snot blowing out of her nose.

"I forgive you" she cooed. "A hundred times, I forgive you."

She fell into Harry's arms, and for a while they enjoyed the security of one another's embrace. Eventually, as her beating heart began to slow and the surprise of it all began to subside, logical thought returned to Lisa's brain.

"When did you do all this? How have you managed to keep it a secret?"

Harry reached for the answer. An odd off kilter sensation swept over him. He had no idea of when he had done this. He had no recollection of ever planning this. All he could recall was knowing that this room was done and waiting for them when they returned from the hospital.

He looked past his wife, recognising none of his own handiwork, feeling like he was looking through the door to somebody else's home.

"I have my secrets" Harry said, trying to hide the new sense of dread that had arrived inside of him.

A quiet whimpering signified Dylan's waking moments. Excitedly, Lisa turned and fetched him from his carrier. Harry remained staring at the room which now seemed to shimmer with unfamiliarity. Lisa stepped past him with Dylan in her arms.

"Look" she cooed. "This is your bedroom. Hasn't daddy done well?"

The new-born lay limp in her arms as new-borns are prone to do. Harry watched Lisa as she gave their son the tour of his bedroom, pointing happily at the fittings that he had no recollection of installing.

Harry stepped back and out of the room. The urge to rush in and take his wife and child from this place was almost too much to resist.

CHAPTER 11
108 SUBSCRIBERS

Lisa recoiled. "She threw up? That's disgusting!"

Harry nodded, fighting the urge to correct his wife. Yes, it had been disgusting, but disgust had been the least of what Harry had felt as he had watched the old woman be overcome by her emotions. If Lisa had only seen the terror and the sadness, the desperation to go back and do something - *anything* - to change the outcome for her neighbour, disgust would have been the last thing on Lisa's mind too.

"She was very shaken up."

"Was she alright? Have you checked in on her since?"

"I think she was fine" Harry said. "She made me leave not long after she'd been sick, but she seemed better once it was out of her system. I'll call round tomorrow and double check she's still breathing."

Harry pressed his foot to the brake pedal for what felt like the fiftieth time in their short journey. Lisa pulled her phone from her pocket and began to scroll. They travelled in silence for a while, and Harry was relieved to do so. He had talked nonstop since picking his wife up from the hospital, and while the need to gush had felt uncharacteristic as it had burned in the pit of his stomach, Harry too felt better now it was out of his system.

"Dinner is more or less ready for you when you get home. It just needs heating up. We're having spaghetti. We can call off past the pizza shop for garlic bread if you like. Saves us waiting for some to cook."

The light of Lisa's phone went out. Her eyes bore a hole in her husband.

"What?"

"Tea is ready? *You cooked?*"

"I cooked, I fixed the hole in the wall, I tidied up, I unpacked, I edited three videos, and I helped an old woman who had thrown up all over herself get to the bathroom." Harry flexed his bicep in a classic strongman pose. "I'm a house husband now. This is just what we do!"

Lisa marvelled at the man driving the car with an open mouth expression that wasn't entirely just for show.

"I'm lost for words. Who are you and what have you done with my real husband?"

"Listen, I know that it wasn't the smoothest start to the move, but what you said yesterday really resonated with me. You're keeping this whole thing afloat at the moment. It's only fair that I do my bit to keep everything ticking over too."

An odd sounding laugh escaped from Lisa's throat.

"What?"

She said nothing. Instead, Lisa wriggling out from under her seat belt and kissed Harry on the cheek. When she sat back, she tried to think of when she had last been this happy.

"If I didn't know any better" she said dreamily, "I'd think you were after something."

And there it was. A weight suddenly dropped onto Lisa's shoulders as heavy realisation came crashing down upon her.

"Everything OK?" Harry asked, sensing something was suddenly up.

"Everything's fine... I just... Did you do all of that because of the way I am?"

"The way you are?"

"You know, the thing I told you about this morning?"

"What thing?"

"You know what I'm talking about Harry."

"Do I?"

Lisa folded her arms.

"You're not going to make me say it."

"Why not?" Harry said, his voice taking on an ugly whine. "It's a baby. Not a tumour."

Lisa's jaw tightened. Her husband had been playing a game all along. The warmth of their intimacy dissipated into the darkness of the car, and Lisa folded her arms against the cold pressure that had become a permanent fixture within their relationship since they had first set foot into number 7 Ragworth Lane.

"I really think it's something we need to talk about" said Harry. "It's not going to go anywhere. At least, not without you doing something to *make* it go away."

"We will talk about it, but only when I'm ready. Right now, I'm not."

"When will you be?"

"I don't know" Lisa said.

A quiet settled over the car that was so loud even the innate back and forth of the radio could not fill it. Lisa got the distinct feeling that Harry was sulking, and then prompted by a watery sniffle, she was met with the terrifying thought that he might be about to cry. Thankfully he did not. Instead, he reverted to default conversation, pointless and irritating.

"How was work?"

"Don't do that."

"Do what?"

"Pretend like nothing is happening."

"Well, what am I supposed to do? We can't talk about the baby, we can't talk about you being pregnant, you don't want to talk about the house or the channel. It really doesn't leave us a lot to discuss."

Lisa pulled her phone back out of her pocket and began absently scrolling through nothing in particular.

"Why do we have to talk?" Lisa asked, catching Harry off guard. "Can't we just *be* for a while?"

"You want to sit here in silence? You? After the ranting and raving that you did on the way home yesterday about *whatshername*?"

Lisa caught her temper before it had a chance to flair out of control.

"You know what?" she said. "I do."

*****

The smell of pasta sauce had mingled with the drying plaster and the general mouldy smell that seemed to occupy the house. The aroma that this created was as heavy as it was thick. Lisa and Harry pulled off their shoes and placed them by the front door. The standoff from the car still lingered between them.

"Well?" Harry asked finally. "What do you think?"

A genuine confusion gripped Lisa for a moment before she followed her husband's gaze to the spot in the wall where the hole used to be.

"Oh, wow." She ran her hand across the smooth surface of the new wall. "This is... Incredible."

"Careful. It might not be totally dry yet."

"It looks good. Really good. Professional even."

Harry shrugged, still annoyed at the way Lisa had dismissed his concerns in the car.

Lisa's eyes ran along the wall and into the kitchen.

"The boxes are gone!"

"I told you. I unpacked most of them, and I put the rest in the box room. You might want to move a few bits and pieces around once we get a little more settled but at least we won't be tripping over them in the meantime."

She headed into the kitchen and leaned over the hob. On it sat a pan of minced beef, mushrooms, and sauce. Pasta sat in a deep pan waiting to be boiled.

"And this smells amazing. It's exactly what I need after a day like today."

Harry twisted a dial under the hob and began to heat the pasta.

"Thank you" she said. "For all of this."

"It's OK."

"And... I am sorry. We will talk about it, but not yet. I'm not ready, and I want to make sure that I know what I want before we get into it. It's only fair on both of us."

"On all three of us" Harry said to no response.

Lisa changed out of her work clothes while Harry worked on the dinner. She came downstairs once she was changed and helped him put the finishing touches to their meal. They ate it in the living room, sitting crossed legged on the sofa with their plates propped up on cushions in front of them, watching the TV as it played nothing in particular.

Toward the end of his meal, Harry extended a hand. The urge to place it on Lisa's stomach where his unborn child was growing came suddenly, and he caught it with just enough time to re direct it to one of her knees.

"That to-do list you made really helped me today. I felt more focused. Do you think you could make me another one tomorrow?"

"I can make you another one" Lisa said through a mouthful of pasta. "Fixing that floorboard would be a great place to start. I feel like a lot of the cold is coming from there."

Harry eyed the dark hole in the corner of the room.

"You might be right" he said, although he didn't really believe this. "Anything else? The weekend is just around the corner. If you give me a couple of jobs that are more urgent than others, I might be able to go out and get the supplies I need ready for Saturday."

Lisa thought this over, quietly crunching on overdone garlic bread. She swallowed, started to speak, and then hesitated. Harry stared forwards, watching the television, oblivious of the nerves that jangled within his wife.

"I was sort of hoping we might go home this weekend."

Harry almost choked on his spaghetti.

"Home? We've just got here! There's so much work still to be done!"

"I know" Lisa nodded, her eyes suddenly shining in the shade of the room. "It's just been a really big week and there's been so much change. I really think a little bit of normality might help me get in a better headspace moving forward."

Harry studied his wife, looking for a subtext that she was not yet revealing.

"We're four and a half hours from home. That's nine hours in the car. If we set off after your shift on Friday it's going to be the early hours of the morning by the time we get there. We'll end up sleeping most of Saturday and then driving back on Sunday. It doesn't seem worth it. And then there's the petrol costs. We're easy looking at over eighty pounds."

"Please" Lisa said, her voice aching with vulnerability. "I really want to go back home. Even if it's just for a day. This place, this whole town, it feels so… cold."

"We can put the heating back on. It's probably fine now. I just wanted to wait until the plaster had completely dried."

"That's not what I mean. You know that."

Harry did. The house was shrouded in a freeze that simply did not want to shift. It was one of the reasons that Harry had bought the house in the first place. It was the foundation of the haunting that Harry had come to experience.

He observed the outline of his wife in the gentle light of the television screen. As she sat huddled on the sofa in the gloom of their living room Harry could just about make out the girl he had married all those years ago. He reached out and laid his hand palm upwards. Lisa placed her own freezing hand in his.

"We can go home" he said. She squeezed his fingers. Her face softened in appreciation. "You do know we can't stay there though, don't you?"

"I know" she said. "It's just going to be nice to get away. Even if it is only for a little while."

"You know what? I agree" Harry said, and this time he was surprised to find that he was not lying.

SUMMER

CHAPTER 12
61,376 SUBSCRIBERS

"Harry" Lisa called, leaning out of the kitchen window that looked out onto their back garden. "The burgers are ready."

Harry set down his beer on the shelf attached to the barbeque and headed over. He took the tray of uncooked meat from his wife.

"Excuse me" she said, sounding annoyed.

"Oh. Thank you."

"No" Lisa said, still sounding annoyed. "That's not what I wanted."

"I... these look really good."

Lisa rolled her eyes. She leaned forward as far as her swollen belly would allow and pouted her lips.

Recognising what his wife was hinting at, Harry leaned through the window and kissed Lisa. She jerked backwards and wiped at her mouth.

"Why was that so wet?" she laughed, her face screwing up in mock disgust.

"I had a sip of beer before you beckoned me."

"Ew." Lisa wiped at her face with the back of her sleeve. "Don't you realise that I'm pregnant? Do you have any idea what alcohol could do to the baby?"

"Oh no! He'll be born a dullard!"

"Just like his father."

"You cheeky-"

Before he could finish, Lisa leaned forward and pulled Harry back through the window, placing another kiss squarely onto his lips.

When she released him, Harry took the tray of meats over

to the barbecue and began placing the burgers onto the grill one by one. Fire licked at their undersides, the fat bursting into delicious smoke that teased the taste buds of everyone in the garden.

"She seems to be handling it well" Guy said. "The pregnancy. She seems happy."

"I think it's the good weather" said Harry. "The winter was tough. Plus, we'd just moved here, and she was still settling in at work. It was all maybe a bit too much of a change all at once."

"I don't know mate. Some women take better to it than others. When Jackie was pregnant, she cried every day. With the first one anyway."

Guy watched his wife as she sat chatting happily with some of the other women around Harry's garden table. A boy of about seven sat cuddled into her, his blonde hair buried into her chest.

"With the second one, all she wanted to do was sleep and puke."

"Sounds like fun" Harry said, flipping a burger that was already threatening to turn black.

Guy sipped from his beer bottle and chuckled.

"Great fun. Really made me want to try for the third."

Guy tipped his bottle again. He paused when he noticed the questioning look on Harry's face.

"I'm joking mate. Two is my lot."

"I think we're probably going to be the same. Two kids seems more than enough."

Guy drained his bottle and tossed it into the recycling bin that he had dragged next to the barbeque.

"One is more than enough mate. This is the thing that nobody seems to understand. You see, you have this little biological clock in your head that's been there since birth, and it's been ticking away quietly in the background. Then, one day out of the blue, this little alarm starts to sound that tells you it's time to reproduce. So, you go and you get married and you breed and then the baby is born, and then the little alarm, that stops ringing. Suddenly, all you're left with is a little voice that just asks *what the hell have I done this for?* I used to have time to myself. I used to be able to do what I want. I used to be happy!"

Harry flipped two more burgers and then handed his spatula to Guy.

"Could you take over for a second?"

"Of course. Where are you going?"

"There's a bridge on the other side of town. I was thinking I might go throw myself off it before the baby's born."

Guy punched Harry hard enough in the arm for Harry to suspect that it was going to leave a bruise.

"I'm not joking" Guy said. "Fatherhood is a nightmare."

"I don't believe you."

Guy sniggered.

"How long until the kid arrives?"

"Four months."

"Alright. Give it seven months, enough time for your paternal hormones to wear off and your sleeplessness to really have an effect. You give me a call then and tell me whether you still don't believe me."

"If it's so bad, how come you have two of them?" Harry asked, watching as Guy's youngest son kicked a football into a tiny plastic goal at the end of the garden.

Guy shrugged. He looked over his shoulder to make sure that his wife was not within earshot and then leaned in close to Harry regardless.

"You want to know the worst thing about all of this having kids malarkey?"

"Please" Harry said. "Because you're doing such a good job are selling this to me as it is."

"It's what it does to your sex life…"

Harry began to laugh. "What *does* it do to your sex life?"

"Kills it" Guy laughed, clapping Harry hard on his bruising shoulder.

"Honestly?"

"Honestly. When the kids not awake, you're too tired to do anything, and on the rare occasion when you're not too tired you can guarantee that the kid is going to be awake. Either that or you'll have spent the day up to your elbows in bottle sanitizers and shitty nappies. You try getting intimate with baby shit under your fingernails. It's not easy. I'll tell you that."

Harry sipped from his beer, deciding the burgers could last another minute before they needed flipping again.

"That still doesn't explain how you have two of them though, does it?"

Harry drained his beer, bent down and kicked open the lid of his cooler. He plunged his hand into the icy water and picked out a bottle that had been nestled at the bottom.

"You want another?"

Guy nodded gravely. He took the bottle from Harry and opened it as Harry picked out one of his own.

"Alright, so picture this. You haven't slept with your wife in weeks, months maybe. It starts to feel like years."

"OK."

"Then suddenly the kid is just about old enough for you to get someone to babysit for it. Like, properly babysit. An overnight deal."

"Yeah…"

"So, you decide you're going to make something special of your time together. You go online, you start looking at hotels, you're going to go away for the night."

"I can see where this is going."

"Oh yeah? Well, how about this for a twist? The night rolls around and you're all set to go, and she looks at you with this really guilty expression on her face. Can you still see where this is going?"

"Not anymore."

Guy checked over his shoulder again. Jackie was now clapping along with Nettie as her son performed some sort of routine for them all. The old woman was smiling so widely that her eyes had wrinkled almost completely shut.

"You ask her what's up. She says she's forgotten to take her pill."

Beer spewed from Harry's mouth. The barbeque hissed loudly as the liquid hit the coal and suddenly both men were laughing in that precious hushed laughter that's only possible between two old friends.

"So, you used a condom then, surely?"

"Are you kidding me? I hadn't known the touch of a woman for over three months and you want me to wear a condom? Mate, it's been a nightmare, but it was absolutely worth it. Best sex of my life. Even if it only did last fifty seconds!"

The two friends broke into a fit of laughter that was so loud it drew disapproving looks from every woman sat around the garden table.

Harry pressed a burger with the back of his spatula and watched the juices run from it. They burst into flame as they hit the coals underneath the grill.

"It must be worth it though, right?" he asked. His insecure tone sounded alien in contrast to their recent jovialities.

Guy was barely paying attention. Instead he was watching his children playing. The younger of the two was throwing his football into the air and unsuccessfully trying to catch it. The oldest one was once again sat on his mother's knee, playing contently with an action figure he had brought with him.

"On a day like this? Absolutely." Guy said.

The women's conversation suddenly flared in volume as a

new couple walked through back doors and out into the garden. Lisa stood with them, her arm on the back of a tall looking man with a thick beard. She waved off the woman who went to her place at table and guided the man over to Harry and Guy, the only two males at the barbeque save for the children.

"This is my husband Harry" she said, "and this is his friend Guy. These two used to work together."

The bearded man nodded in acknowledgment.

"Boys, this is Andrew. Andrew is married to Ruth who I work with. I'll introduce you to her later."

"Hi Andrew" Harry said extending his hand. Andrew took it in his own and squeezed a little too tightly for what the occasion called for.

"Now then" Guy said. Harry watched him recoil as Andrew crushed his friend's hand in turn.

"What's on the menu?" Andrew asked.

"Burgers" Harry said. "Lisa's put them together from scratch."

"Oh" Andrew said. He leaned over and inspected the grill. "And what's the veggie option?"

Harry's mouth opened but he made no sound. A smirk broke out across Andrew's face.

"I'm only kidding you mate. I'm not a lefty. I wouldn't be caught dead eating any of that shite."

All three men broke into a cautious laughter as the ice of their introduction began to thaw.

"Beer?" Guy asked, already opening the cooler.

"That would be great. *She's* got me on this diet that means I can't really drink but I've already had a word with her and warned her that I'm going to get completely bladdered today."

"Feel free" Harry said flipping each of the burgers over in quick succession. "I think these are about done, don't you?"

Both Guy and Andrew leaned forward. Andrew pressed his

thumb deep into the middle of one of the burgers, wincing only slightly as the boiling fat caught on his skin.

"They need a couple more minutes" he said. "Is this the first time you've barbecued?"

"You mean at this house?"

"No" Andrew said, "I mean is this the first time you've *barbecued?*"

Harry looked to Guy for some reassurance but found only a puzzled expression.

"No... Am I doing it wrong?"

Andrew opened his beer and sipped from the neck of the bottle. He lowered his eyebrows and shook his head dismissively.

"You're not doing badly at all. Are they beef?"

Harry suddenly got the feeling he was being backed into a corner. "They are" he said.

"You'd have been fine then" Andrew said. "Beef is more forgiving than say... pork. If they were pork you would need to give them a lot more time."

"What difference would it have made?" Harry laughed thinly in an attempt to lighten the quickly darkening mood around the grill.

"Well, if they'd been pork they would have been undercooked and you'd have poisoned everyone. Gastroenteritis is really nasty you know."

"Yeah, I'll bet it is. But they're not pork."

"But if they had been, they would have been undercooked. That's all was trying to say mate."

"But they're *not* pork. They're beef. Guy, pass me my beer, would you?"

Guy passed a half empty bottle to Harry who quickly drained it in one.

"Do you think they'll be ready now?" Harry asked.

Andrew threw his hands up defensively. "Hey" he said.

"It's your barbeque."

"Great. Get them off the grill would you Guy? I'll go and collect some buns."

Harry was oddly relieved to walk out of the glorious sunshine and into the gloom of his home. He made his way through the living room which had become a dumping ground for people's shoes and passed into the kitchen where Lisa stood preparing salad.

"Are you still in here? Your friends are all out there. Why don't you go and enjoy yourself?"

"They're just people I work with. I wouldn't say any of them are friends" she said, chopping tomatoes.

"They seem to like you enough."

"I suppose they do. It's nice to have people round that I get on with."

"Which is exactly why you should be out there. Let me worry about the side salads" Harry said.

"It'll give me a chance to get away from that idiot for a moment anyway."

"Guy?"

"Obviously not Guy" Harry said. "That idiot who came with whatshername. Andrew."

Lisa suddenly stopped chopping.

"You be nice to him" she warned. "Ruth is the head of HR. She's already slumming it coming to this part of town anyway. I don't want her to go home to find that my husband has been rude to hers."

Laughter bubbled at the back of Harry's throat.

"You're worried about *me* being rude to *him*? He's already tried to accuse me of trying to poison everyone with my cooking."

Lisa continued to work on the salad. The gentle chopping of her knife seemed somehow a little faster than it had been before.

"I'm sure he didn't mean it like that, whatever he said."

"You weren't there."

"What do you want Harry?"

"The burgers are ready" Harry said. "I need the buns."

Lisa opened a cupboard above her head and took out a stack of buns still in their plastic wrapper. Harry took them from her, sensing that his wife was happy to see him leave her kitchen.

As Harry entered into his hallway, he found Nettie with her hand on the front door handle.

"Oh" Harry said, surprised. "Leaving so soon?"

"I... no love. I need to use the toilet."

Harry smiled uncertainly at how the old woman's face was suddenly turning a deep shade of red.

"You know we have a working bathroom upstairs, don't you? This place might not look like much but all the essentials work."

"I know they do love" Nettie said, her face growing redder by the second. "It's not that. I just..."

"You don't want to go up there alone…"

The old woman nodded sheepishly.

"I'll see you in a few minutes" he said warmly. The old woman left, her face slowly turning back to it's natural colour.

When he arrived at the barbeque, Harry slid the burgers into the buns and then carried them over to the garden table. The women broke out in appreciative applause. Harry bowed theatrically and then headed back to the barbeque to begin cooking the sausages that Lisa had dropped off on her way back outside.

"What sort of graphic design?" Andrew was asking Guy with a distinct lack of genuine interest.

"Whatever our clients need really. We've worked with everyone from PlayStation to tiny little indie businesses that need a bit of extra sparkle on their social media output. In an industry like ours you can't be too picky about who you work with. You take the jobs that you can get."

Andrew nodded thoughtfully.

"So, it can't be that lucrative then?"

This time it was Guy's turn to fix Harry with a disbelieving look.

"Well, I wouldn't say that. I'm pretty high up in the company so the money is pretty good. Don't get me wrong, I didn't come here by private jet, but I do alright. Ask Harry. He used to work with us. In fact, I took his old job after he left."

"It's true" Harry said. Strangely, he felt the need to persuade Andrew that Guy was not lying. "Working that job allowed Lisa and I to buy this place and keep our place back home at the same time."

Andrew craned his neck to look at the crumbling exterior of Harry's home.

"Yeah, but how much could a place like this cost?"

Harry was dumb struck.

"Could you and your wife afford to have a home in the south and buy one of these houses too?"

Andrew looked back toward the house.

"It depends how much a house like this one cost."

"I'm not going to tell you how much my house cost" Harry said.

"OK" said Andrew, seemingly nonplussed. "I'll just find out online."

Harry considered asking Andrew not to do this. He thought of explaining that to do so would be to massively overstep a social boundary with a man that Andrew had only just met. In the end however, Harry decided it would be simpler to ask Lisa never to invite this man to his home again.

"It's just a place for us to learn our new trade I suppose."

"New trade?" Andrew asked from under raised eyebrows

"Flipping houses. Lisa and I aren't planning on living here, we bought it so that we could do it up, renovate it and sell it on."

Andrew considered this for a moment, his eyes searching Harry's face. "It didn't look like much renovation had happened when I walked through it."

"You cheeky-"

"You should have seen the place when he bought it" Guy said, swooping into the conversation before Harry could end it once and for all with a selection of choice four letter words. "It was barely standing then, was it, Harry?"

"No" Harry muttered. The heat that rose from under his collar now outperformed the heat from the barbeque.

"Well, it's tough, doing up houses" Andrew offered. "A lot of people try it and a lot of people fail. In fact, a lot of them do such a bad job of it that they end up selling their own houses to help float the ones they were intending to rent. It's a bit of a mugs game really when you think about it."

"We're doing alright" said Harry. "We're under budget and pretty much on schedule. In a couple of months we should be all done."

"A couple of months? Are you doing it alone or have you got someone to help you with it?"

"I get people in here and there when I need them but most of the time it's just me."

Andrew drained his beer and then opened the cooler to take out another. He did not bother to offer one to either Harry or Guy.

"Take it from me. If you are not done within a year, you never will be. That's when you need to cut your losses and get out of here. It'll just become a money pit after that."

"Have you flipped houses before?" Harry asked.

"No" Andrew said.

Guy bent down and took out another much-needed beer and handed it to Harry. The three men stood and watched the sausages cooking, Harry turning them intermittently and Andrew supervising closely as he did. By the time anyone spoke again, all three of their bottles were empty.

"The renovation isn't the only reason Harry bought the house though" Guy said.

"Guy..."

"Why else would you buy a place like this?" asked Andrew.

"Guy. Come on."

"Harry has a YouTube Channel too. It's all about the house."

"A YouTube channel?" scoffed Andrew. "How old are you?"

"A lot of people my age have YouTube channels" said Harry, lamenting the fact that he was being pulled into an argument he wanted no part of.

"No they don't. Name one."

"Dean King" Harry said.

"Who's Dean King?"

"He runs *King of the Haunt*. It's a pretty massive channel. Have you seriously never heard of it?"

Andrew shook his head. Harry was not surprised.

"What's it about?"

"Guy just told you. It's about the house."

"But what about the house?" A broad grin was beginning to cross Andrews face.

"It's about fixing it up."

"It is not" Guy said. Harry snapped his head in his friend's direction, his fury rising as he found Guy to be wearing an almost identical grin across his own lips. "Tell him what it's really about. Don't be shy."

All eyes were suddenly on Harry. He rotated the sausages again, doing his best not to look as betrayed as Guy had made him feel. The pressure to answer built to an unbearable level.

"It's about ghosts" said Harry. "The house is haunted."

Harry was horrified when both men fell about laughing. The icy impasse that Andrew had built around himself was now thawing in Guy's direction as they shared in Harry's perceived naivety.

"No it isn't" Andrew said.

"Oh, sorry Andrew. I hadn't realised that you had conducted your own investigation on the walk from the front door to the back garden. I'm glad that you managed to come to such a quick conclusion though. Sterling work."

Both men continued to laugh.

"But it can't be haunted. Ghosts aren't real."

The beer that sloshed in Harry's empty stomach was quickly shortening his temper.

"Again, I hadn't realised that you were a parapsychologist. You really should have told me that ghosts weren't real before you got here and saved me the effort of buying the house in the first place, you fucking clown."

Andrew's laughter abruptly stopped.

"Alright mate, I was only winding you up."

"Yeah, well it worked didn't it? This is really serious stuff. I've put a lot of effort into that Channel, so for you to come in here and start slagging it off without even seeing it seems a bit of a shitty thing to do."

Harry turned the sausages one last time.

"Do these look good?" he asked Guy quietly.

"I don't know."

"They look done to me" Andrew said.

"Thanks Jamie Oliver."

Harry picked the sausages off the grill with his bare hands and placed them onto a plate. He carried the plate to the table and put them down in the centre to further applause. This time Harry did not bow.

"You'll have to get your own buns from the kitchen" Harry said.

"Are you OK? Lisa asked, sensing her husband's unhappiness.

"Fine" he said, before heading back to the barbeque where the cooler housed his next beer.

"I'm sorry if I offended you" Andrew said as Harry arrived. "I didn't mean to upset you. It's the beer. It makes me hostile. This is why I don't drink it as much these days."

"Don't worry about it" Harry said. He picked another three beers out of the cooler and handed one to Guy, one to Andrew and kept the third for himself.

"So, how long have you had the channel?"

"You don't need to feign interest on my behalf" Harry said. Weirdly, Andrew looked hurt enough for Harry to consider that he was now genuinely interested in his work.

"Since January" Harry said.

"So... six months? Is it doing alright?"

"Sixty thousand subscribers. I'm closing in on a million views."

Andrew's beer caught in his throat. Harry was quietly satisfied when he choked and coughed by way of response.

"Bloody hell mate" Andrew sputtered. "I didn't realise that you were getting those sorts of numbers. Fair play to you!"

"He's not as stupid as he looks you know" Guy said. "Harry usually makes a success of the things he turns his hand to."

"Let's hope you can make the house work for you after all then" Andrew said. Recognising the annoyance on Harry's face he quickly added "I'm kidding. It's a joke. How many videos have you uploaded?"

"I'm not really sure. I put out one a week. I run an Instagram and a Twitter account alongside it, and I post on those every two days."

"Now you can see why the renovation is taking so long" Guy said. Neither Harry not Andrew laughed at this.

"What sort of things do you post?"

Despite the influx of questions Harry still found it hard to believe that they were anything other than a different form of antagonization from Andrew.

"Updates about the house. Whatever happened that week. I cover some stuff that's happened off camera too. YouTube shorts were made for that sort of thing. The main channel is where the money is though."

"You must be making a decent cop with those sorts of numbers then, are you?"

"I do alright. It's not quite as much as my wage was when I was working with Guy but-"

An explosion of sound cut Harry off mid-sentence. All three men leapt back from the barque that was pushed up against the fence as the dog next door began to bark furiously from the other side. In the commotion, Guy's beer bottle slipped from his hand and shattered onto the decking at his feet.

"Fucking thing" Harry raged at the top of his voice.

The women at the table gasped loudly at Harry's profanity, but he did not hear it, so loud was the animal's onslaught.

"Jesus Christ" Guy cursed. "I nearly leapt out of my skin."

Thick ropes of saliva flowed through the slats in the fence. Harry approached cautiously and glared at the dog through his fence. Its eyes were wide and darting as if it was somehow trying to work out a way to get through the fence.

"Simba" he yelled. "That's enough."

The dog took no heed. It continued to bark, forcing its face tightly between the fence slats. Harry kicked at it. This time he did hear the gasp from the women's table which was closely followed by the stomping of Lisa's feet.

"What are you doing?" Lisa yelled over the barking of the dog.

A garden full of outraged expressions trained directly on

Harry. Suddenly, he felt the veil of his anger lifting, revealing the true mean-spirited nature of his actions. The venom in his veins however still refused to dissipate.

"That bloody thing nearly made me fall into the barbeque."

"It's just a dog" Lisa said. "It's just a stupid dog."

"I…"

The dog continued to bray against the fence with enough force for the whole thing to rattle. It forced its face up against the fence again, its wet nose pushing through the gaps in the wood.

Without stopping to think, Harry kicked at the animal again. He caught it hard on its nose. A pained squeal simmered from the dog.

"What are you doing!?" Lisa yelled. She grabbed her husband and pulled him away from the fence. Beer sloshed down Harry's front as the motion of Lisa's grasp nearly pulled him off his feet. "We have a garden full of guests! How many of those have you had?"

"It's nothing to do with the beer" Harry said. His voice carried the wine of a child caught out by its mother.

Lisa took the beer bottle from Harry's hand.

"I think you should go inside for a while. I'll deal with the barbeque."

"I think you should give me my beer back."

Without breaking her husband's gaze, Lisa held the bottle of beer up and turned it upside down. Cold liquid ran down onto the decking, splashing up Harry shins and coating his sandals.

"Why don't we go inside and you can show us that YouTube channel you were telling us about? I'm sure Andrew would love to see what you've done."

Ignoring Guy's words, Harry calmly bent down, opened the cooler and took out another beer. He offered one to both Guy and Andrew who awkwardly turned him down and then he made his way past the embarrassed women sitting around his garden table and went into his living room. As he shut the back door behind him, Harry's anger found a new boiling point.

"That fucking dog" he spat, his words wrapped in a significant slur. "It never stops. It does that all day long."

"You should poison it" Andrew said.

"You know what? That's not a bad idea."

"Yes, it is" Guy said.

"Antifreeze in a sausage would do the trick. Or better yet you could get hold of some rat poison."

"There used to be a shed in that back garden that was full of rats" Harry said. "If the dog somehow found some of the poison that I'd left lying around, that surely wouldn't get back to me."

"Of course it would" Guy said. "What you're talking about is incredibly illegal."

A drunken smile was now spreading across Andrew's face. "There'd be no way to trace it back to you. If the dog died, I doubt the police would even bother doing a toxicology test on-"

"Can we stop discussing how to murder the neighbour's dog?" Guy suddenly looked furious.

"I'm only joking" Harry said, forcing a laugh which sounded oddly similar to the kind a cartoon vampire might utter right before it sank its teeth into someone's neck.

"It's not a funny thing to joke about. I'm being serious. If you did do it and you got found out, you'd go to jail Harry."

The seriousness of Guy's words threatened the delicate courtesy that they had achieved in the back garden. Guy shifted uncomfortably as he searched for a way to push the conversation forward.

"So" he said finally. "Are we going to see this YouTube channel or not?"

"Yeah, good idea." Harry pulled his phone from his pocket. The idea of poisoning the animal next door still played through his mind. He ushered the two men through to the living room and followed closely behind.

Guy and Andrew sat down on the plush sofa by the window. The room was bright and clean, a stark contrast to the state Harry had found it in. The hole in the floor had been fixed over a stressful couple of days in the depths of winter, and since that time a plush grey carpeting had been laid. The walls had been skimmed and then painted a happy shade of white. *A blank canvas*, that's what Lisa had called it as she had stated with absolute confidence that white paint not only made rooms look bigger, but that they also conjure positive vibes from people entering the room.

Modern light fixtures had been fitted into the ceiling which had also been freshly plastered and painted. The room sat like an oasis of modernity in the still crumbling desert of the rest of the house.

"Wow" Andrew said, his eyes darting around the room. "You have at least started renovations then."

"There's far more happening in this house than could be seen with the naked eye" Harry said. "A lot of stuff behind the walls and under the floors had to be done before I could do any cosmetic stuff. We got this room done first because we needed somewhere comfortable to spend our time."

"It looks great" Guy said.

"It should do" said Harry. "It cost a fortune."

Harry switched on the TV that had been fixed to the wall over the newly renovated fireplace and he cast his phone to the device. The YouTube app sprung to life on the screen.

"Who the hell is *King of the Haunt?*" Andrew's tone was mocking. Harry felt oddly embarrassed by the zany thumbnails that Dean King insisted on applying over his YouTube videos.

"I told you about him in the garden. He's another

paranormal investigator. There's quite a few of us on YouTube."

"*Investigator?*" Again, there was mockery in Andrew's tone.

Harry navigated to the search bar and began to type.

"Our Haunted Home? Is that you in the thumbnails?"

"Yeah" Harry said.

"It looks nothing like you. Why are you pulling those stupid faces?"

"I was trying to look scared. You have to provide some sort of hook to pull people in to watch the videos. Unsubscribed viewers decide in less than a second whether to watch your video based entirely on your thumbnail. I have to play the game."

Andrew chuckled. "If you say so."

"Which one would you recommend that we watch?" Guy asked, sensing another confrontation bubbling just below the surface of Andrew and Harry's conversation.

"Take your pick. What sort of thing do you want to see?"

"I want to see a ghost" said Andrew.

"I haven't got any with actual ghosts on camera."

"Really? There's enough cameras stuck up around the place. I would have thought that if this place was really haunted you would have caught something by now."

"What about that one?" Guy asked quickly.

"That one's just about when the water pipe burst."

Andrews quiet chuckling escalated into full condescending laughter.

"There's some decent stuff in this one." Harry said through gritted teeth.

Harry loaded up a video called *Ghost Voice Caught On Camera*. Andrew's breath caught in his nose.

"I thought you said you hadn't filmed any ghosts yet."

"You don't actually see the apparition. You hear it, or you will do if you can be quiet for long enough."

The video opened onto Harry's title sequence. Shots of the house under a grey filter crossfaded on the screen to the sound of an ominous drone. An exterior of the house took over the screen. Smoke faded up from the bottom of the frame and eventually culminated into the words *Our Haunted Home*.

"Slick" said Guy, dusting off a phrase the pair of them had used frequently in their graphic design days.

"Cheers. I paid a guy online to make that for me. I can shoot well enough, but video effects are a totally different animal for me. I suppose I could have used A.I. to generate one but that seems a little-"

"When do we hear it?" Andrew asked impatiently. Harry sighed.

"There's an intro first. YouTube pays out different amounts of money based on your viewing hours. It doesn't make sense to just upload the sound bite and leave it at that. If I can get people to watch the video to the end I make far more ad revenue."

"So, you pack it full of filler?"

"It's not filler" Harry said. "It's an introduction to what happened. There are updates on other videos in there too. Nobody cuts straight to the action. Without context it won't make any sense."

Andrew groaned. "Can we skip to the ghost voice?"

Harry wondered whether Andrew was now intentionally trying to get under his skin. Given that his eyes were still fixed on the TV and that there wasn't even the hint of a smile on his face, he reasoned that he was probably just incredibly impatient.

"Did you not hear what I just said? Without context it won't make any sense."

"Just tell me what the context is then."

"Are you serious? I'm literally on the screen explaining it now if you'll just watch."

Begrudgingly, Andrew watched the on-screen version of Harry explain some of the developments on a previous video, replaying clips and going over them with a deeper level of analysis.

"I can't follow this. Can't you just tell me?"

"Are you five years old?"

"I just want to hear the voice."

Harry snatched up his phone and found the section of the video that had been most replayed by the thirty-eight thousand people that had watched it. His thumb held the slider in place while he tried to properly prepare Andrew for what he was about to hear.

"What you need to remember is that there was nobody else in the house. In fact, you see me leave through the door camera. Then if you listen really carefully you can hear a voice that-"

"Can't you just play it?"

"-you can hear a voice that seems to say something. I can't quite make out what it is, but it sounds like it's either wait, or afraid. There's a lot of debate in the comment sections. That's actually how I generate a lot of my traffic, through people tagging each other in to see what their friends think."

Andrew said nothing, now electing to be so polite that he looped all the way around to becoming rude once again.

With huge reluctance, Harry let go of the slider. The TV screen came to life. On it, a grainy version of Harry walked through his hallway, put on his shoes and sat on the bottom step, and then left through the front door. The abrasive sound of the lock twisting in the door frame was heard before a quiet hiss seemed to pass in front of the camera.

"There!" Harry said simultaneously with his onscreen doppelganger. "Did you hear that?"

"Hear what?"

"Don't tell me you didn't hear it. It's going to play again in a second. Just listen carefully."

The on screen version of Harry appeared again with a solemn expression on his face. The drone in the background intensified as he stared directly into the camera and then uttered the words "Did you catch that?"

"That's actually become a bit of a catch phrase of mine now" Harry said.

The grainy footage replayed on the screen. The words *Volume Plus 100* appeared in an archaic looking font.

Again, Harry left through the front door. The lock clicked and then the hiss floated across the sound of the speakers once again.

"There."

"I don't hear anything."

As if responding to Andrew's doubt, the video replayed, this time with the words *Volume Plus 200* displayed in the bottom corner. The hiss this time took on a more human tone. Although it wasn't entirely clear what was being said, there were definite vowels and consonant sounds being arranged into some sort of intelligent order.

A subtitle popped up under the hiss. *Wait / Afraid.*

"I didn't hear anything."

"You did. You heard *something*." Harry felt his patience finally give way to a deluge of frustration. "Whether you thought that it was words or not is neither here nor there, but you heard something."

"I genuinely didn't."

"Bloody hell! You did. Guy, tell me you heard something."

Guy smiled uncomfortably.

"I'm not sure it was a voice, but I heard something on the tape."

"See."

Andrew shook his head.

"He might have done, but I didn't."

Without even realising that he had moved, Harry found himself on his feet and pointing an accusatory finger into Andrew's face.

"Then you need your ears testing mate because there's a voice there as clear as day."

"I'm sorry" Andrew said. "I just don't hear it."

"Listen!"

Harry dragged his finger across his phone and replayed the clip again. When it had played out, he replayed it again, and again, and then again.

"Do you mean that sound just after the door locks?"

"Yes!"

"Oh! I didn't realise that was what I was supposed to be hearing. Yeah... that's just wind noise."

"Wind?" Harry laughed in disbelief, completely exasperated by this point. "It's an indoor camera! How could it be wind?"

"It could be a draft from when you opened the door."

"But it was closed when the sound happened."

"Yeah" Guy said. "I'm not sure that's wind sound to be honest with you."

Andrew thought this over for a moment. Harry's heart pounded loudly in his chest. His blood made whooshing sounds in his ears. The way this man had not even had the decency to meet Harry at this emotional peak was infuriating.

Andrew rubbed his hand over his mouth.

"No" he said in his abrasive northern accent. "I'm not having that. What other videos have you made?"

"You'll have to find them for yourself when you get home" Harry said. "Why don't you head off there now? I'm not going to sit here and defend each of my videos to a man who is quite obviously a moron."

"I'm a moron?" Andrew shouted, standing up from his place on the sofa and instantly looming over Harry. "You're the one that bought a house because you thought there was a ghost in it! I mean, you're what? Forty years old? With a baby on the way? Isn't it time you started making better choices for you and your wife? Grow up."

"Get out of my fucking house!" Harry screamed. When Andrew did not move, Harry instead stormed out of the room.

Venturing into the garden, Lisa could already see the rage etched across her husband's drunken face.

"Now what?" she asked as he stormed past the table of women.

Music drifted over the fence from next door. Simba began to bark the instant Harry approach the beer cooler.

"Hey!" he shouted at the top of his lungs.

"Simba…" came the blonde woman's voice from next door. "Calm down darling."

Harry gripped the top of his fence, braced his foot against the wood and hoisted himself up enough to glare at the woman. She was sprawled on a garden chair, half dozing in the sun.

"Hey!" Harry shouted again. The woman sat up in shock, covering over her bikini top behind her folded arms.

"What the hell are you doing?"

"Keep your fucking dog under control would you?" Harry raged. "It's done nothing but bark all day! We've got guests over you know."

Suddenly Lisa was tugging at Harry's shirt, trying unsuccessfully to get him down from the fence.

"If you don't keep that thing under control from now on, you are going to be sorry. You can trust me on that one."

"Are you threatening me?" the blonde woman snapped.

"Get down" Lisa growled. Harry gripped the fence tightly, refusing to back down until his rage had been spent.

"No, I'm threatening that thing" Harry said, pointing at the dog that was now leaping up towards him.

"Leave me alone or I'll call the police" she said.

"And whose side do you think they'll take? Mine, or the scumbag who chooses to live in a shithole like this full time?"

"Harry! Get down! Right now!"

With an almighty effort, Lisa dislodged her husband from the fence. He fell backwards, spilling out into the decking and knocking over the beer cooler and the barbecue in the process. The women at the table screamed as hot coals spread across the wood only to be instantly extinguished by the spreading ice water from the cooler. Despite the enraged barking of the dog, the garden felt silent.

Harry rolled in the water and then got to his feet. Guy's wife was stood shielding her children under each arm, her hands draped over each of their ears.

From the house, Guy watched on with a look of utter confusion on his face. Andrew was smiling smugly at the scene.

"What are you smirking at, you smug cunt?"

"That is enough!" Lisa screamed. "Get into that house and get yourself cleaned up! Don't you dare come back into this garden until everybody has left!"

Harry was planted to the ground, stunned by the fury in Lisa's voice.

"I am so sorry everyone" Lisa said.

"Don't you apologise for me" Harry slurred. Lisa did not even acknowledge that he had spoken.

With growing embarrassment, Harry collected up one of the few beer bottles that had not smashed when he had knocked over the cooler and then began his short walk of shame back into his crumbling house.

THE HOUSE

Harry opened his eyes into stifling darkness. The temperature in the room was so high that for a moment, he felt like he was choking. The light bed sheets that Harry and Lisa had draped over their bed in place of their usual thick duvet had twisted around his limbs as he had slept, adding to the feeling of suffocation that Harry felt.

He kicked wildly at the sheets wrapped around his legs and then rolled onto his side, laying his arm across a naked and sweating Lisa.

She grunted, annoyed, and then in the darkness of the room she muttered "It's your turn."

"My turn to what?" he said to the back of his wife's head.

A scream tore him out of his half sleeping state. Harry sat up, his eyes widening against the gloom of his surroundings.

"Did you hear that?"

Lisa moaned and twisted in place, rolling over onto her side to face Harry. She reached out and shoved him.

"It's your turn" she hissed. "Go and see to Dylan."

The scream rang out again from the end of the hallway. Now Harry recognised it for what it was. The hungry cries of his infant son.

He ran the back of a hand across his sopping forehead. Harry thought of his son, dressed in a thick nappy and a tight baby grow and realised that across the hallway his child was very likely in an extreme state of discomfort.

The thought drove Harry to his feet. As he walked around the bed, Harry pulled up the curtain. The sky beyond the window was relinquishing its inky blackness in favour of a deep shade of royal blue. A new day was breaking. With a sinking heart Harry realised that it would be too hot to get Dylan back off to sleep now, and so despite the fact that Harry seemed to be suffering a hangover without having touched so much as a single drop of alcohol the night before, he would need to pull himself round and get ready for the day.

He crept quickly across the landing and pushed against Dylan's bedroom door.

The room glowed a serene shade of green from the baby's night light. Harry dropped to his hands and knees and quietly crawled up to the side of his son's cot.

Inside, the sound of Dylan's cries rang loud and true.

Summoning every ounce of his resolve, Harry forced a cartoon smile onto his face, got ready to spring over the lip of the cot and said. "I think somebody might be-"

Harry leapt to his feet.

"Awake!"

Harry stood and stared.

"Dylan?"

Dylan's voice wailed from the centre of the cot but despite how many times Harry rubbed his eyes in sheer disbelief, he could not see his son.

"DYLAN!?"

Harry tore past the cot and snatched at the curtains, whipping them open and letting early morning twilight mingle with the green of the room. It was still not enough. He still could not see his son.

Harry sprinted to the door and batted at the light switch. Now, hard white light flooded the space with enough ferocity to double the pain from Harry's phantom hangover. He hurried back to the cot where Dylan's voice continued to wail.

It was empty. Dylan wasn't there.

Harry reached in and snatched at the baby blanket, ripping it off the tiny mattress and hurling it over his shoulder. He lifted the pillow and in a moment of sheer surreal panic he squeezed it, hoping to find a warm hard lump at its centre. Dylan was not in it. He was nowhere to be seen.

"Lisa!?" Harry called; his voice infected with the absolute panic. "Lisa! Get in here!"

The pitch of Dylan's crying escalated. He sounded more frightened now, or worse than that, he sounded to be in an increasing level of pain.

Thunderous footsteps shuddered across the hallway. Harry could hear Lisa already complaining about being woken up despite the pounding of his heartbeat in his ears.

"Honestly, can I not get one morning when I get to sleep in at least until the sun has fully come up?"

She stopped in the doorway when she saw the look on her husband's face.

"What is it?"

Harry found that he could say nothing. Instead he pointed to the cot.

Lisa rushed to his side and peered into the crib. The crying continued as clearly as if Dylan was lying in the middle of the mattress.

"Where is he?" she asked, grabbing the tiny sheet that shrouded his mattress.

"I don't know."

"Where is-"

"I DON'T KNOW!"

Lisa pulled the sheet to expose the naked mattress and then, upon seeing that Dylan was not there, she dropped to the floor and looked under the cot.

"He's not here!" she cried. "My baby's not here!"

"This doesn't make any sense!"

Harry reached in an felt the mattress. To his surprise a hard lump shifted within it.

"Lisa?"

Dylan's cries suddenly changed. Where before they were clear and unobstructed, now they were muffled and tight. They were coming from inside the mattress.

"He's in there!" Harry screamed. "My God, he'll suffocate. Dylan is in there!"

"Get him out" Lisa shrieked.

Harry grabbed the mattress, tearing at one of the seams of its fabric and pulling tightly with both hands. The material held. Dylan's crying began to waver.

"Get some scissors or a knife, or a fork! Something! Anything!"

Lisa bolted from the room. Harry pulled at the material of the mattress again, pressing his thumbs together over a seam and then pulling them apart. His fingernails groaned with the pressure and threatened to lift out of their nailbeds, but Harry did not even feel this. All he could focus on now was getting his son out of the mattress before he suffocated on his own cries.

The fabric split just enough to reveal the bottom half of Dylan's face. His blue lips parted and inhaled a thick whoosh of air before he let out another deafening cry. Harry leaned in, his ribs bending against the lip of the cot. He tried to pry his fingers into the gap between Dylan's skin and the fabric wrap of the mattress but found his son was compacted so tightly into his bed that there was no room for him to do so.

Harry leaned further in. Unable to quite get the purchase he needed to begin tearing elsewhere, his ribs began to creak against the hardwood of the cot. The lip of the crib ground against his chest, crippling his ability to breathe.

In a last-ditch effort to gain more purchase, Harry lifted one of his legs and heaved himself over the cot. He leaned deeper and deeper until-

Suddenly Harry was falling. His arms stretched out in front of him, desperately reaching for the cot that had disappeared before his very eyes. The darkness of his stairway unfolded before him.

Harry's body collided with a step midway down the stairs and then bounced into the air again. He twisted in mid-air and then came crashing down onto the exposed floorboard of his hallway.

An odd sensation, like the bursting of bubble wrap, ran

across his lower leg. When his body came to rest, a pain - the likes of which he had never considered could even have been possible - exploded throughout his body.

Harry screamed loud and unashamedly. He was laid face down at the bottom of the stairs, his nose pressed hard into the musty smelling floorboards. He rolled himself onto his back, his vision glowing white despite the darkness of the hallway, and he gripped his leg just above the knee. A crunching sensation sent a new wave of pain throughout the entirety of Harry's being.

"Oh my God!"

Lisa's steps thundered down the stairs, but Harry barely heard them, such was the volume of his agonised screams.

"Harry, what the hell happened?"

Harry tried to tell her how he had fallen down the stairs, but a scream from the pit of his stomach interrupted his words. It ejected from him with such force that he feared his throat might tear.

"Where does it hurt?" Lisa was saying. Her voice echoed as if it was coming from the far end of a tunnel.

Harry pointed to his lower leg. Tears began to roll down his face as his agony somehow intensified. It possessed every inch of him, throbbing with inaudible volume throughout his body. He hurt so badly that he could see the hurt glowing across his vision.

"Your leg?"

Harry nodded, sobbing loudly between the screams that hijacked his throat.

The dog next door began to bark and the woman beyond the wall began to shout.

"I'm going to need to take a look at it" Lisa said.

Harry's hands remained clamped tightly around the space above his knee. To touch any closer to where that awful bursting sensation had occurred was to risk adding to the agony that he felt, and despite the illogical nature of this thought, Harry felt that the pain might kill him if it were to get any worse.

Lisa dropped to her haunches, her professionalism holding her in a clear and calm state. She lifted Harry's leg by the ankle.

A sickening crunch ran through his shattered bone. Fresh shards of misery tore into his body.

Harry's vision began to tunnel. Suddenly his mouth was dry. He fought against the urge to let his eyes roll back into his head. "Harry?" Lisa said, releasing his leg gingerly and tapping him hard on the side of his face. "Harry, do you feel like you're passing out?"

Sweat began to force itself from between his pores despite the fact that he felt freezing cold.

"Yeah" he managed, his voice thick and unfamiliar.

"You're going into shock" she said. "You need to try and calm down. Can you breathe for me?"

"I... am... breathing" Harry said.

"You're hyperventilating" Lisa said. "You need to slow down. Come on. Breathe with me. *In*..."

Together, they took a breath.

"And *out*..." Harry and Lisa exhaled together. Lisa's breath was significantly steadier than Harry's.

"There we go" she said. "I'm going to get you some water and then I'm going to call an ambulance. I'll have to leave you for a moment. You're not going to go to sleep if I leave, are you?"

Harry shook his head.

"Say *no*."

"No."

Lisa sprung to her feet and darted into the kitchen. She switched on the landing light. Harry heard the sound of water pouring into a glass. He brought his head forward bracing himself for the mess he expected to find when he looked down at his broken leg.

It looked completely normal, as if nothing had happened at all.

Lisa sloshed water across Harry's face as she put the glass to his lips. He coughed and spluttered as it caught in his throat.

"Sorry" she said. "I need you to drink some of this though."

Harry sipped minutely from the glass. The water tasted odd, like it had been held in a metal bucket before being poured into the glass.

"Jesus, Harry" she said watching him drink. "What were you doing at the top of the stairs?"

"I was..."

What *was* he doing?

Harry distinctly remembered a feeling of panic and of needing to find something, but he could not remember exactly what that something was. He recalled tearing at something and how he had been willing to lose every fingernail in his hands if he needed to, but the memory felt distant, as if it had happened a lifetime ago.

Harry took another draw from the glass. This time it was more of a gulp than a sip.

"You were what?" Lisa's phone was in her hands and she was holding down the power button, trying desperately to switch it back on after turning it off to go to sleep.

"I was... *Dylan*! I was looking for Dylan! My God, is he alright?"

Harry tried to push himself into a sitting position on a leg that crunched every time it moved.

"Who? Who's Dylan?"

"Our..."

Harry trailed off, noticing the pregnant belly of his wife for the first time since he had fallen down the stairs.

Lisa's phone glowed to life. She hammered her thumbs

across the screen and held the device to her ear.

The world around Harry seemed to fall into place. The hangover that he had felt as he had leaned over Dylan's cot was real. It was a remnant of the countless beers he had drank at the barbeque earlier on in the day, the day which had ended when Lisa had effectively kicked him out of his own party.

"Ambulance please" Lisa said. "My husband's had a fall. He has a broken leg, and I think he might have a head injury too."

"Head injury?"

Dylan - if their baby was indeed a boy - had not been born yet. The spare bedroom was very likely still a spare bedroom and nothing more. Certainly, it would not be the nursery he had imagined it to be.

"I really thought that I saw our son" Harry moaned. Fresh tears began to collect in his eyes.

Lisa looked down at him, confusion and anger mixing with concern to create an ugly expression across her face.

"Shush" she said. "I'm on the phone."

CHAPTER 13
64,277 SUBSCRIBERS

The steady beep of Harry's heart rate monitor began to creep up again. A nurse, who had been busying herself with paperwork, stopped and squeezed his shoulder.

"It'll be over before you know it" she said, unconvincingly.

"That's easy for you to say" Harry said. "Is there any chance of a drink before we do this?"

The nurse looked across at the doctor. The doctor shook her head.

"Sorry. You're not supposed to take anything on board over the next twelve hours."

"I thought you said I could sip water? I'm really thirsty. I think it's the nerves."

The nurse glanced at the doctor. She was stood by a large metal basin, washing her hands. The nurse passed a small plastic cup to Harry. He shuffled himself into a sitting position and drank quickly, certain that the doctor wouldn't see.

"I saw that" the doctor said, still facing away from Harry.

"Sorry."

The doctor shook her head. "Has the procedure been explained to you by one of our consultants?"

"Yeah" Harry said.

"Good. And the patient has signed all the relevant paperwork?"

"He has" said the nurse.

"Good. Good. Listen..." the doctor checked over Harry's wristband, the one that had his name and patient number printed across it in bold black writing. "I'm afraid this isn't going to be very pleasant. Your condition I going to get momentarily worse before it gets better."

"Yes. I've been warned."

"Good. Good. I can see you've already got your gas pipe."

Harry picked up the mouthpiece to his nitrous tank and shook it. "I do."

"Yes. Yes. I'm afraid you're going to need that. Shelly, do you have the morphine to hand?"

As if following Harry's lead, the nurse picked up her syringe and shook it for the doctor to see.

"Good. Good. We're just waiting on a couple of porters to arrive before we can start."

Harry shifted on the bed. A crunching sensation ran through the bottom of his leg sending shards of pain throughout the whole of his lower body. The beep of the heart rate monitor shot up again. The nurse squeezed Harry's shoulder by way of response.

"You'll be fine" she said quietly. "Take a hit from your gas tank."

Harry obliged. The room began to swim pleasantly around his head.

The doctor typed something into her laptop and then leant forward towards the screen, squinting over glasses that perched on the very end of her nose.

"I must say, you've really done a number on yourself. How did this happen?"

"I fell down the stairs" Harry said, electing to leave out the part where he had hallucinated losing his unborn son inside of his own cot.

"Nasty" said the doctor. "Was alcohol involved?"

"A little bit. We were having a barbeque."

"I see. Ah, here they are..."

Two burly looking porters entered the room. The doctor smiled in greeting.

"This is Felix and Ken. They'll be assisting during your

procedure."

"OK."

"Essentially, they're going to hold you in place while I pop that ankle back into its joint. I'm afraid this isn't going to be very pleasant."

"You've said that."

"Yes, well, I really want to hammer that home. You have your gas pipe for when you need it and Shelley will be on hand with the morphine for if things get really bad."

"You said that too."

"I see. Well then, shall we begin?"

The two porters walked around the bed and stood either side of Harry. Each man gripped Harry under the armpit and over his shoulder. The beep of Harry's heart rate monitor quickened. Nurse Shelley held the morphine syringe in her hand. Her body stiffened as if in anticipation.

The doctor lifted Harry's ankle tenderly. The crunch that rippled through Harry's leg sent fresh waves of panic through his system. The beeping heart rate monitor hastened again.

"Deep breath…"

With tremendous force the doctor pushed Harry's ankle toward him. His leg folded sending bright white lights dancing across his vision. Then she pulled.

Harry reeled in agony as hot pain shot through his system. A lazy numbness swam through him as nurse Shelley pushed morphine into his veins, but this did little to reduce the pain he felt. The doctor pushed Harry's leg into a foetal coil again, and then once again heaved with all of her might.

"*Jesus Christ!*"

Harry screamed as splinters of his broken bone dug into the muscles in his leg.

"*Come on*" the doctor hissed. "This is an awful stubborn one."

"Take a pull on your gas" the nurse said. She handed Harry

the gas pipe that had fallen out of his hand and onto the floor.

Harry followed instruction. The room span again. He began to hope that he might black out.

"One more go" said the doctor. She pushed Harry's leg up under his chin and then with a tremendous effort wrenched it toward her as hard as she could. Harry slid down the bed. The porters' hands dug into his armpits as they fought to hold him in place. A loud and agonising pop rang out from the bottom of the bed.

All at once the hands that had gripped him let go. The doctor placed Harry's leg gently back onto the bed and took a step backwards. She was out of breath with the effort, and a fine sweat had broken out across her forehead.

Harry's vision melted around him.

"Are you alright?" nurse Shelley soothed, running her hand across Harry's own perspiration-soaked forehead.

He nodded, for he was unable to speak.

The doctor returned from washing her hands in the nearby sink. When she spoke, she was still struggling to catch her breath.

"Good. That went well. Good. You did well."

"Thanks" Harry croaked. His words felt like sandpaper in the back of his throat.

"So, only sips of water for the next twelve hours. I'm afraid you won't be able to eat anything in that time though. There is some good news though. We've managed to get you booked in for surgery this afternoon. You should be good to go home after that."

"Great."

"Is there anyone waiting for you out there? I saw a lady looking rather nervous in the waiting room."

"Lisa."

"Wonderful. I'll send her in and then the porters will take you both up to the ward."

"Great" Harry said again, barely clinging on to consciousness.

Lisa followed as the porters wheeled Harry to the ward and then she helped transfer him from his temporary bed to a more permanent one. She thanked the two men for their help, and they took their leave.

"How was it?"

Harry opened his mouth, ready to tell his wife what a stupid question that had been. Instead a thick sob escaped, and this gave way to an unexpected but very much needed emotional outpouring.

When Harry regained his ability to speak, he apologised to his wife for the difficulty he knew that he had caused.

"What do you have to be sorry about?" Lisa asked, not wanting to put much pressure onto her husband in his emotionally fragile state.

"I'm just sorry" Harry said. "This is going to be a real burden on you, you do know that, don't you?"

Lisa smiled softly. "Aren't that what husbands are supposed to do, be a burden for their wives?"

"I'm serious" he said. "I'm going to need help with showering. I won't be able to get my cast wet, and I can't exactly climb in and out of the bath on my own."

"You never bothered showering before. Why start now?"

Harry could not bring himself to smile at his wife's poor attempt at humour.

"We'll just tie a bag around your leg and I'll heave you in and out of it as best as I can. It's not exactly rocket science is it? Honestly, I don't mind."

Harry searched his wife's face for a sign of insincerity. She smiled gently, sympathy etched across her thin lips as she sat perched on the end of the bed. Still, guilt ran through Harry's veins.

"What about the house? I won't be able to walk for a while,

and then I'll be on crutches after that. Then I'll have to go through rehab. It's probably going to be weeks before I can work on the house again."

"Oh." A sudden realisation flickering across Lisa's eyes. "I suppose you're right."

She instinctively traced her hands over her swollen belly, feeling the curvature where their unborn child was growing.

"How long will it be before we can get the renovation up and going again?"

Harry mulled the answer over his head, trying to find just the right set of words to properly sugar coat his less than desirable response.

"Six weeks recovery time. Call it another two weeks once my cast is off to start getting up and walking around unassisted again. We're probably looking at just over two months."

Harry watched as Lisa did the maths in her head.

"Do you think the house will be done by the time the baby arrives?"

The question conjured a fresh batch of tears behind Harry's eyes.

"I don't think so."

"I don't want to raise my child there."

"I'll just keep working for a couple of months after the baby is born and then we can go home. You won't be raising the baby in the house."

A sigh escaped Lisa that seemed to deflate her almost entirely. She rubbed her hands across tired looking eyes, now reddened by the events of the day and the interrupted sleep of the night before. "God" she said, "what a mess."

Harry pulled himself forward. The pain that erupted underneath his cast forced him back down almost instantly.

"What on earth were you doing at the top of the stairs Harry?"

"I told you. I was looking for Dylan. I heard him crying,

and then I went to see him, and when I looked in his cot he wasn't there. I could hear him, but I couldn't see him."

"Harry, there is no Dylan. We don't even know if we're having a boy yet."

"That doesn't mean anything" Harry said. "I saw him, or at least I heard him. But I had seen him before. I saw your waters break, and I saw his birth, and I'd made him a bedroom. It was all there in front of me. I saw everything."

"You dreamed everything" Lisa said.

"I didn't dream it."

"Look around" Lisa said, sounding annoyed. "Do you see a baby? Look at my stomach. It hasn't even been born yet. How could you have seen it? It has to have been a dream. You have to have been sleepwalking."

Harry felt frustration at his inability to properly explain the reality of the things he had witnessed.

"When have you ever known me to sleepwalk?"

"I can think of one time. In fact, I can think of two."

"When?"

"I don't know the exact dates if that's what you're looking for, but there was this one time when you'd been out with Guy and some other people from work, and you'd come back steaming drunk. I woke up in the middle of the night and you were gone. I got up to go to the loo and I found you staring into the airing cupboard. You were pissing all over the towels."

"What?"

The slightest flicker of amusement spread across Lisa's face. This only served to make Harry feel more frustrated.

"I grabbed you and I asked you what you were doing, but it was a total case of the lights being on and nobody being home. You stared right through me. You didn't even know I was there. You even peed on me a little bit. I was so angry. You're lucky that I find it so funny now."

A mocking giggle broke from Lisa's throat. Harry stared at

her from under a furrowed brow.

"I wasn't sleepwalking. It wasn't a dream."

"Oh for God's sake Harry. How could you explain any of this then?"

"Maybe it was a premonition?"

"That our unborn son is going to disappear in his cot?"

"Spirits have been known to-"

"Fucking hell" Lisa cursed, loud enough for a nurse to poke his head around the door. "I knew you were going to bring it back to this bullshit."

"Spirits have been known to show people glimpses into the future."

Lisa pressed her face into her palms. Her voice now sounded muffled. "Our house is not haunted."

"Are you serious? What about all the evidence?"

"What evidence? You have no evidence that anything remotely unusual is going on in that house!"

"The YouTube channel-"

"-Shows nothing" Lisa said. The conversation paused as Lisa left her words to hang over her husband. "Your channel doesn't show a single scrap of evidence that anything is happening in there."

"Over sixty thousand people-

"-Are seeing what they want to see."

Betrayal clawed Harry from within. Lisa had watched all of Harry's videos since he had begun uploading and until this moment, she had said nothing to suggest that she was anything other than impressed with the evidence he had put forward.

"You said you liked my videos."

"And I was telling the truth. But I didn't say that I believe them. They're entertaining and I'm proud of what you've managed to do, but Harry... come on. It's a lot of..."

Lisa suddenly looked panicked as her words failed her.

"Nonsense?" asked Harry.

In a moment of true horror, Lisa simply let the silence speak for itself.

"I'm sorry Harry. I just don't believe in ghosts."

"Alright" Harry said, pulling himself into a sitting position despite the pain that shot through his leg. "I'm going to tell you something that I haven't told another living soul. I want you to make sure that you listen to what I'm telling you, and you'll need to stick with me, because this was honestly the scariest moment of my life."

Lisa shrugged. She looked exhausted.

"Do you remember when the pipe burst, and we had that big hole in the wall?"

"How could I forget?"

"Do you remember we called a plumber to fix it?"

"Yeah."

"That day I saw something that I can't explain."

"I know you did. You've already told me about this. You told me that night when we were buying new towels. You saw figure in our house."

"No" Harry said, shaking his head, pain throbbing in his broken leg. "That wasn't the truth. Well, it was partially the truth, but it wasn't the full story."

"So, you lied to me?"

"No" said Harry. "I didn't tell you the full truth. There's a difference."

Lisa suddenly looked angry. "Why would you do that? I would never lie to-"

"Just listen. The day that the plumber came, something else came first. It looked just like a real person. It was pretending to be the plumber that I'd called. It even had the same van as the real plumber did, but he was never really there."

"Harry…"

"He showed up, and he started working on the broken pipe. He had me help him and he asked me to hold the pipe while he used this big saw thing to cut into it, but once he got going it was too powerful and it cut off a part of the pipe that came flying out. The metal-"

"Harry..."

"-the metal came flying out and it hit him right in the neck and it cut his throat and he fell back and started to bleed out. It was honestly like he was dying, so I ran off into the house to get something to use as a bandage, but when I came back downstairs after getting the curtains to help stop the bleeding he was gone."

"*Harry...*"

"When the real plumber arrived he told me that his uncle or his brother, I forget which, was called John, and that he died not long ago and I truly think that was him. That was his spirit in our house. I saw the whole thing."

Harry was surprised to find that he was shaking when he had finished telling the story. The pain in his leg had become almost unbearable, but he gritted his teeth against it. Lisa coiled her hands around her swollen belly and rubbed gently, watching her husband as he grappled to get his shakes under control.

"Harry" she said, finally able to respond now his story was over. "That didn't happen."

Harry's mouth dropped open.

"How can you say that? After everything I've just told you, how can you say that I'm, what... *lying* to you?"

"I'm not saying that you're lying, but you could be confused, or maybe you thought you saw something that you didn't. I don't really know. But what you say you saw, you did not. You can't have Harry. Ghosts don't exist."

"I swear I saw it"

"Prove it."

Lisa's words dug into Harry and twisted his insides. The eternal question of proof felt more crushing coming from his wife. The reality was that he had no proof. What he had seen could never be proven.

"I shouldn't have to" he said. "You're my wife. You should just believe me."

Lisa's hand stretched across Harry's bed and found his knee. She squeezed. A look of what seemed like regret settled across her tired looking face.

"How could I believe something like that?"

Harry fought to find a response. Anger coursed through him, mingling with a deep sense of betrayal. He felt like grabbing his wife by her shoulders and shaking her. How could she not believe him? After all he had told her, and all she had seen, both on the Mrs Fisher tape and on the channel he had painstakingly constructed, how could she still not believe him? In the end, Harry simply laid back and stared at the ceiling, his jaw clamping tightly against itself. The sound of his teeth grinding consumed his ears.

"I think I'd better go. I start working an hour. I need to go home and freshen up before I can get back here."

"Uh-huh"

"I'll come and see you on my breaks."

"Right."

Lisa leaned across the bed to kiss Harry. He turned his head away from her and faced the wall.

CHAPTER 14
64,277 SUBSCRIBERS

Harry woke from surgery to find Lisa waiting by his side. For a moment his eyes struggled to focus, and Harry could have sworn the face of John Masterman was staring down at him. Lisa's soft voice murmuring of his name brought clarity to his waking, and suddenly he realised exactly where he was.

Harry looked down at his leg. The clumsy temporary cast had been replaced by one made of rigid white plaster. The pain that had throbbed in his leg right up to the moment the Anaesthetist had lulled Harry into a deep and dreamless state had now vanished. A terrible taste resided in his mouth.

"Can I..."

A pain in the back of his throat sent shockwaves through Harry's body. He grabbed at his neck, feeling for an external injury that was not there. Rather than speak, Harry motioned for the pitcher that was at his bedside.

"You want some water?" Lisa asked. She picked filled small plastic cup for him without waiting for an response.

Harry grabbed the hoist that hung suspended over his bed and pulled with all his might. He squirmed under his sheets, trying desperately to get himself into a sitting position. Lisa placed a hand behind his head and pulled him forward.

Harry drank the full glass in one go and then held it out to his wife by way of asking for another. Lisa filled it and then watched as he drained that one too.

"More?" she asked.

Harry shook his head. The gravely pain in his throat was too severe for him to even try and speak through it.

"The surgery went well" Lisa said brightly. "They put six

screws and one pin in there. The doctor said that your leg was in a worse state than they had initially thought after looking at your X-rays."

Harry nodded. The odd floaty sensation that had shrouded him since waking was beginning to shift and reality became more tangible. Somewhere in the back of his mind a quiet anger was gaining in volume, calling for Harry to do something. But what? He was not sure.

"When... home?"

"The doctor said that they're going to keep you in for the night so that they can keep an eye on you. Then I should be able to get you home in the morning."

Harry nodded. Exhaustion pulled at him, making him feel impossibly heavy against the bed. He yawned deeply and a fresh wave of pain tore at the back of his throat.

"Is it sore?"

Harry nodded again.

"I think they had a bit of trouble getting a breathing tube down there. It was quite a long operation. You were there for maybe six or seven hours."

Harry grunted.

"Are you alright?" Lisa placed the back of one of her hands against Harry's forehead as if checking for a fever. "You don't look great."

"Tired" Harry managed. The niggling anger that thronged in the back of his mind began to flare at his wife's line of questioning. Had she done something to upset him? Harry found that he did not have the energy to start searching his memories for the answer.

Lisa stood and pulled Harry's sheets up tight around his neck.

"You should get some rest" Lisa said. "There's nothing doing tonight. In the morning I'll come and get you and we can go home."

Harry nodded, fighting the urge to yawn for fear it would aggravate his throat all over again.

Lisa bent down to kiss him. Her lips found the middle of his cheek and this time Harry did not move away. He did not have the energy to put up a fight, even if he wanted to.

CHAPTER 15
64,421 SUBSCRIBERS

"She doesn't believe me" Harry said as he flipped meat over on the barbeque.

Guy thought about this while he sipped from a beer bottle. "It is a tall ask. I mean, can you really expect her to believe you based on the evidence you've provided?"

"But the channel-"

"-Is shit" Guy said, smiling in a holier-than-thou kind of way. "Yeah, you've got decent viewing figures, but the internet is full of idiots who are far more gullible than your wife. Most sensible people need a little more persuading before they're going to believe that you're living in a genuine haunted house."

Harry looked up at the building that he had bought. Something moved beyond one of the windows. He thought about pointing this out to Guy but knew that even this would not be enough to persuade him.

"What can I do to make her believe me?"

Guy sipped from his bottle and mulled this over, sluicing beer between his lips.

"You have to get proof" he said. "And quickly."

He stared back up at the house. It looked entirely normal now, much to Harry's disappointment.

"These things take time. I can't force something supernatural to happen, can I?"

Guy flashed that holier-than-thou smile once again. "Can't you?" he asked.

Suddenly it seemed simple. Suddenly Harry felt stupid for not recognising this before.

Guy made a surprised sound and stepped back from the grill. "Careful! You're gonna burn those!"

An acrid smell invaded Harry's nose. He looked down at the grill to find that the sausages he had been cooking had been replaced by the severed fingers of his unborn son.

"Good morning!"

The voice dragged Harry out of his slumber and into a harsh bright hospital room. He struggled to focus before finding the smiling face of a woman he didn't recognise at the side of his bed.

"You look like you were having quite the dream there Harry" the nurse said, setting his chart back on the end of his bed.

Harry looked beyond his cast to find a pair of crutches laid neatly at the bottom of the bed.

"Care for a stroll?"

"I'd love to" Harry said. The remnants of his dream were already fading to nothing in the depths of his mind.

By the time Lisa arrived at the hospital, Harry had walked up and down the ward seven times and had made it up and down a flight of hospital stairs twice.

"Wow" she said, discovering Harry standing by the window. "Look at you up and about!"

"I can't get very far" Harry said almost apologetically, "but I can move under my own steam."

"I can see that" Lisa smiled. She was wearing her uniform and looked oddly well put together given she had just finished her shift. "Are you ready to go?"

"Yes. Get me out of here."

Harry collected the bag of pills that the doctor had left for him at the ward reception. He winced as a nurse produced an angry looking needle and informed him that he would need to inject himself with one of those every day if he didn't want his body to reject the metal that was holding his bones in place.

"There's a six-week supply of these in your bag" the smiling nurse told him. "You need to make sure that you use them all. One a day."

"Great" said Harry.

Travelling from the ward to the car park was an exhausting ordeal. Harry found that using his crutches for any real distance was not only tiring but also incredibly painful. The plastic of the handles bore down into the soft flesh between his thumb and forefinger. He stopped several times, sitting on hospital benches and catching his breath as he quietly apologised to his wife. Lisa assured him that he had nothing to feel sorry about ,but this did nothing to soothe the guilt that was growing inside of him.

Lisa helped him into the car, shielding Harry from the rain with the back of her coat. He flopped tiredly onto the passenger seat and struggled to catch his breath.

"We're going to have to call off past the supermarket" she said quietly.

"What for?"

"You're going to need a few things" she said, tapping the NHS logo on her uniform. "Trust me. I know what I'm talking about."

Lisa waited patiently while Harry struggled to his feet and onto his crutches once they had parked up. The weight of his cast pulled tremendously at his back, twisting him into an awkward position that hurt his shoulders and his hip all at once. Lisa walked slowly beside Harry as he hobbled from the car to the entrance. By the time he arrived, he felt like his hands were on fire.

"Are you OK?" she asked him. An expression of pain was rippling across his face.

"It's just taking a bit of getting used to."

Lisa screwed her face in sympathy. Harry leaned up against the entrance to the supermarket while Lisa went to collect a shopping trolley. He watched her with disbelief as she returned, already laughing at what she had found.

"There's no way you're getting me into that thing" he said. Lisa's smile inspired an almost identical one to spread wide across Harry's face.

"Why not?"

"Because I'm not-"

"- A cripple? An invalid? Call it whatever you want, that's exactly what you are. I don't think you really appreciate how defenceless you are right now. You more or less have to do what I say."

Harry handed over his crutches to Lisa with great reluctance and sat back into the wheelchair-trolley combination she had wheeled over to him. She laughed heartily as she began pushing him across the supermarket floor. He tried to hide his own amusement behind one of his hands.

They glided through the aisles happily, revelling in the novelty of the situation. Lisa picked up a flask and placed it into the trolley.

"I can set you up with a full flask of tea in the morning and then you can have hot drinks whenever you want them."

"I've got a broken leg. Not broken hands… or brain damage for that matter."

Lisa pulled the trolley over to the side of the aisle and leaned over her husband. Harry suddenly felt like a child that was asking too many questions.

"And just how were you planning on carrying these cups of scalding hot liquid from the kitchen to the living room? You'll have both hands clamped around your crutches. Were you planning on carrying mugs with your teeth?"

She was right. Harry had not appreciated just how helpless his injury had rendered him.

"I'm going to get you some microwave meals too. We can bring the microwave through to the living room and just leave it there. Honestly, what a pain in the arse this is going to be!"

"I'm sorry" Harry said, before noticing the mischievous smile resting on his wife's face.

Harry did not question any more of Lisa's suggestions as she pushed him around the supermarket. For now, he was grateful that for whatever reason she was revelling in the new power balance that had been established within their relationship. Perhaps, Harry mused, it was because Lisa was familiar in her role as a caregiver. Looking after the sick and the infirm was just what she did, and now Harry was simply another patient under her charge.

Perhaps Lisa's mood was somehow the result of the little bit of certainty that had been forced upon them. In this state Harry no longer had the capacity to make changes to the house, or *not* to make them, as the case may be. Maybe she was comfortable in the fact that her expectations of the renovation would be met for the next six to eight weeks. Each day she could go to work and know that nothing would be done, rather than returning home to find Harry had made less progress than she had hoped he would.

On the other hand, maybe she was simply amused at the sight of her husband sitting behind a shopping trolley, looking like an overgrown boy on a trip to the shops.

Whatever the reason, Harry was pleased that his wife was coping well.

He paid for the groceries using the bank account he had promised would only be used for renovations and then Lisa wheeled Harry back to the car.

They ate their evening meal on the living room floor. Once they had finished, Lisa helped Harry up the stairs and into bed. She cuddled into him as he lay on his back and stared up at the ceiling, trying to fall asleep in this unfamiliar position.

"Thanks" he whispered into the darkness. "For looking after me."

"No problem" Lisa said. Her voice was heavy with the early stages of sleep.

Harry's wife shuffled closer, her pregnant belly pressing into his side as she kissed him on the cheek. "I love you" she whispered into him, and Harry whispered the same back.

All he could think about however, was the churning desire to somehow humiliate this woman through proving her wrong, despite everything she had done for him earlier in the day.

CHAPTER 16
64,421 SUBSCRIBERS

Harry scooted down the stairs slowly, lowering himself into a sitting position on each step, before turning, bringing his crutches down, and then repeating the process all over again. The sound of Lisa's ablutions rang out from behind the closed bathroom door. By the time Harry arrived at the bottom, the same spot in which he had broken his leg in the first place, he was exhausted.

Using the bannister for leverage, Harry pulled himself up onto his crutches and then he hobbled into the kitchen.

He flicked on the kettle and then tried to steady his breathing while he waited for it to boil. He poured most of the water into his flask along with three large scoops of coffee, and then poured the rest into Lisa's favourite mug.

The bathroom door creaked, and the sound of Lisa's footsteps thudded overhead. Harry listened as they first went into the bedroom and then arrived at the top of the stairs.

"Harry?"

"Down here" he called back.

"How did you get down the stairs?"

"On my arse. And with great difficulty."

Lisa finished up what she was doing while Harry finished making the coffee. When she came down, Lisa looked surprised to find him in the kitchen.

"I've made you a cuppa" he said with a smile.

"You shouldn't have."

"I've said it before and I'll say it again, I'm not an invalid."

"No" said Lisa, picking up the cup before deciding that it was still too hot to drink. "I mean you shouldn't have bothered. I don't have time to drink it. I need to get to work."

"Already?"

Harry looked at the space on his wrist where his watch usually was. He had forgotten to put it on this morning in all the novelty of his first proper day getting around on crutches.

"Debbie from work lives fairly close by. She said that she can come to get me if I promise to pay half of the petrol money."

"Debbie? As in Debbie from the engagement party?"

Lisa stopped her rushing momentarily and stared confusedly at her husband.

"What engagement party?"

Of course, Harry thought. *That wasn't real. Or, it hadn't happened yet.*

The sound of an engine pulled up in front of the house and was closely followed by three succinct pips of a horn.

"Looks like she's here." Lisa tried unsuccessfully to have at least one sip of her coffee before gathering her things and making a beeline for the door. Harry snatched at his crutches so he could see her out of the door.

"You've got your flask. Microwave is in the living room. Dinners in the fridge."

"OK."

"I'll see you when I get home. I might be late tonight. Debbie likes to work over."

"Really?"

"Really."

With that, Lisa stepped out of the house and closed the door behind her. Silence reigned supreme.

Harry stood in the kitchen for a while, taking in just how empty the house suddenly felt. It was as if the space inside the building had somehow become smaller, like the walls that he had worked so hard to tame had closed in on him in some sort of revolt.

"Alright" Harry said to himself. "Time to get to work."

He placed his flask into a small bag that he draped around one of his wrists and then stumbled into the living room. Harry crashed onto the sofa, threw his crutches to one side and then lowered himself onto the floor.

Taking out his laptop from its place underneath the couch, Harry felt an urge of motivation. He thought of all the people who had refused to believe him, many of whom were his own family and friends, and how sweet it would be to finally prove them wrong.

Harry might not have captured his most compelling experience to date, the cameras he installed only coming as the result of the Masterman haunting, but he was almost certain that his upstairs camera would prove some insight into how he had come to fall down the stairs.

Harry booted up his camera app with a physical excitement. His hands quivered lightly as he tracked through the footage on his laptop screen, watching in reverse as he exited the house with Lisa, lay at the bottom of the stairs, and then finally tumbled from the bottom to the top.

Harry squared the footage up a few minutes prior to him appearing in the frame and pushed his computer's volume up to its maximum. The gentle hiss of his upstairs ambiance flowed through the speaker system.

"Come on" Harry whispered to himself. "There has to be something. A voice. Dylan crying. An apparition. *Anything.*"

He sat and watched. After several minutes Harry saw the bright white image of himself track across the night vision footage, stand at the top of the stairs and then lean forward over the top step. A split second later the onscreen version of Harry was falling, his body colliding with almost every step before a meaty thud rang out from the hallway below. A moment later Harry listened as his own cries of agony began.

Annoyed, Harry rewound the footage and watched it all over again. He leaned forward, the shift in his body weight adding significant pressure to the inside of his cast, and he listened intently for anything he could use to prove that his falling down the stairs was a supernatural event.

Again, a bright white outline of Harry appeared. It stood at the top of the stairs and then fell forward without any intervention from any outside force.

"There has to be something" Harry said out loud. As much as he despised admitting it to himself, Harry could see how the footage would look to the untrained eye. It looked like an image of a man deep in the throes of a vivid sleepwalk simply becoming confused by his surroundings, taking a wrong turn and then falling down the stairs. It hurt Harry to admit it, but it looked exactly how Lisa had said it would.

Harry pulled open the camera feed from the hallway camera and hit play. Although the frame looked beyond the bottom of the stairs and was more focused on the front door than anything else, Harry still found himself wincing as he watched himself landing in a crumpled heap at the bottom of the stairs.

"Shit" Harry hissed as his onscreen doppelganger began to wail. The footage was showing nothing compelling. For all anyone would be able to tell, Lisa could have been exactly right. He would need to spin the footage for anyone to believe that this was anything more than a simple accident.

Harry dug his phone out of his pocket and held it at arm's length. For a moment he toyed with the idea of crawling across the room to collect his tripod, but then he thought better of it. Better to strike while the idea was hot, while the petty one-upmanship that churned away against his heart was motivating him to make the most compelling video of his life.

He held his camera at arm's length, and without even a hint of an idea as to what he was going to say, Harry began speaking into the lens.

"Hey guys, it's Harry from Our Haunted Home. This video is going to be a little different to the usual content you'll get from me because... well, it's probably easier for me to show you than to tell you. Look what I've got..."

Harry turned his phone camera and framed up the cast in the viewfinder.

"Guys! I've broken my leg. Or at least, that's what my wife would have you believe..."

Harry stopped the recording and allowed ideas to whirl around his mind. Amidst the inspiration Harry found a quiet but nagging doubt. In all his time running the channel, Harry had never really discussed much of his personal life other than the fact that he had bought number 7 Ragworth Lane with his wife and that they had worked together to pay for the renovations. Never had he mentioned her by name, nor had he given any insight into their relationship. Now though, Lisa had made this more personal. She had become a figurehead in Harry's mind for all the people who did not believe in what he was trying to do. She had stuck her flag in the ground and made her opinions very clear when she had said that she did not believe his story about John Masterman. She had chosen a side, and she had forced Harry to choose his. A little conflict, Harry realised, may just be what this channel needed to push it into the mainstream.

With this thought in mind, Harry's thumb found the record button and he rolled his camera again.

"See, my wife Lisa thinks that I was sleepwalking, and that when I fell down the stairs it was the result of too much alcohol causing a sudden bout of somnambulism. The truth is that *I was pushed*..."

Harry let the words hang, building tension into his monologue.

"I'm going to show you some security camera footage from the night I broke my leg. What you are about to see is graphic, so if you are one of the many people who watch this channel with your family, particularly if you have young children, you might not want them to see this."

Harry pictured the video in his mind. Here he would splice in the footage of his fall, letting the images tell their own tales. He envisaged the image of his body crumbling into a heap at the bottom of the stairs against an intense droning soundtrack. The thought sent goose bumps across his skin.

"OK" Harry said into his camera with a voice that was softening. "I know what this looks like. To an outsider it looks like I'm sleepwalking and that I take a misstep, but friends, *believers*, do I have a story for you!?"

"For weeks I've been having these... visions. I guess that deep down I want to call them premonitions, because I've been seeing a time that hasn't happened yet. It all began when my wife told me that she was pregnant..."

Harry sat in the centre of his living room and spoke for a solid twenty minutes. He spilled his guts into his phone's tiny lens. He spoke about how Lisa had fallen pregnant and of how she didn't know whether she wanted to keep the baby. He talked about the party where Lisa's waters had broken, and how she had cried on the journey home because she did not want to come back to this house to raise their child. He explained everything that had happened the night he thought he had lost Dylan, and he told his viewers how he categorically knew that all of this had been real.

When he was done, Harry uploaded the footage to his laptop and began pulling the threads of his tale together in his editing software. He infused ambient flourishes of dark sound under his words and overlaid his security camera footage perfectly, creating a story that was engaging and terrifying all at once. He played and replayed the footage of him falling at various angles and speeds and multiple levels of zoom. He rerecorded the parts of his monologue that he thought weren't quite convincing enough and then he uploaded his film to YouTube. He sat, and he waited.

The views began to roll in instantly, but at this stage this was not an unusual occurrence. Harry had worked hard to build his six hundred thousand strong fan base and knew anecdotally that many of them watched his videos the moment they were released. He poured coffee from his flask into its waiting lid and drank, anticipating the arrival of the comment section discussion.

The first few comments were asinine. Phatic communication by definition, the majority of them did not push beyond simple congratulations on another video well done.

Harry refreshed the page. A new discussion had filtered its way to the top.

"I don't know dude" Harry read out loud. "You look like you're sleepwalking to me."

Harry clicked a dropdown, expanding on the replies.

"Right?" said the first.

"100%" said the next.

Annoyed, Harry refreshed the page. Surely the next few comments would be in support of his story. Surely the case he had put forward had been compelling enough for his audience to believe.

Harry was alarmed to find that yet another new discussion had taken the top spot of his comment feed.

"Does anybody else think that this guy has lost it? I mean, some of his early videos seemed to be really going somewhere, but now... I don't know. It all just seems a bit... desperate."

With a growing horror Harry read the replies to this thread.

"I totally agree" he read aloud in a wavering voice. "Some of the earliest stuff gave me chills but it's pretty obvious that whatever was happening in that house is over with."

"Pathetic" read another. "Now he's just trying to pass off his dreams as ghost stories? Maybe I'll start a channel and I'll just explain my nightmares if that's what passes for a paranormal investigation these days!"

Harry flung his laptop off of his lap in a moment of abject fury. It clattered against the bottom of his cast sending shock waves of pain coursing through his leg.

"FUCK!" Harry screamed at the top of his lungs. "FUCK FUCK FUCK!!"

The dog next door began to bark. Harry gripped one of his crutches and hurled it at the shared wall before he had even had time to think of his actions.

"Shut up!" he screamed. Harry's cries only served to rile the dog further. Harry threw his other crutch. It hit the wall with enough force to leave a huge gouge in the plaster he had installed only weeks before.

The edges of Harry's vision began to turn red. He crawled across the living room floor like some loathsome worm and snatched up his crutch is from the ground. The gouge in the wall looked worse from this new perspective. The dog beyond the wall continued to bark.

Harry struggled to his feet as quickly as he could, his cast bearing much of his weight as he stood. Harry trudged into his kitchen fuelled by a boiling rage and tore open the fridge door. He snatched at a packet of sausages from the top shelf and took two of them from their wrappers. With great difficulty but a dogged determination, Harry opened the cabinet under the sink and began rummaging through the containers that Lisa stored away in there.

He pushed a large bleach bottle to one side and peered into the darkness.

"There you are" Harry said as he reached for a yellow box of rat poison.

The box felt heavy, still half full after he had scattered the first half across his lawn in the days after he had torn down his shed. He had spent the days after that collecting up the corpses of the rats who had taken his deadly bait. At the time he had been quietly horrified at the agonised expressions that had been frozen across their tiny dead faces. Now, the idea of that expression on the face of the dog next door brought Harry immense joy.

Harry dragged himself to his feet and took a bowl from the drainer. He mushed the cold sausage meat into the ball and then scattered a generous helping of the rat poison over the meat.

A fleeting doubt flashed lightning fast across Harry's mind. A fresh bout of barking from the dog cast it away as quickly as it had occurred.

Harry stepped into his back garden with incredible difficulty. He held the bowl in one hand and a crutch in the other, hopping his way out onto the lawn.

The sound of a doggy door clattered and the barking that had been dulled by the wall between the two households found its full potential behind Harry's fence.

Simba bounded across his garden and leapt up at the fence just as he had during Harry's ruined barbeque.

"Simba" Harry called in a soft and caring voice. "Simba. Dinner time."

The dog's barking continued. It forced its face up against the fence, its muzzle protruding through the gap between the two panels. Harry looked up at his neighbour's house, observing that the woman who lived there was either too apathetic to care what her dog was up to or that she had left the house. Either way Harry knew that he would need to work quickly if he was really going to do this.

The dog snarled through a slot in the fence.

"Simba" Harry soothed again. "I've got something for you."

He dipped his hand into the bowl and produced the poisoned meat. With great care he extended it towards the dog's snarling maw, holding it as close to Simba's nose as he dared.

The animal suddenly quieted. It sniffed the air in front of its face. Simba's wet nose twitched at the prospect of a free meal.

"Good boy" Harry whispered. "Here you go."

He pushed his free hand closer to the dog. Simba greedily lapped at the meat from Harry's hand.

"There you go" Harry said. "Was that nice? Did that taste good?"

Loud chewing stemmed from behind the fence as Simba made quick work of the last of the meat. When he was done, he pushed his muzzle back through the fence slats and greedily waited for more. Harry backed carefully away from the fence and the dog resumed its barking once it realised its free meal was over.

"That's it" Harry said, stealing another glance at the apparently empty house next door. "Make all your noise now. In an hour you won't be making so much as a fucking *peep*."

He turned, revelling in the satisfaction of giving into his murderous rage and made his way back to the house. Behind Harry, Simba's barking was already taking on an odd quality that he had not heard in the animal before. It was as if he was somehow recognising that he was in serious danger, and that the sounds he produced now may be some of his last.

Harry did not stop to listen to them. Instead, he hurried back into his house and closed the back door, suddenly feeling like he was able to face his critics with a renewed sense of serenity.

CHAPTER 17
62,243 SUBSCRIBERS

Harry had struggled through a growing sense of unhappiness as he had poured over the comments on his latest post. While the views on the video had grown at a faster rate and in a greater number than any film he had uploaded so far, the comment section this time seemed alive with people quick to dismiss his story as nothing more than make believe.

Harry had responded to the positive messages of support that he had received, thanking his viewers for their continued allegiance to his cause, and then against his better judgement he had begun to challenge his critics.

Arguments swelled in the comment section, most of them starting out relatively civil before inevitably devolving into name calling and petty point scoring. Engaging in these conversations did nothing to stunt the growth of his swelling suspicion that he might be losing his audience, despite what the viewer figures would indicate. And yet, Harry found himself unable to resist. He simply could not sit and let people call him a liar, especially given just how terrifying the events that led to him breaking his leg were.

Harry had hunched over his laptop for hours, responding back and forth with his supporters and his critics, working away until his legs had grown numb from sitting too long on the floor. A hunger began growing in his stomach. He was just about to stop for lunch when a notification emerged that stopped Harry in his tracks.

It was a message direct to his inbox. With a great sense of trepidation, Harry opened it to find that it had come from *King of the Haunt*, the very channel upon which Harry had modelled his own.

Harry sat and stared at the unopened message for a few seconds, not quite sure he was believing what he was seeing. Another red notification pulled him out of his stare. A second message had just landed from *King of the Haunt*.

"Hi Harry. I get why you're doing it, but you should probably stop responding to the people hating on your content. They're going to use anything you say as ammunition to make you look like a bad guy, so it's best just to ignore them altogether. Regards, Dean."

Stunned, Harry opened the second message.

"PS, love the channel. Fantastic content."

Pins and needles began to burst through Harry's fingers. This was it, the message he had been waiting for. Dean King had been watching his content and had decided that he liked what he saw.

Harry prepared to type his response only to find that his fingers had frozen over the keys. How on earth would he even start to respond to a person of such magnitude? Dean King's channel, *King of the Haunt*, had over four million subscribers and had become the leading paranormal UK channel in a little over a year of him starting it. Since this time, Dean had enjoyed a level of wealth and success that Harry had only dared dream about in the most fantastical recesses of his own mind. King had been the man who had made Harry aware that turning his passion for the supernatural into an income stream was even a possibility. Now, almost three years after Harry had ascended him onto a pedestal so high that its peak was almost invisible from the ground, Dean King had landed in Harry's inbox. It was no surprise then that Harry's hands shook as he began to type.

"Hi Dean" Harry sounded out loud as he typed. "Thanks for the message and for the sound advice. I think I've just let a few negative comments push me over the edge, which is not something I would normally do. I suppose I'm still quite new to this YouTube personality thing. I haven't had as much practise as you. Keep up the good work. Your channel is forever an inspiration to me."

Harry's fingers hovered over his keypad. The message he had typed was fine. It was light in tone, and polite and informal enough to mask the starstruck nausea that was now pulsing in Harry stomach. Still, Harry feared that it was closed ended and would likely kill the conversation dead.

Without thinking it over, Harry typed out his closing words.

"Thanks for getting in touch. I'd love to collaborate on a project with you someday. Best. Harry."

He hit send, sat back, and then worried that he had been too formal.

He stared at the screen, hoping to find a way to unsend the message.

A notification flashed across his screen. Harry opened the message to find a succinct response.

"That would be great mate. What's your number? I'll give you a call to discuss."

With a sudden growing suspicion that this must be some sort of prank, Harry typed his phone number into the response and hit *send*. His phone began to ring almost instantly.

"Hello?"

"Harry. It's Dean."

The voice that Harry heard sounded surprisingly like the one he had listened to countless times when watching *King of the Haunt*.

"Dean?"

"Yeah mate" said the voice in a thick London accent. "How's it going?"

"It's fine" Harry heard himself saying, "Things are fine."

His clipped response sounded disbelieving to the point of rude. Despite this, the voice on the end of the line laughed.

"Glad to hear it mate. Have you managed to calm down a bit yet?"

"Calm down?"

"After those twats in your comment section. Honestly mate, you give them hours of free entertainment and all they can do is criticise. That's the great British public for you though, isn't it?"

"Yeah" Harry said. "Is this really Dean King?"

More laughter. "Yeah mate."

"It's just… well… you're massive, not just on YouTube, but to me as well, you're massive. Are you sure this isn't a wind up? If it is and you just tell me I won't be angry."

Dean laughed heartily once again, graciously accepting the flattery that Harry afforded him.

"It's me mate. We could video call if you like but I've not had a chance to do my makeup."

"Excuse me?"

"It's a joke Harry. I was making a joke."

"Oh."

"Listen mate, are you alright? You don't sound alright."

"No" Harry said, only now feeling like he was starting to find his feet. "I think this is all just a little surreal. It's all a little bit out of the blue."

"I can call you back at a different time if you'd like?"

"No" Harry snapped. He felt like the opportunity of a lifetime was slipping through his fingers. "Now's fine. Sorry. I'm just a little shocked, that's all. What can I do for you?"

"Well," Dean said, he himself now sounding a little lost, "You mentioned a collaboration in your e-mail, and I thought that sounded like a great idea. Buddying up with likeminded people to make content is the best way to get new followers."

"Great" Harry said. "So, you'll be coming here, to my

house?"

"That's right. You have actually seen my channel haven't you Harry? That sort of thing accounts for a good eighty percent of my content."

"I've seen it, yeah. Sorry, this is all still a bit-"

"Surreal" Dean King interrupted. "Yeah. You had mentioned that."

"Sorry."

"Listen" Dean said, his voice flattening out, the jovial tone of overly sunny small talk giving way to one of sincerity. "Harry mate, I'm just a man like you are trying to gain a following on YouTube. I want to make a bit of money and have a few laughs on the way. I get that I've been doing this longer than you have but seriously, you need to drop this starstruck act that you're putting on."

"Sorry."

"And you need to stop apologising" he added.

"Sorry. I will do."

"Great." The bright bouncy tone had returned to Dean's voice. "When are you free to get this done? Obviously, I've seen what you've done to your leg. Terrible business all that. Great content though."

"I'm free pretty much whenever" said Harry, eager to seal the deal before Dean had a chance to pull out of it.

"Alright. Let me check my diary and I can get back to you. In fact, I've got it here. I was thinking maybe-"

An explosion of sound rattled through Harry's hallway. He threw himself forward as if trying to avoid a physical impact from the racket. Pain shot through his leg as the pressure from his body folded over it, grounding his cast into the ground.

"What the hell was that?" Dean asked on the other end of the line.

"I have no idea" Harry said.

"Blimey. Is that part of the haunting?"

The sound exploded through the hallway again, only this time Harry recognised it as a fist pounding against his front door. The horrifying sound of a woman's indistinguishable screaming accompanied it, setting Harry's hair on end and his teeth on edge.

"Harry, it sounds like-"

"I'm going to have to go" Harry said. "Will you send me a message once you checked your-"

More pounding. Another bout of ferocious screaming.

"No worries" Dean said. "Send me a message will you? Let me know that you're still alive after-"

The pounding this time was so loud that Harry feared his door was about to go through.

Harry killed the call and began the painful task of clambering to his feet. He pulled his crutches closer to him and made his way to the front door.

The woman from next door did not even wait for the door to fully open before hurling her accusations at Harry.

"You killed my dog!" she shrieked.

Harry was stunned. The woman before him was a mere shadow of her former self. Her eyes were stained red, presumably from the salt of her own tears. Her hair stood at a mess of odd angles. Her clothes were covered in mud. Down her front was an off-white spew of some quickly drying liquid that looked foamy and toxic.

"What on earth are you talking about?"

"Don't lie to me" she yelled. "You killed Simba. He was lying in the mud by your fence! You poisoned him. Didn't you?"

"Who the hell is Simba?" Harry asked. An ache began to rumble through his stomach as the weight of his actions suddenly registered. Harry had hated that dog and, in a very real way, he had hated the woman who owned him too, but he had somehow not anticipated ever being confronted with the consequences of his actions. Despite how he felt about the woman standing on his doorstep he couldn't help but feel a pang of guilt at seeing her in her heartbroken state.

"Simba was my dog!" the woman screamed at him. "The dog you tried to kick in the face a few days ago. Did you think I wouldn't put two and two together and realise this was your handiwork?"

"Look at me" Harry said, motioning to his cast and his crutches. "How could I have hurt your dog? I've got a broken leg."

"That doesn't mean anything. I'll be calling the police you know. They'll find out whether it was poison and then we'll know that you did this."

"Oh piss off" Harry said. "I had nothing to do with this and I want nothing to do with you. So, if you'd kindly step off my doorstep, I'd like to go sit down now."

Rather than leave, the woman began to weep loudly. Her legs visibly weakened in her state of distress. At that very moment, the low rumble of a car's engine underpinned the woman's cries. Debbie's car pulled into place across Harry's drive. Lisa stared wide eyed out of the passenger side window before getting out.

"I won't let you get away with this" the woman sobbed, pointing an incredibly long fingernail into Harry's face. "I'll make sure you pay."

"What the hell is going on?"

Concern was etched across Lisa's face as she realised that the woman on her doorstep was in the middle of a complete emotional breakdown. Debbie watched on from her idling car, not even bothering to hide the fact that she was rubbernecking the confrontation happening outside of number 7 Ragworth Lane.

"This idiot says I killed her dog" Harry said, refusing to show even an ounce of compassion for fear that it may be misinterpreted as guilt.

"You *did* kill my dog. I know you did it."

"Easy now" Lisa said to the crying woman. "That's a very serious allegation. Do you have any evidence at all that proves he might have been responsible?"

"Simba died next to your fence. There was sick all around him. Your boyfriend must have poisoned him."

"Firstly" Lisa said, "he's my husband, not my boyfriend. Secondly, just because your dog died near our fence does not mean anything. He could have choked to death on something from inside your house and made his way out into your garden before he passed away. You're going to have to do better than that if you're going to pin this on Harry."

"This is bullshit" the neighbour said. "You're both in on this together. I'm going to call the police and let them sort this out."

"Alright" said Lisa, "you do that."

With that, Lisa pushed past the woman and helped Harry step back into the hallway before shutting the door. There was a rattling boom as the woman on the other side kicked the door and then headed back to her own house.

"My God" Lisa said once quiet had resumed. Harry stared at his wife in awe. He had been impressed by how quickly she had defused the situation. If it had been up to him, he would have let the argument go back and forth until the woman had admitted fault or left of her own accord.

"You'll never guess who I spoke to on the phone today" Harry said.

"Did you kill her dog?"

The bluntness of Lisa's question caught Harry off guard. "No."

"Do NOT lie to me. I'm going to ask you one more time. I promise that I'll believe whatever you tell me, but if I somehow find out that you've lied, I swear to God I'm going to leave you. Do I make myself clear?"

There was a fire in Lisa's eyes that Harry did not recognise. Standing before him, Lisa looked exhausted. It was as if the stress of the move and the new job and the neighbour had all crashed down on her at once and had pushed her toward the edge of some metaphorical cliff.

"Crystal" Harry said.

Lisa inhaled deeply.

"Did you kill that woman's dog?"

"No."

Lisa searched her husband's face while her own remained entirely expressionless. She headed into the house.

"Wait" Harry called after her. He struggled to turn on his crutches and keep pace. "You believe me, don't you?"

"I said I would."

"Don't get me wrong, I hated that dog, but I wouldn't kill it."

"OK" said Lisa.

Against his better judgement, Harry let a wry smile break out across his face. "Just because I don't feel that bad that it's gone, doesn't mean that I killed it. Let's face it, if I had done it, I'd have been doing us both a favour. That animal was a nightmare. I mean, most people would have had the good grace to teach it to stop making noise by that point. Even she must have been annoyed by it."

Lisa stopped still behind the open fridge door. When she closed it, her face had turned ashen white, almost as white as the neighbour woman's face had been.

"That was her dog" Lisa said.

"Yeah, but she had to have been annoyed by it too. It was a prick, and there's no way it's safe to have an animal that big around a kid."

"Her son is disabled" Lisa said, slowly closing the fridge and backing away from Harry. "She got the dog to help him develop. It was more or less his only friend."

A sinking feeling gripped at Harry.

"How on earth do you know that?"

"Because I speak to her" Lisa said. "Or, at least, I did. I probably won't get the chance now because she thinks you've killed her dog."

The colour continued to drain from Lisa's face as she battled with something within herself. A question caught in her throat and she swallowed it down only for it to rise up again and force its way out of her mouth.

"Harry. Please tell me you didn't kill her dog.

"You said you believed me."

"Just tell me again..."

Carefully, Harry took a step towards Lisa. He was startled to see her take a step away from him.

"I didn't kill her dog."

"LIAR!"

"I'm not lying" Harry said, trying to take hold of his flinching wife.

"I can see that you're lying Harry! What the hell is wrong with you?"

"I didn't do anything!"

"Get away from me!"

Lisa pushed past her husband, almost sending him crashing to the floor.

"Stay away from me!"

"Lisa, I'm not lying to you."

An aura of betrayal had settled over Lisa. "We should have never come here" she screamed. The void in which Simba would usually bark at such an outburst seemed suddenly deafening. Another pang of guilt hit Harry hard in his stomach.

"I wish you'd never talked me into buying this house. Since we've got here you've gotten lazy, and you've gotten selfish, and you've started to lie."

"I have not."

"There you go again. You can't help yourself."

"Lisa, I-"

Harry's wife hurried past him. One of her feet collided with the bottom of his crutch and the shift in balance sent Harry spilling onto one of the kitchen worktops.

"What the hell are you doing?"

"I want to go" Lisa said. "I want to leave this place and go back to our own home. I'm done with this house."

"We can't leave" said Harry, righting himself to his feet. "The house still isn't ready."

"Sell the house. We'll take the loss. Harry, it's not worth it anymore. It never has been."

"You don't know what you're saying. We can't just up and leave. It doesn't make any sense."

"No. you can't talk me out of it." A vicious shake had taken over Lisa. To Harry she looked very much like a woman on the brink of losing her mind. "I'm not bringing my child into this house. Harry, if you won't leave then I'll go without you."

"Lisa."

"Stop trying to talk me out of this. I want to go home!"

True silence reigned in the kitchen for the first time in what felt like an age. The house around them was still and yet it felt oddly brooding, as if this conflict was what it had really wanted all along.

"I'm going home with or without you" Lisa said.

"What about work?"

"I'll transfer back. Hospitals need nurses. There'll still be a place for me."

"But you hate everyone there."

"Not as much as I hate being here."

"So you're going to leave me stranded here? How am I supposed to get around without you? I have a broken leg!"

"I'm not leaving you stranded. You can come with me."

"What about all the stuff you've brought with you? You won't fit everything into that little car."

"I'll leave it here."

"This is ridiculous" Harry spat at his wife. He twisted on his crutches and tried to approach her once again, but Lisa backed away, never taking her eyes off Harry the whole time. She reacted to him like he was a stranger who had barged his way into her home. Her face was drawn into a permanent look of panic. Her hands had balled into fists as if she were expecting to have to fight him off at any moment. Harry's cool temperament was beginning to wear thin.

"You're not going anywhere" he said, hobbling forward on his broken leg.

"You can't stop me."

"The hell I can't. You're my wife and you'll do as I say. You aren't going anywhere, and I want you to get that stupid... No, that pathetic thought out of your stupid head. You are mine. Do you hear me? MINE!"

Harry launched himself forward. He reached for Lisa as he fell clumsily through the air. She fell backwards, pulling away just in time. Harry's hand grazed her NHS uniform with only the slightest of touches. His leg clattered to the ground with tremendous force.

"Get away from me" Lisa said, pulling herself to her feet. She hurried around her husband and began rushing up the stairs. With great effort, Harry rolled onto his back and watched her disappear into the darkness of the hallway.

"Get back here you bitch! You can't do this to me! I won't let you go anywhere!"

Harry had pulled himself into a sitting position by the time Lisa had made her way back down the first few stairs with an overnight bag slung loosely over one of her shoulders. Her pregnant belly obscured her view of her husband sitting with his back to the door until she was halfway down.

"Move" she said.

A low cackle bubbled in the back of Harry's throat. "Where are you going to go?"

"I'm staying in a hotel tonight. I don't feel safe being around you. Get out the way of the door."

"Which hotel?"

Lisa pressed her lips tightly together.

"If you don't get out of the way of the door, I'm going to call the police."

She dismounted the steps with a jittery caution. Lisa let her overnight bag slip off of her shoulder and then she held the strap in both hands. It hung heavily at her side. Harry's eyes tracked it as it swung back and forth.

"You're going to hit me with that? Is that the plan?"

"Get out the way of the door."

"If you leave, I'll make sure that you-"

The bag hit Harry hard enough to knock him onto his side. He lay disorientated until the bottom of the door clattered against his back. Lisa was trying to force herself through the small gap she had managed to create.

Harry grabbed at her ankle as she tried to squeeze through the door. Above him, his wife screamed something, but Harry could not hear exactly what it was. All he could do was try to pull her back into the house. Lisa kicked her legs and suddenly broke free. She spilled out onto the street, crying hysterically, dragging her bag behind her.

Harry clambered to his feet, pulling himself up onto the door handle and leaning against the door frame. His broken leg pressed hard into the ground sending jolts of pain through his still healing bones.

"You'll be back!" he screamed into the night. "You can't stay away for long. When you do come back, I'll make sure that you're sorry you ever left!"

Lisa didn't look back. She ran beyond the gate and then down the street. Her strides looked lumbered as she struggled against the weight of the bag and the child that was growing in the depths of her stomach.

Harry watched her movements with wild eyes. When she was finally out of sight, he noticed that Nettie was watching him from her doorstep.

"What the fuck are you looking at?" he said, his voice ugly and malicious.

The old woman watched him with tired eyes. Her hand did not leave the door handle to her home.

"You sound just like he did" she said, and then she went back into her home.

CHAPTER 18
61,896 SUBSCRIBERS

Harry had spent the hour before he forced himself into his bed drinking the last of the alcohol he had bought for the barbeque. When that had dried up, he had tried to phone Lisa, unsure of what he wanted to say to her but sure that he wanted to say it nonetheless. She predictably did not answer, and the only correspondence between the two was a text from Lisa that read "Stop calling me."

Harry had fallen into an uneasy sleep. Images swirled in front of his eyes, first of Lisa, and then of Nettie, and then of himself as he fell down the stairs. He watched himself fall over and over again from a vantage point at the top of the stairs, the images of his dream taking on a security camera quality until he eventually awoke.

Now a hangover twisted his brain.

Harry swung his broken leg over the side of his bed and reached for the crutches he had flung across the room. He hurried himself towards the bathroom where he vomited into a waiting toilet bowl. His sickness was spurred on by the regret that had taken a place next to the previous evenings booze.

When he was done, Harry saw that dawn had broken and the day had begun.

He took himself back to his bedroom and unlocked his phone. Lisa had not tried to contact him since she'd asked him to stop.

Fine. She would still be sleeping anywhere. Best leave her to rest and then speak to her when she got home. She would be starting work in a few hours and Harry waking her early would not do much to placate the ill feelings she harboured toward him.

He brushed his teeth and got himself dressed, stretching jogging bottoms over the sizable cast that gripped his lower leg. When he was done, Harry took himself into his living room and began the difficult task of concocting a plan to win his wife back.

"Guy?" Harry said, holding his phone to his ear.

"Harry? What the hell are you doing calling at this hour? It's not even seven in the morning."

"I know" Harry said. "I'm sorry. Have you gone home yet?"

"I was going to go back today" Guy said. His interrupted sleep added weight to his voice.

"So you're still in the northeast?"

"I'm still at the Travelodge. Harry, I'm exhausted. Can this wait?"

"Not really. I need your help. I've broken my leg."

"You've what? Jesus, Harry, call an ambulance! What are you phoning me for?"

Harry began to laugh, suddenly appreciating how that must have sounded to Guy.

"I did it a couple of days ago, right after the barbeque. I fell down the stairs."

"Why didn't you tell me?"

"Are you a doctor?"

"I work in marketing."

"Then why would I call you? Listen, I want to do something for Lisa but obviously I can't drive. I was wondering if you'd be able to help me out today. I just need a couple of lifts here and there, then if you fancied getting stuck in on a couple of DIY projects, I'd really appreciate the help."

There was a reluctant moment of quiet on the end of the line. Harry heard a shuffling sound and then:

"Harry, I really need to get back home. I have work in the

morning and it's a long drive. It was great seeing you the other day and I'm sorry about your leg but-"

"She's going to leave me" Harry said suddenly. "I need to make a grand gesture to really pull her back in. I can pay you if money is the problem."

An unspoken insult drifted down the line.

"You're my best friend Harry. I'm not going to charge you for giving you a ride here and there."

"You'll do it then? You'll help me out?"

Harry listened to the sigh of a man who knew he had been backed into a corner from which he had no way out.

"How on earth do you manage to do this every time? I need to be gone by three. I'm meeting some of the lads from work at eight and I want to get showered before I go out. Especially if I'm going to be doing DIY."

"Thanks Guy, I mean it."

"What do you need me to do?"

*****

Guy watched Harry hobbling to the car with a mixture of pity and that schadenfreude pleasure that men experience from seeing their best friends enduring significant hardship.

"What the hell have you been up to?" he asked, getting out of his car and helping Harry into the passenger side.

"I told you. I fell down the stairs."

"Shame you didn't break your neck" Guy said. "Waking me up at seven on my last day off."

Harry reeled off the whole grisly story of how he fell down the stairs on the journey to the hardware shop. He did not hide from the details of how he had seen his unborn son trapped in his mattress, nor did he skirt around the fact that he had all but threatened his wife as she fled from their home. Guy sat and listened to the whole tale, never judging or asking questions. Instead he listened to the story and when it was over, he agreed that Harry would need to plan something spectacular if he had any chance of getting his wife back.

They pulled into the broken-down car park adjacent to the crumbling town centre. Guy physically winced as he exited the vehicle.

"It's rough round here" Harry told him as his friend helped him get to his feet.

"You're telling me" said Guy.

The old woman in the hardware shop smiled upon seeing Harry come through the door, and then her face contorted into an expression of concern upon seeing his cast.

"My goodness" she said as she hurried out from behind the till. "What on earth has happened to you?"

"DIY accident" Harry said before realising that his joke had only served to concern the old lady. "I fell down the stairs."

The old woman tensed, her eyes lingering on the cast that clung tightly around Harry's leg. "You need to be careful. A young lady who lived near me died from falling down the stairs when I was a girl."

Harry wondered if she too had grown up on Ragworth lane.

Harry handed the woman a list of the items he would need for the rest of the day. She took it, affixed her glasses to the end of her nose and read, nodding as she did, occasionally murmuring to herself.

"I think I have most of these things" she said. "And I can put you in the right direction for the things that I don't have. The bigger things like the carpet, when do you need those by?"

Guy and Harry exchanged anticipatory smiles.

"Today" said Harry. "It's a surprise for my wife. We're having a baby."

"Is it due tomorrow?" the old lady asked sarcastically.

"What's all the rush?"

"It's a long story" Harry said, shifting uncomfortably on his crutches. "Ideally I need to get this nursery pulled together today."

The old lady looked back over the list, took her glasses off her face and ran a dry hand over a wrinkled forehead.

"Alright" she said eventually. "Let's get you what you need."

*****

It took three trips to get everything that Harry needed brought back to the house. On the last trip Harry stayed home after Guy told him he was actually more of a hinderance than a help. As if to confirm what Guy had told him, Harry watched on helplessly as he struggled to drag a rolled of carpet up the stairs.

"I really think we should have paid to get a professional to install this thing" Guy wheezed. He dropped the carpet onto the hardwood floor of the spare room with a satisfying thump. He picked up the fibres that now clung to his sweatshirt with a thinly veiled annoyance.

"I can't afford it" Harry said. "Our credit cards are pretty much maxed out for this month. Plus, there's no telling whether they'd have been able to come and do the job today."

Guy looked at the carpet and the bundle of jagged carpet grippers in the corner of the room.

"Have you ever installed flooring before?" he asked dubiously.

"No" Harry said. "But it's nothing that a couple of YouTube tutorials couldn't explained."

They sat in the middle of the spare bedroom floor and watched two tutorials on Harry's phone. Harry swiped away the little red notifications that alerted him to the new comments springing up on his video. He found that a rigid deadline was giving him all the motivation he needed to maintain his focus.

"What time is Lisa due back today?" Guy asked once they were done watching the final tutorial.

"About six" said Harry.

Guy exhaled. "Alright then. Let's get cracking."

The two men worked quickly. The carpet was installed with only a minor issue - a bunching of the fabric that swelled like an air pocket in the middle of the room - but both Harry and Guy were satisfied that this could be hidden by the cot once they had built it.

They spread sheets across the floor and painted the dark brown walls a gentle shade of white with an expert display of teamwork. Harry painted from a sitting position, covering the walls up to Guy's waist height, and Guy took the top half of the room, using a step ladder to reach up to the mottled ceiling.

Once they were done with this, Guy used a paint roller on a broom handle to mask the stains on the ceiling while Harry assembled the cot in the centre of the room. By the time lunchtime had rolled around neither man noticed the hunger that had grown in his belly. Instead, they enjoyed the feeling of a job well done.

"What time is it?" Harry asked as they loaded the mattress into the newly built crib. Guy checked the watch that he had covered with tape in an attempt to stop it becoming spotted with paint.

"Ten past three" Guy said.

"Oh shit. I'm sorry mate. Didn't you need to be away by three?"

A look of determination melted across Guy's face.

"I did, but it doesn't matter. The lads can wait. I want to see how this place turns out in the end."

The pair set to work applying the finishing touches to the room, hanging bright pictures on the wall and installing light curtains adorned with a duckling pattern. By the time the men were done, another hour had passed and each of them now reeked of the sweat of their labours. This was overpowered by a heavy sense of satisfaction that ebbed from each man in great blossoming plumes.

"Hey" Harry said, working one of his hands free from his crutches. "Put her there."

Guy took Harry's hand in his own and shook it vigorously.

"We've put in a hell of a shift today" Guy said, marvelling at the room in its completed state.

"I'll say. Same time tomorrow? We'll get the hallway done."

"Piss off" Guy said, slapping Harry hard on the back. "I'm going home."

Guy went down the stairs and Harry scooted along behind. They said their goodbyes at the doorway.

As Harry watched Guy's car pull off the drive he noticed that Nettie was returning home with a heavy set of shopping bags in her arms.

"Nettie" Harry shouted, waving as best as he could with his crutches attached to his wrists.

The old woman glanced in his direction and then quickened her pace to her front door.

"Wait!"

Harry stepped out of his house. His socks became instantly saturated with the dirty water that seemed a permanent fixture of his driveway. He hurried to the old woman's side, his crutches digging into the soft mud of her front yard.

"Nettie! Please, wait!"

"What do you want Harry?" she said without stopping. The old woman placed her bags down on her front porch and began rifling through her handbag for her keys.

"I wanted to apologise. I shouldn't have spoken to you like

that last night."

"No, you shouldn't have."

"I'm sorry."

"OK."

Nettie continued to rummage through a purse that looked fit to burst, eventually producing a small set of keys attached to a modest looking keyring. Harry bent clumsily to pick up her bags.

"What are you doing?"

"I'm helping you."

"I can do it myself. Don't touch my things."

Harry stood up straight. The old woman continued to avoid his gaze.

"Nettie. I said I was sorry."

"That doesn't mean I still can't be angry" she said. "The way you spoke to me last night was disgusting. I haven't been spoken to that way since...Well, for a long time. Put it that way."

"I'm sorry."

"You should be."

Nettie put her keys into the lock and opened the door. She stepped inside the house and pulled her bags over the threshold behind her. Harry turned to head back into his own house and change his sodden socks.

"Do you know what the worst of it was?" the old woman shouted after him as he walked away.

Harry's progress stopped.

"The way you spoke to that young lady last night, that was the really unforgivable thing. It made me feel like I was a girl all over again, listening to that brute tormenting that other poor girl behind the walls. If you ever speak to your wife that way again, I'm going to call the police. They might not have done anything about it back then, but times have changed now. I'll see you taken away if you do it again. Do I make myself clear?"

"Crystal" Harry said with an odd feeling of déjà vu. He was surprised to find that he didn't feel even the slightest annoyance at the way the old woman was speaking to him.

"Again, I'm very sorry."

Nettie nodded and then closed her door.

*****

When five o'clock rolled round, Harry set himself on the bottom step and waited patiently by the door. He had no idea whether Lisa would be coming home, but given the fact she had only taken a small overnight bag with her when she had left, and given the fact that all but one of her work uniforms was hanging in their shared wardrobe, there was every chance that she would need to come back for practical reasons alone.

He sent her a text asking if she knew what time she would return. Harry did not receive a reply. This did nothing to diminish Harry's determination to meet his wife the moment she stepped through the door. He would wait all night if he needed to.

An hour later the sound of a car's engine idling at the end of the driveway brought Harry out of a near slumber. He sat himself up, smoothed out the sweatshirt he had put on after he had struggled out of the shower earlier in the day and got himself unsteadily to his feet.

The door handle twisted, and Lisa entered the house.

"Lisa, I-"

"I have nothing to say to you."

"No, wait, I want to talk to you."

"Leave me alone Harry."

"Please" Harry pleaded. He tried to turn on his crutches as Lisa went by him in the hallway. "I know I've done wrong but I-"

"Done wrong? Do you know how frightened I was of you last night? I have put up with a lot lately. I've been frustrated and angry, but I never have been *frightened* of you before."

"I know" Harry said. Lisa opened up a drawer in the kitchen and took out a small but sharp looking knife. She walked towards her husband holding it ahead of herself, forcing a barrier between them.

"What are you doing?" he asked incredulously.

"I'm making sure you can't do anything stupid."

The urge to argue his case, to tell her that she was being ridiculous tugged at Harry from the inside, but he swallowed this feeling and pursued his wife as she hurried upstairs.

"I'm sorry. I was way out of line."

"You can say that again" Lisa called from the bedroom.

"But I've spent the day trying to make it up to you. I have something I want to show you."

The sound of cupboard doors opening and closing came from the bedroom. "I don't think flowers are going to smooth this one out Harry."

"It's not flowers."

Amazingly, a small spark of excitement ignited in Harry's chest. The anticipation of seeing his wife see the nursery that he had painstakingly put together was enough to bring a spring to his otherwise hindered step.

Lisa came out of the bedroom with her work uniform strewn unceremoniously over one of her shoulders. The small knife was no longer in her hand, apparently it had been forgotten in her hurry to retrieve her scrubs for the following day.

"Debbie is waiting in the car outside" she said. "Whatever you have to show me, just do it so I can get back to her house."

"You're staying with Debbie?" Harry asked. "I thought you were going to stay at the Travelodge."

"So did I. They rejected all of our credit cards. When I

checked the recent transactions it said that you'd spent nearly a hundred pounds on books on the occult and nearly four hundred on a new camera. What the hell are you doing Harry?"

"What? I don't remember doing that. What new camera?"

"Harry..."

"OK, never mind. Please, would you just follow me?"

Harry led his wife down the cramped hallway and stopped outside of the spare bedroom door. The small spark of excitement was beginning to find kindling deep within his chest.

"Some of the paint might still be wet and there are a couple of snagging issues, but you need to remember that we did all of this in a day."

"We?"

"Me and Guy."

Lisa faltered. Her eyebrows stitched together in a look of confusion.

"Guy helped you?"

"Yeah, listen. I want you to know that I would never do anything to hurt you or the baby, despite what I said and did yesterday. I love you both so much, and I want you to remember that every time you go into this room. OK?"

"OK..."

"Go on then" said Harry excitedly. "Open the door."

Harry thought he recognised the faintest of smiles on Lisa's face as she opened the door. Her hand reached into the darkness and flicked on the light to reveal the spare bedroom just as it always had been, filled with boxes, largely derelict, surrounded by brown ugly walls.

Lisa searched the room from the doorway.

"Am I missing something here?"

A cold wash ran through Harry's heart. His eyes widened against the sight of the neglected space. The dusty smell of an unused room hit him hard in the face.

"What is this?" Lisa asked.

Harry stepped forward into the room. His mouth dropped open as he gawped at the undoing of his hard work. Gone were the soft white walls and the childlike pictures. Gone was the plush carpet and the duckling patterned curtains. Gone was the cot that he had built today.

"What the hell?" he asked nobody in particular. "Where the hell has it all gone?"

"Is this supposed to be some sort of joke?"

"How... how could this be a joke?" Harry's skin began to tingle with the illogical nature of what was happening. In a tired and frightened voice, he asked Lisa "Where has everything gone?"

She stepped into the room and picked up a stack of books that sat atop a case for a brand new camera.

"*A Practical Guide to Demonology. Contacting the other side.* This is what you spent the last of our money on?"

Harry said nothing. Instead he continued to gawp, staring wide eyed at the camera case he had no recollection of buying.

Lisa shifted behind Harry, turning off the light and stepping away from the room. Harry's head continued to swirl in the darkness, grasping for answers that it could not possibly find.

"I don't have time for this Harry. I have to get back to Debbie. She's waiting outside."

"No" Harry said, becoming angry now. He shook his head in defiance of the reality he was facing. "This isn't right! I spent all day turning this into a nursery. There was a cot and a carpet, and we painted the walls. It was finished."

"Who painted the walls?"

"Me and Guy."

Lisa was found anger of her own.

"Harry, Guy went home after the barbeque. He's back in

the South."

"He was here today."

"No" Lisa said. "He wasn't."

Harry swayed unsteadily on his one good leg. A ringing sound seemed to emanate from the walls, overpowering Harry senses, enveloping him in its unpleasant tone.

"You need to get out of here" she said. "This house, it's not good for you. It's not good for anyone. It's changing you Harry."

"I swear I decorated this room. It was beautiful. I did it for you."

"You didn't" Lisa said softly. "You can't have. Look at it."

"But..." Much to Harry's chagrin, he found he had nowhere else to go.

Lisa collected her things and headed down the stairs. Harry continued to stand alone in the dark of the room.

"I'm going to call you tomorrow" Lisa shouted up from the hallway. "Please think about what I said. I'm going to go home. I still love you enough to let you come with me."

The front door closed loudly behind Lisa. A hollow silence took its place.

Harry gazed drunkenly around the room, his eyes picking up the boxes and general clutter of the abundant space in the darkness. The house was toying with him, making him out to look like he was losing his mind. It was lashing out, annoyed that Harry was exposing it for what it was, a place of illusion, a place of malice and madness.

"You can't do this to me" Harry said into the emptiness of his home. "I won't let you keep hiding this from everybody. I'm going to show the world what you are, or I'm going to burn you to the ground. Either way, you are not going to get the better of me."

Harry exited the room and closed the door behind him, promising himself he would decorate it again. He would pull it into the perfect shape it had been in when he had left it this afternoon.

He tracked out onto the stairs and began the arduous task of descending to the ground floor on his hands and his one good leg. In the quiet moments between Harry's determined grunts, he was almost certain that he could hear the sound of mocking laughter.

CHAPTER 19
62,052 SUBSCRIBERS

With a dogged determination, Harry rushed towards his front door as quickly as his crutches would allow. A guttural rumble filled his hallway. The sound intensified when Harry tore open the door.

Dean King noticed Harry, nodded in acknowledgement and then held up a finger. His car's engine continued to rumble as it idled in the driveway. Loose paving slabs shook along to the sound.

A palpable excitement rattled through Harry's chest. He gripped the handles of his crutches, almost as if trying to stop himself from floating up into the air.

Dean put down the phone which had been clamped to the side of his face, and then killed the engine. The car shuddered to a stop. He opened his door and climbed out of the low driver's seat of his electric blue sports car.

"Wow" Harry said from his place in the doorway. "Nice car."

Dean flashed a crooked smile.

"What? This old thing? This is just a run around. You should see my weekend car."

Not knowing whether to believe him or not, Harry simply laughed along with Dean. He leaned into the car and then took out a black holdall bag.

"How's the leg mate?" Dean asked as he walked across the cracked driveway slabs.

"Broken" Harry said.

Dean nodded, watching Harry over the sunglasses he wore

despite the day's gloomy weather.

"I can see that mate. Great job in turning that into a tasty bit of content though. You'll go far in this business, take it from me."

Upon entering Harry's home, Dean pulled off his sunglasses and perched them on the top of his head.

"Hey" he said, marvelling at the hallway. "Great aesthetic. It's rundown but relatable. The kind of thing the great unwashed can see themselves living in. How long did you say you've been living here for?"

"About seven months" Harry said. The urge to touch Dean King and verify his authenticity pulled at his fingers. Dean looked almost surreal in this fleshly state, so used was Harry to watching him in two dimensions broadcasted to his phone and laptop screen.

"Great find." Dean said. "Places like this are great little starter houses for channels like ours. You can pick them up for a steal and just dump them off on someone else when you're done. How much did it set you back?"

The question felt intrusive. Strangely, Harry contemplated lying, telling Dean he paid less for the house than was strictly true.

"Seventy-seven" said Harry. Dean pulled air through his crooked teeth.

"Fair enough" he said. "Has it done you well?"

"Yeah. It's cosy enough. My wife doesn't like it for some reason. She's chosen to go back to our actual home in the south. It's a bit complicated really."

Dean poked his head through the living room door on his way to the kitchen. He pushed a pellet of chewing gum into his mouth and began to chew loudly.

"It's probably not as complicated as you think mate. She doesn't like it because it's a shithole, pure and simple. But that's not what I meant by has it done you well. I meant financially.

How much money are you making off the channel?"

"Oh" Harry said, feeling an odd sense of invasion for the second time in as many minutes. "I do alright."

"Fucking hell mate, what does alright mean? Five grand a month? Ten? What is it?"

The urge to lie returned.

"About a thousand a month" Harry said meekly. "Give or take."

"Jesus."

"Is that not... good?"

Dean pulled his sunglasses back over his eyes.

"No, but don't worry about it" Dean said. "We all have to start somewhere."

Harry cringed at the feeling of his face turning red. He moved to the front door and nudged it closed with the end of one of his crutches. Dean hurried to catch it before it closed fully.

"That's OK mate. I have a few more bags I need to bring in first. I don't suppose you'd be able to help me with them, would you?"

Harry looked down at the weighty cast on the end of his leg.

"I'll take that as a no then." Dean said. "You're neither use nor ornament." He left the house and trudged back up the cracked driveway, opening the boot of his car to reveal a pile of black bags and silver cases.

"What is all of this?" Harry asked.

Dean dropped one of the bags onto the hallway floor with a loud grunt.

"Lights" he said, "Studio lights."

He went back out onto the drive and collected more of the cases, bringing them into the house and dropping them onto the hallway floor. Harry watched helplessly as the equipment piled up, moving quietly onto his bottom step once the floor space of the hallway had been taken up.

"Why all the equipment?"

"I thought you just used a handheld camera. That's all I see you use in your videos."

Wheezing, Dean shook his head. He produced a vape pen from inside his jeans pocket, inhaled from it and then breathed out a plume strawberry scented mist into the air.

"That's because I only *want* you to see the handheld camera. There's a lot more that goes on behind the scenes. Relatability. That's the key to a show like mine. I have to let the audience believe that I'm just a normal geezer, just like they are. If they knew the cost of the stuff I was using to make these videos it would drive a wedge between me and the everyman that makes up my audience. Does that make sense?"

Harry thought it over for a minute, trying to ignore feeling that he was peeking behind the curtain that he did not actually want to see behind.

"Sort of."

Dean exhaled another plume of strawberry vape into the hallway. "Look at it this way mate. Audiences expect a certain level of quality when it comes to their YouTube content, right? That's why the shows that look like shit track like shit in the algorithms. You following me?"

"Yeah."

"I knew you weren't as stupid as you looked. At the same time, the people who watch these shows are after a certain level of authenticity. They want to feel like the things I show them could happen in their own houses, so I can't exactly show them my thirty-grand camera - which is in that case by your feet by the way - so be careful, would you?"

Harry looked down to find that his crutch was now resting on the strap that was attached to the expensive looking carry case Dean was pointing at.

"Sorry."

"Don't worry about it. So, I can't show them the camera all the lights or the gimbals or the massive editing suite that's taken over my spare bedroom because then they'd see the truth of the matter, wouldn't they?"

Harry's head was spinning. The information seemed to be leading him to a conclusion that he did not want to be led to. Regardless, he felt backed into a corner, forced to ask the follow up questions that sat on the tip of his tongue and sent bitter sensations through the sense of reality he had come to believe.

"And what exactly is the truth of the matter Dean?"

Dean scoffed, catching his laughter in the back of his throat. He allowed himself a brief crooked smile.

"Well, come on Harry mate. Play the game. You're not going to make me say it are you?"

With a serious hesitation, Harry shrugged his shoulders.

"I'm not sure I'm following you."

Dean took another drag from his vape and then put it back in his pocket.

"Come on Harry. It's not real, is it?"

"What's not real?"

"The whole ghost thing. Not all of it, anyway. There's a lot of smoke and mirrors that goes into shows like ours."

A hard lump formed in the back of Harry's throat. Suddenly his arms felt numb and he had to look down at his hands to make sure that he was still in fact holding onto the handles of his crutches.

Recognising the upset his words seemed to be causing, Dean quickly tried to backtrack on his sentiment.

"Don't get me wrong, a lot of it is real. It's just that not all of it is. I mean, on your channel, you must stretch the truth, right? Sure, you fell down the stairs, but at the end of the day *you fell down the stairs*. Twisting it to give it a paranormal spin, that was clever, but you can't really believe that a ghost forced you to see your unborn son so that you would fall down the stairs, can you? The moans and the knocking and the shit moving about on camera, that's your wife making the noise and pulling strings isn't it?"

Harry found himself too stunned to even speak. He stared open mouthed at the man he had so idolised when he had started this journey. It was as if Harry could see a mask physically slipping away from Dean King's face. Gone was the serious paranormal investigator that he thought he had known from the videos he poured over. Instead he now saw man who amounted to little more than a cheap illusionist, a peddler of campy found footage with no goal other than turning a quick profit.

"No" Harry said, "That's not what happened. All the stuff I've filmed has been authentic. Everything is real in my videos."

Dean King chewed his gum like a cow chewing cud. He watched Harry carefully, looking for signs of a crack in his facade. When he found none, he simply resorted to his trademark crooked toothed smile.

"OK mate. This video should be easy enough to make then. Less smoke and mirrors for us to install, eh? Do you have anywhere I can charge this camera battery?"

Harry motioned to the living room with numb arms. Dean went in, seeking out a plug socket with his camera case in hand. Harry followed, feeling like he had been punched in the gut.

"Are you telling me that all the houses you visited in your videos, and all the churches, and all the abandoned prisons, that they weren't really haunted?"

"I didn't say that" Dean said. "I believe in ghosts, and I believe that those places are haunted, but what I'm saying is that sometimes I have to spice up the truth with a little well-placed fiction. Our audiences want the extremes mate. What am I supposed to say? *I visited the Jolly Sailor Pub, the most haunted pub in England but I didn't come away with any evidence, so you'll just have to take my word for it?* How would that look?"

"It would look like the truth" Harry said.

Dean stopped what he was doing, stood up straight and locked Harry with a concerned look.

"Look mate, I really thought you were on the same page as me. Don't get me wrong, I'm open to finding real evidence of ghosts, but so far, I just haven't. If you're saying that this place is haunted and can give us some real evidence then that's great, bring it on. All I'm saying is, if we can't get anything in the limited time that I'm here then we're going to have to make something happen. Alright?"

This was not alright. Harry contemplated kicking Dean King out of his house and revealing to the world the heart-breaking secret this man had just shared. This thought however brought with it a tremendous sense of an opportunity lost. Dean was Harry's ticket to finally proving to a massive audience that his home was haunted. The chip on Harry shoulder suddenly began burning brighter than it ever had before.

"Alright" Harry said. "You're right. We'll just have to make something happen."

"There you go mate" Dean beamed. "I knew you'd get it. You're a class act mate. A real class act."

Harry did his best to tidy the hallway as Dean set his camera battery on charge. His mind continued to work as he struggled against a heavy bag that got entangled in his crutches.

"Dean? Did you bring your investigation kit with you? The one with the Ouija board, and the EMF reader and all that?"

"I brought the lot mate. Like I said, just because I add a bit of flair into my videos doesn't mean I'm not serious about finding proof of the other side. It's just that some of the places I visit with the channel are owned by... How should I put this?"

Harry waited, his sense of excitement starting to return, overshadowing the betrayal that had clutched at his heart.

"I guess I would call them *idiots*." Dean laughed, easily amused by his own escapades. "Honestly, so many people find the paranormal where there's just nothing. I get calls from people all day long swearing up and down that their home is the next Amityville and when I get there all I'm finding is noisy water pipes and overactive imaginations. It's a wonder anyone actually watches my videos at all. They probably wouldn't if I didn't work a bit of magic through them before release."

"But don't people mind you faking their experiences? Hasn't anyone ever refused to let you undermine their hauntings?"

A deep look of suspicion enveloped Dean King.

"Nobody has ever complained. Think about it. Everybody wants their fifteen minutes of fame. I never promised to exorcise any of these homes, and I don't say I can help bringing the haunting to an end. I only promised to show them to the world. People just want to be seen and heard. That's why everyone is on Tik Tok and Instagram and Facebook and all that other shite. Speaking of which, you really should get a Tik Tok mate, it's great for engagement."

"Yeah" Harry said distantly, "I suppose I should."

Dean finished setting up his camera battery and began unloading his lights. Once he was done, he pulled his phone from his pocket.

"Right" he said with one of his arms outstretched, "I think it's about time we start promoting this little video of ours. Let's go live. I usually get great engagement on Insta at this time of the day"

Dean flicked on the lights and stepped into frame. Harry trundled toward Dean, leaning into the shot and smiling broadly. Dean's thumb hovered over the record button and then stopped.

"Don't smile mate. It doesn't set the right tone. Try to look serious, like I do."

"Sorry" Harry said, forcing the smile from his face. Dean hit the record button and stared into the camera. Harry did the same, an expression of curiosity bleeding out of his stoic frown.

"I'm here with Harry from Our Haunted Home in what he says is one of the most haunted houses in all of Britain, if not the world. Me and Harry are gonna be working on a video tonight which I'm really excited about. Harry, tell them the sort of things you've experienced while you've been living here. What can our viewers look forward to seeing?"

A sudden boldness stirred in Harry. His skin puckered under the goose bumps that erupted across his arms. His mouth started to move before he even knew what it was going to say.

"Well, I think that our viewers can expect to see the realest video that *King of the Haunt* has ever made. I don't want to say too much, but Dean has just told me something pretty unbelievable about his previous films, and I think that his viewers would be interested to know that-."

Dean killed the recording, nearly dropping his phone in the process.

"What the hell was that?"

"I was answering your question. What else was I supposed to do?"

"Are you trying to throw me under the bus?"

Dean was scrolling through his phone feverishly.

"My comment section is going fucking mad."

"Great"

"Yeah" Dean said, "*Great*. What the hell is wrong with you?"

"What's wrong with me? You're the one who's been lying

to everyone this whole time!"

Dean laughed bitterly. For a moment Harry thought he was going to square his shoulders, back him into a corner and beat him for what he had said. In the end Dean backed down, stuffing his phone into his pocket and collecting up his things.

"I'm off. This was your big chance Harry. All you had to do was play the game and you could have had everything you wanted."

"All I've ever wanted is for people to know the truth."

"Yeah, well now you'll have to let people know the truth alone on your own channel. You're not using mine as a sounding board for your silly little beliefs."

Harry watched calmly as Dean started pulling collecting up the bags he had strewn on the floor as he made his way to the front door.

"Are we not doing this anymore?"

"So that you can call me a liar on my own channel? Absolutely not."

"If you don't do it, I'll tell everybody what you said."

Dean laughed again. His crooked teeth stood like tomb stones in his gums.

"And I'll deny it."

Dean opened the front door and trudged out to his car. He popped open the boot, stuffed his bags into the car and then went back to the house for more. Harry was waiting for him in the hallway, a smug grin spreading across his lips.

"You look happy for a man who's doomed to be a nobody for the rest of his life."

"I don't think that I'll be a nobody once our video airs. We're going to show the world exactly what's been happening in this house."

Dean faltered.

"Are you deaf? I said we're not going to be making any videos together. I'm not going to be pushed around by some little upstart. What in the world makes you think I would work with you now?"

Without saying a word, Harry looked up to the ceiling. Dean's eyes widened when he saw the camera hanging in the corner of the hallway.

"My wife went mad when she found out how much money I'd spent on those things, but they were totally worth it. They're actually really good cameras. They record video and audio. But the feature I like best is that they never stop recording."

Dean tensed under Harry's gaze as he realised that he had been played expertly.

"You dick."

Harry shrugged his shoulders.

"That seems to be the general consensus these days."

"So, what? You want money?"

"I want to work with you on this video, but I want to show the truth this time. No tricks. No special effects. We roll the cameras and we put out what we capture."

Dean thought this over. His eyes darted from Harry's steely gaze up to the black lens of the camera above him. He ground his teeth as he contemplated his next move. In a sudden flurry of movement, Dean headed to the door.

"Where are you going?"

"To the hotel. I need some sleep. We're gonna be up all night at this rate."

"So, we're doing it then?"

Dean stepped out onto the driveway and looked up at the crumbling house around which Harry had built his life.

"I don't have much of a choice, do I?"

CHAPTER 20
62,052 SUBSCRIBERS

Harry opened the door to find an exhausted looking Dean King waiting on his driveway. The street behind him was lit only by a flickering lamppost and yet its darkness was still surpassed by the darkness of the circles under Dean's eyes.

"I haven't slept at all" he said stepping into the house without waiting to be invited in. "I spent all day tinkering around with special effects software. I want to show you something and I want you to be honest about how it looks, alright?"

"We're not using special effects in this video."

"But Harry, we need to at least show something for our audience to-"

"We won't need it."

"How can you be so sure?"

Harry closed the door behind Dean. He had not slept either. The events of the day had played over and over in his mind, keeping him from resting. The more Harry had thought about Dean and his suggestion that they should create false signs of the haunting he clearly did not believe existed, the more Harry had come to realise that just like Lisa and Guy and Andrew and Debbie and the thousands upon thousands of people online, Dean was just another non believer that Harry desperately wanted to prove wrong.

"You'll see."

Dean followed behind Harry, grunting loudly as he lugged his lights up the stairs. When they eventually reached the landing, Dean was surprised to find the place in complete disarray.

"What the hell is all of this?" he asked, squeezing past the boxes that were now stacked in untidy piles across the landing floor.

"Just some bits and pieces that I needed to move out of the spare room" Harry said. "We never really unpacked them after we moved. You know, this room was going to be a nursery. My wife is having a baby."

"Fascinating."

Harry opened the door to the spare bedroom and went in. Dean followed, then stopped on the threshold between the hallway and the spare bedroom. His eyes widened and his skin turned pale.

"Harry. What have you done?"

"I made the room a bit more conducive of an investigation space. Like I said, I think we need to try really hard to make something happen tonight. I figured this way we have the best chances to make something happen."

The interior of the room looked like a scene from a cheap horror movie. It was empty aside from a small table and the two chairs that were neatly tucked under it. Harry's new camera - the one he had no recollection of buying - sat on a tripod next to the table. A wide, wet pentagram was painted onto the floorboards, shimmering in the light of the black candle that burned in the middle of the table.

"Is that...blood?"

The question sent a throbbing sensation across the fresh scars that tracked up and down Harry's arms in the shape of inverted crosses. He tugged at his sweater sleeves, ensuring the bandages he had clumsily wrapped around these open wounds were out of sight.

"It's just paint" Harry lied.

Dean King seemed to lose another shade of colour.

"Harry. This is too much. It's not going to look real on

camera. The whole thing is going to look staged."

Harry chuckled to himself as he hopped over the pentagram and settled himself into one of the seats.

"I know, ironic, isn't it? It's going to look totally fake but in reality this is going to be the realest footage you've ever recorded."

Dean watched the light dance across Harry's face. The candlelight contorted Harry smile into an ever-churning patchwork of expressions. Carefully, Dean crossed the pentagram and sat himself down at the table.

"Have you got your camera?"

Dean set the heavy case he had been carrying onto the table and took out his camera.

"I wish you'd let me use my GoPro. It's what people are used to seeing me use."

Harry shook his head.

"No, it's what people are used to seeing you *pretend* to use. It's like you said, people expect a certain quality from your films. When the action starts, you're going to be glad you brought that all singing all dancing piece of kit with you. You are not going to want to miss a second of the action."

Harry pulled his own camera closer to the table. He angled it so that it was picking up the dark outlines of Dean and himself and when he was happy, he pressed the record button on the back of the device. The camera beeped quietly. A red light began to flash.

"You're going to need to talk me through how to use the Ouija board" Harry said. "I've watched you use it hundreds of times on your channel, but I've never actually used one myself. Is it really as simple as putting my finger on the pointer and waiting for it to move?"

Dean reached down and took his board from his bag. He placed it in the middle of the table, moving the black candle to one side, sending yet more elongated shadows stretching across the room.

"It's called a planchette mate, but yes. It is as simple as that."

Harry marvelled at the lettering that sat around the rim of the Ouija board. In the dim light of the room it seemed to take on an almost mythical quality.

"Sometimes you just have to give the planchette a quick nudge, just to get the ball rolling, if you get me?"

Harry realised that Dean was whispering to avoid the cameras picking up his incriminating words and exposing him as the fraud that he was.

"How about tonight we just wait and see what happens? I'll promise not to push the planchette if you do the same. You just need to trust me. I've done a lot of preparation. If there was ever a night when something paranormal was going to happen, this would be it."

The scars that throbbed across Harry's arms caused him to wince inwardly. Dean watched Harry in the darkness, noticing the tiny pained expressions that played out across his face. He seemed now like a different man to the one he had met earlier in the day. There was a vacancy about him that had not been there before, but at the same time there was a good chance that Harry was displaying the exact opposite. Was it a vacancy, or was it like Harry was possessed by something that had not been there before?

Dean smiled politely, trying not to give the impression that he was searching for something in Harry, analysing his demeanour, digging for what lay just below the surface.

"Shall we get the ball rolling?"

"I thought you said it was called a planchette" Harry smiled. Dean did not even fain humour at Harry's joke. The two men placed their fingers on the small wooden pointer.

Dean exhaled. Harry did the same. Dean's voice wavered as he began to speak into the darkness.

"If there is anybody-"

"You haven't hit record on your camera yet."

"Oh" Dean said, "So I haven't. How could I forget that?"

His hand left the planchette and he reached over to the camera, pressing the record button. The camera beeped. Dean returned his hand to the board.

"If there is anybody with us tonight, we would urge you to speak if that is your desire. You can use this board as your voice and our bodies as your vessel."

The room fell into a silence. The house became still. A wave of impatience washed over Harry.

"No. If there are any spirits, or entities, or demons or whatever in my house, we *command* that you speak to us. You shouldn't be here."

"What are you doing?" Dean asked.

"I'm trying to provoke a response" Harry said. He closed his eyes again. "I order you to use this board and explain to me just who the hell you think you are terrifying my family like this? Was that you that pushed me down the stairs? Was it you that burst my water pipe? Are you the coward who hid behind an image of a dead plumber so that you could try and drive me from this house? Well guess what, I'm still here you fucking coward-"

The planchette shifted under Harry's finger. He looked to Dean, who was currently staring at his host with a horrified look on his face.

"Was that you?"

Dean King shook his head. Excitement swelled in Harry.

"Was that it?" Harry asked. "One little twitch? I offer you up my blood-"

"- your blood?-"

"- a perfectly good animal sacrifice and the promise of yet more lives and all you give me in return is one tiny twitch of such a small piece of wood? You are pathetic-"

"Harry..."

"- I honestly expected more from-"

The planchette slid quickly across the board and then stopped over the letter G.

"There we go" Harry said contently. "Have you got anymore, or is that really it?"

Dean watched with wide eyes as the planchette shot across the board and settled on the letter E.

"Oh..." Harry said, sounding suddenly disappointed. "Are you about to tell me to *get out*?"

The planchette moved again, this time settling on the letter T.

Harry sighed. "How predictable" he said. "How disappointing."

"Harry, are you doing this?" Dean asked. Harry withdrew his eyes from the board and locked him with the darkest gaze Dean had ever seen. There was a hopelessness in Harry's eyes that made Dean feel as if he was staring into the darkness of his own grave.

Dean took his hand from the planchette. Instantly Harry reared back. His throat swelled. His back arched. He spoke in a voice that sounded like it had come from the depths of hell.

"Get your hand back on the board!"

Tears welled in the corner of Dean's eyes as he placed a trembling finger gently onto the planchette. He was nearly pulled from his seat as the small wooden pointer began to careen across the board.

O
U
T
G
E
T
O

U
T
G
E
T
O
U

"Harry, is this you!?" Dean asked again. Carefully, Harry removed his hand from the planchette leaving Dean to cling onto it alone. An energy crackled up Dean's finger as the pointer dragged his hand across the board with ferocious force.

"How are you doing this!?"

"Keep your hand on the board."

Dean's camera whirred as it recorded the events that he could not possibly explain.

"Harry, I don't like this. I'm going to take my hand off."

"No. Don't!"

Dean lifted his hand off the planchette. In the moments before the flame atop the black candle extinguished itself, both Harry and Dean watched in disbelief as the planchette continued to slide on its own.

Darkness, complete and all-consuming filled the room. Dean sat frozen in his chair listening to the gentle scraping of the planchette moving autonomously in the blackness. He opened his mouth to speak just as the scraping came to a stop.

"Dean?" Harry asked.

"Yes?"

"Does your camera capture night vision?"

Heavy breathing, then "No."

"Mine doesn't either... Is anybody there?"

Both Harry and Dean tensed as the planchette slid delicately across the surface of the wooden Ouija board once again. The sound came to an abrupt halt.

"Did you see what it said?" Harry asked.

"Harry. Is that you moving the planchette? I won't be angry if it is, I just want you to tell me the truth."

"It's not me" Harry said into the pitch-black room.

"We can't read what you're saying" Dean said, cautiously.

The gentle sound of wood sliding across wood sounded in front of both men again.

"We need to relight the candle."

Harry reached into his pocket slowly, as if any sudden movements might startle the spirit that possessed the board into fleeing from the room. He felt the small plastic lump of his lighter and began carefully prizing it from his pocket. If he were to drop it now, he would likely never be able to find it without getting up from the table. Breaking the pentagram he had painted across the floor would almost certainly break the lines of communication, or so he assumed.

With a quietly shaking hand, Harry held the lighter out in front of himself and flicked the igniter.

A choked moan escaped from Dean's throat. Harry watched it in a state of surprised confusion as Dean looked up from below with horror on his face. Dean on the other hand struggled for breath as he observed Harry, still sitting in his chair, floating some four feet off the ground.

Realisation crashed in on Harry.

"Oh my-"

Suddenly Harry was falling. His lighter went out, plunging most of his rapid descent into complete darkness. His chair hit the ground and then flipped backwards, sending Harry crashing onto the hard wooden floor of his once pristinely decorated nursery room. White light exploded across his eyes as his head collided with the ground. The wounds across his right arm opened with the impact of his fall.

Harry rolled onto his stomach. Somewhere in the room Dean was screaming, his feet or hands clattering loudly against the floor in his attempt to put distance between himself and Harry.

"Dean!" Harry called. "I'm alright. You need to calm down! Don't break the circle! It's really important that you don't break the circle!"

"I'm getting my camera and I'm getting out of here Harry. Put your lighter on. I want to get out!"

"But this is proof" Harry said. An ill placed smile started to spread across his face in the bowels of the room. "We finally have proof of the paranormal!"

"Fuck proof" Dean moaned. "Light the candle, I'm getting out of here."

Harry pushed himself into a crawling position. The pressure this sent through the wounds in his arm and the shattered bone of his leg was excruciating, but Harry found he simply did not care. He had levitated. His camera had surely captured the moment before the candle blew out on its own and the planchette had moved across the Ouija board of its own accord. This was undeniable proof of a haunting. It was as concrete as could be.

What Harry and Dean's cameras had captured would outperform anything that Dean had faked in the past. It was so visceral that it would likely become national, if not international news. And not just on the internet, but through mainstream media too. Harry would feature on the front page of any tabloid he chose to speak to. He would do the rounds on the talk shows, picking and choosing which ones he wanted to appear on. This would open up book deals and documentaries and movie deals and-

"Harry, what's that sound? Is that you?"

"What sound?"

Harry strained against the silence. The sound of his blood whooshing in his ears and the short gasping breaths of Dean King were all he could hear.

"Harry, put your lighter on."

Harry held out his lighter and rolled his thumb across the igniter. A bright white spark illuminated the room for the briefest of moments, brief enough for Harry only to make out the cowering shape of Dean King.

There was a marked change in Dean's breathing.

"Dean? Are you still there?"

Harry rolled his thumb across his lighter again. Another bright white spark leapt from it, illuminating the room for merely a fraction of a second. It was more than enough time however for Harry to see that Dean and he were no longer alone in the room.

"Dean?"

A deep and terrified scream permeated from Dean's throat. Harry tried desperately to light the lighter again as the scuffling of Dean's feet across naked floorboards rattled throughout the room. The sound curved around Harry from the front, ran behind him and then swooped round from the back.

Harry rolled his thumb across the lighter again. Yet another flame burst into life and died to nothing, showing Harry that Dean was still sat firmly in place.

"Who's running around?"

Harry flopped onto his stomach and began dragging himself toward his camera. He pulled himself along, sliding across the floor, reaching out into the darkness until his hand found the plastic leg of his tripod.

Harry tipped the tripod over and the camera atop it clattered to the ground hard enough for Harry to worry he might have broken it. He pulled the tripod toward him and unclipped the camera. Feeling for damage with sweat soaked fingers, he slung the camera's strap over his neck, turned it in the direction of Dean King and rolled his lighter again.

The brief flame revealed him sitting cross legged, rocking backwards and forwards with his hands over his face. The fire died out and the room was cast into darkness once more.

"Can't you get it to work?" Dean begged.

"It won't stay lit" Harry said. He pressed his throbbing thumb down against the metal cogs of his lighter and flicked it as hard as he could. A bright orange flame burst into life and this time it held, sending warm comforting light flooding into the room. Harry's brief respite from the horrors of the evening disappeared instantly when he realised that Dean was gone.

"Dean?"

Nothing, and then Dean fell down from the ceiling above. The camera that was slung around Harry's neck captured the stomach-churning moment that Dean's belly flop came to a painful halt across the hardwood floor. He snorted loudly as several of his teeth were dislodged and went scattering across the floorboards.

Harry trained his camera onto Dean in the last fleeting moments before he was dragged kicking and screaming out of the room.

The door slammed shut behind him.

Heat from the lighter bore down onto Harry's thumb, forcing him to drop it. Harry slung his camera around his neck and then felt for his crutches, pulling them toward him and forcing himself to his feet. He hurried for the door, reaching out into the darkness, feeling for the handle.

Harry pulled open the door and hopped out into the landing. He ran his hand along the wall, feeling around the space where the light switch should have been. He found it, flicked it on and then squinted against the startling bright light of the naked bulb above him.

Dean King was stood at the top of the stairs. His eyes were fixed on some unknown point at the bottom of the steps. He swayed gently in time with his shallow breathing.

"Dean?"

His stare broke. He turned to look at Harry. Harry framed

the YouTuber with his camera.

"What is this?"

Dean's voice sounded hopeless.

"Dean! Wait."

The man that Harry had so once admired leaned forward and spilled into the darkness of the stairway. Thick slabs of impact were underpinned by the quiet grunts and groans of a man feeling his bones break inside of his body. The sound of the fall stopped abruptly, and a wet gurgling sound begun to echo in the darkness.

Harry threw his crutches down onto the ground and began the arduous task of shuffling down the stairs. As he lowered himself from one step to the next, the dark outline of Dean King's motionless body became clearer. Harry called out to him but got no response other than the wet plunger sound that seemed to be coating Dean's gasps for air.

The copper smell of blood invaded Harry's nose. As he reached the bottom step, Harry could make out a vast pool of it forming around Dean's head in the minimal light that made it down from the landing.

"Dean. Can you hear me?"

Predictably, Harry got no response.

Forcing himself to his feet, Harry stepped over Dean's body and reached out for the light switch. He hammered the heel of his hand into it. The orange glow that filled the hallway illuminated what Harry suspected to be Dean's dying minutes as he lay bleeding to death at the bottom of the stairs.

Harry threw himself forward. He clattered to the floor and then clambered towards Dean. As he came face to face with the man he had once idolised, Harry found himself grappling with an almost crippling sense of disgust. Dean's neck was broken, twisted almost all the way round on his shoulders, and yet somehow he was still breathing. The twist which had turned Dean's head had put tremendous strain on the flesh around his throat and so it had ruptured, and it was now pumping blood into the hallway in time with the slowing pace of Dean King's heart.

Harry leaned forward to shake Dean, but then stopped himself. Any movement could sever his spinal cord and then what little chance there was of saving his life would be gone completely. Instead, Harry gently grasped Dean's hand and brought it up to the tear in his throat. He lay it gently against the wound and then watched hopelessly as Dean's blood simply spilled through his fingers.

Harry reached into his pocket with a slick hand and produced a phone that had at some point been smashed to pieces. The memory of his brief levitation and even briefer fall back to the hard floor of his spare bedroom sent fresh aches and pains through Harry's tired bones. He would need to look for help elsewhere.

Rolling onto his back, Harry tried to ignore the hot blood that saturated his shirt. He picked up a crutch and held it over his head like a lance, drew it back and then drove it into the dividing wall between house and the one next door.

"Nettie" Harry called at the top of his lungs. "I need your help!"

There was no response. A sudden and terrifying thought suddenly occurred to Harry.

There was a very real chance that Nettie could hear him, even through the dulled sense of hearing that the old woman had, but there was also a very real chance that Nettie did not believe what she was hearing. She had said it herself when they had first met. Nettie had heard voices calling her before and they had all ultimately amounted to nothing. It had been another of the house's tricks, lulling Nettie into itself only for her to be discovered by Harry as he had returned from the shed covered in rat blood. Harry imagined her now, lying in her bed, hearing his calls but dismissing them as just another symptom of the haunting at number 7 Ragworth Lane.

Dean King sucked another liquid breath into his lungs.

"Nettie!" Harry screamed, driving his crutch into the wall with tremendous force. "Nettie! Please! I need your help! It's Harry, it's really me, please come to my door! I need you to call an ambulance, I need-"

A sound from next door. The distant echo of a woman's voice. Had she heard him? Harry did not wait to find out.

He drew back on his crutch again and hammered it into the wall with a new determination. He reared back and did it again, twisting his body and straining with every muscle he had. He would punch a hole right through to the old woman's house if that's what it took.

"Nettie" Harry called again. His own laboured breathing now matched Dean's. "I need your help! Please hear me. I need you-"

"Harry?"

Harry froze.

"Nettie? Is that you?"

"Harry, what's the matter love? Are you-"

"Nettie" Harry shouted, barely able to believe that the old woman was really stood behind his front door. "There's been an accident. I need you to call an ambulance."

"What's happened?"

"Please" Harry pleaded. "There's a man bleeding to death in here. I can't stop the blood. I need an ambulance."

"Oh my God" Nettie said. Her voice trailed off. The sound of loose paving slabs rattling in Harry's driveway was enough for him to realise that she had run back to her home to call for help.

Harry turned his attentions back to Dean. He was a ghastly shade of white. The deep red blood that was spilling out onto the hallway floor made him seem even paler by contrast.

"Hold on" Harry said through gasping breath.

Dean's eyes rolled out from the back of their sockets and settled on Harry. He tried fleetingly to speak but found that he could not. Harry was relieved to see there was still a tiny flicker of hope in the dying man's eye.

Nettie's voice gained in volume the further up the driveway she came.

"Harry" she called. "I've called an ambulance. They're on their way. Help is coming. What's going on in there?"

"My friend. He's fallen down the stairs. He's bleeding to death in here. I can't stop it. I think he's broken his neck."

"Jesus" the old woman said. "Let me in. I can help"

Harry traced his path to the door, the one that was paved in the blood of Dean King.

"I don't think I can get to the door."

"You have to. The door is locked."

A new wave of panic spread throughout Harry. Abandoning his crutches altogether, he pulled himself onto his feet and began the excruciating short walk to the front door. The weight bearing down on his broken leg sent shockwaves through his body. The sensation he felt transcended pain and instead Harry felt something entirely different, something much more akin to an electricity each time his bone separated from itself inside of his cast.

With a great relief, Harry found that he could simply fall the final five feet of his journey. His head narrowly missed the front door, flying by it with only inches to spare.

"Open the door Harry!"

Harry reached for the lock. His fingers grasped for a key that somehow wasn't there.

"There's no key in the lock Nettie. I can't open the door."

"You have to" Nettie said through the letterbox. "You have to get the door open. The paramedics are going to need to come in when they get here. You have to open the door."

"But I can't find the key." A thick veil of hopelessness was now settling over Harry. His eyes skimmed over his surroundings, searching for anything that he might use to break open the door or knock the handle off it and let Nettie inside.

Dean King took another rattling breath. He was fading quickly.

"There has to be something you can do" the old woman called. In the distance, Harry could hear sirens wailing.

"There's nothing that I can-"

The camera that was slung around Harry's neck seemed to suddenly take on a new weight.

"*No*" he said to himself.

Dean moaned quietly, his voice now carrying an almost ethereal quality. Looking around, Harry could see nothing else that would have the weight needed to knock the handle off the door.

Gingerly he lifted the camera's strap from around his neck and took the device in his hands.

"Open the door Harry" Nettie called.

Harry held the camera, ready to bring it crashing down onto the door handle, but he found that when it came time to do so, he simply could not.

The footage on this camera was proof to everybody who had ever doubted him that ghosts existed. There was a lifetime's worth of validation saved into the camera's hard drive.

A rattling sound came from the back of Dean's throat. He was dying now, the light of his life no brighter than the sparks that had burst from Harry's lighter. His mouth formed a word. The blood that coated his lips made it sound thick as he bubbled his final plea for help.

"Fuck it" Harry said to himself.

With a tremendous effort Harry swung the camera into the door handle. Both the handle and the camera exploded upon impact. The door swung open almost before the shattered pieces of the camera's hard drive had a chance to hit the ground.

Flashing blue lights filled the room, spilling in from the ambulance that had parked across Harry's drive. Nettie rushed to Harry side, throwing herself toward the ground and cradling his head in her hands as quickly as her elderly frame would allow.

A paramedic burst through the door.

"My name is Emily" she said in a voice that verged on shouting. "I understand you sustained a neck injury."

"Not me" Harry said. "Him."

The paramedic looked past Harry with furrowed brows.

"Him?"

"Dean."

A heavy lead ball settled in Harry's guts. The warmth of his blood seemed to drain. Harry felt like he might pass out as he realised now that he was all alone.

"No" he said, struggling to get to his feet. "No, not again! It can't have happened *again!*"

"I think you should sit back down" the paramedic said, but Harry did not hear her. He pushed her grasping hands away from himself and walked unsteadily on his broken leg. His cast cracked with every step, but Harry again did not even notice this. All he could focus on now was the empty space where Dean King had lay dying only moments before.

"Not again!" he cried, tears spilling from his eyes, "You can't do this to me twice! It's not fair!"

"Sir, can you come and sit down for me? I think you might have hurt your head."

"You did it again!" Harry called into the house. "You tricked me again!"

Both Nettie and the paramedic watched Harry with the same concerned expression on their faces.

"I filmed it" he said, bargaining with the women to believe what he was telling them. "I can show you. I filmed the whole thing on my... my camera."

The paramedic issued a loud yelp of surprise as Harry fell to his knees. Pain exploded through the wounds that were carved into his arms, but this paled in comparison to the pain in Harry's breaking heart.

He scooped up the broken pieces of the camera, hoping against hope that the hard drive might somehow have survived the impact against the door handle. Harry found only the jagged pieces of an utterly destroyed video camera.

His tears came quickly now. Thick raking sobs pulled through his body. Nettie hurried to comfort him, content not to ask questions just yet, perhaps because of her own experiences with number 7 Ragworth Lane. The paramedic, much more hardened to this sort of thing, was much more eager to get to the bottom of exactly what was happening.

"I'm sorry. Who did you say has sustained the neck injury? Do you have a catastrophic bleed?"

"No" Harry said through quaking sobs. "It wasn't me. My friend was here but now he's gone."

"Do you mean that he's left your home?"

"I mean he's vanished. He's left the house. He was probably never here."

The paramedic looked more worried the more she spoke to Harry. "I think maybe it's worth you getting into the ambulance and coming to the hospital for a little check-up."

"No" Harry said. "You think I'm crazy but I'm not. This house, it plays tricks on people. Nettie will tell you. My friend was here, and he was bleeding to death, but now he's gone. It was all on my camera. I swear. But now that's gone too because I smashed it and now nobody... nobody is going to believe... believe..."

A fresh bout of tears interrupted Harry.

The paramedic stood over him, trying to decipher exactly what Harry was telling her. She found little success. Harry scooped up more of the broken camera and clasped it tightly to his chest.

The paramedic ran her hand through his hair, concern etched tightly across her face. She looked around the room, and then her expression flattened with the first murmurings of a bright idea.

"What about that camera up there?" she asked, pointing to the security camera in the corner of the hallway. "Do you think the footage on that one might explain what's been going on?"

EPILOGUE
ACCOUNT DELETED

Stephen could tell that they were a couple of time wasters from the moment he pulled up outside of the property. As he arrived to the viewing some fifteen minutes late (something which he had never done in his whole career as an estate agent prior to taking on the listing for number 7 Ragworth Lane) he noticed the couple filming the house on their phones and laughing giddily at their own antics.

Nevertheless, Stephen straightened out his tie using his rear-view mirror before flattening out his hair with the palms of his hands. *Who knows* he thought, if he could put on a good enough show he might just be able to shift this place, even if it was only on a temporary basis. Number 7 never seemed to stay off the market for long.

He got out of his car and approached the women. They had inconsiderately parked over the driveway rather than on it. The two women inside jumped at the sound of Stephen knocking on their passenger side window.

He smiled, quietly satisfied to have been able to sneak up on them and interrupt their video without them noticing. Stephen motioned for the passenger to wind down her window.

"You can pull onto the drive if you want" Stephen said, not even bothering to ask their names.

"That's OK" one of the girls laughed. "I think I'd rather leave it here. You know, in case we need to make a quick getaway."

Her partner began to laugh anew. Stephen smiled through his growing annoyance and set off for the house. He clipped the toe of one of his new shoes on an unsecured driveway slab, cursing himself for not remembering that particular feature of the house from last time.

The two women clambered out of their cars and walked quickly up the driveway, each of their phones held out in front of their faces, their camera apps capturing every moment of their visit to the house that had been seen all around the world.

"I'm afraid you won't be able to film whilst on the property" Stephen said. "Data protection."

"Oh" said the larger of the two girls. "I was hoping to film so that I could show my mum the inside of the house. She said that she wants to see it before helping me to put a deposit down."

She was lying. Stephen could tell.

"I really must insist that you do not film the property. If you can't promise not to do so then I'll have to end the viewing now."

"And lose a potential sale?"

Stephen smiled smugly.

"The interest in this property has been unprecedented after the media attention its received. I have another five viewings today, and today is my quietest day of the week."

With reluctance, each of the women put their phones back into their purses and stood waiting for Stephen to open the door.

He turned the key and opened the door into the narrow

hallway that led to the tiny kitchen at the back of the house. Stephen stepped in first. He did not bother to take his shoes off.

The larger of the two women was next to step in. Stephen watched as her initial wonder at walking into a place that was a genuine viral sensation melted into a gentle disappointment.

"Oh" she said. "It's quite..."

"Normal?"

"Well, I was going to say *small*, but I suppose yes, it is quite normal really."

"Are you from out of the area?" Stephen asked, noticing the southern twang in the younger girl's accent.

"Yes. We're actually from Surrey."

"Surrey? Wow. And you travelled down just to see this property?"

The younger woman nodded. "We're looking to get onto the property ladder. House prices in this part of the world are a lot cheaper than where we're from."

"They certainly are" Stephen said. "And is this going to be your first property?"

"Yes" the larger lady said, moving through the home, paying particularly close attention to the spot on the floor that had now been seen the world over due to a video the previous owner had uploaded to the internet. Her hand went instinctively to the pocket where she had stored her phone. Stephen's watchful eye prevented her from taking it out.

"As you can see it's a compact little property, but it isn't without its charms. It comes fully furnished, which is an added bonus to anyone on the market to buy."

The younger of the two girls gasped.

"So, we'd get to keep all of this stuff?"

"The previous owner is quite adamant that he doesn't want to keep any of it. He is the very definition of a motivated seller."

"Wow..."

"And it's very affordable too" Stephen said. "The asking price has come down from under seventy-five thousand to just over fifty thousand in a matter of weeks. Think about it. You could be moving into this home this week for the tiny down payment of just over five thousand pounds."

"Wow" the larger girl said, echoing her friend's sentiment. "Can you imagine *living* here?" A dull shudder ran down her spine.

"Shall we see the upper floor?"

Stephen led the women upstairs, paying close attention to their movements as he moved in and out of the bedrooms. Both women tried to sneak their phones from their pockets, but each time Stephen caught them and firmly reminded them that this was strictly prohibited.

When they were done looking around the home Stephen walked them back onto the uneven driveway, putting himself between the house and the women to prevent any last-minute snaps of the house that the mainstream media had dubbed *"Britain's Most Haunted Home."*

"You've given us a lot to think about" one of the women said. Stephen hated to admit it, but she had done a good job of looking like she was seriously considering buying the house.

"I'm sure I have" Stephen said. "If you would like to make an offer on the property I could call the owner now. Although the price has been reduced significantly, he is still open to offers."

The two women shared a look that verged on fanatical.

"You mean you could speak to Harry now? You have his number in your phone?"

"Of course" Stephen said.

"Can I speak to him?"

"Or better yet, can we meet him? I'd feel happier putting an offer in on this place if I could ask a few questions first."

Stephen had been here before.

"I'm afraid that won't be possible" he said. "The owner is a very private man. He does not want to meet with anybody."

"Private? He's spoken to pretty much every talk show host that there is."

Stephen shrugged.

"We'll be in touch."

The women turned and headed for their car, stopping to take one last look at the building. Stephen remained between them and the house, now feeling an incredible sense of determination to stop yet more people filming and photographing the building for their own social media clout.

The younger girl stopped - a look of wild determination on her face. She asked the question that Stephen had been anticipating since the moment they had arrived.

"Is it true? Is the house haunted?"

"I don't know what you're talking about."

"Oh, come on" the bigger woman chimed. "You do. It was all over the news. Number one trending story on Twitter. The guy went on all the talk shows and all the news channels. It split him and his wife up."

"Is it true that she still doesn't believe the house is haunted?" the younger girl asked.

"I heard they lost the baby with the stress of it all" the bigger woman said. "You must know that this is the house, right? Is it true? Did the guy who owned this place end up homeless?"

"I heard his wife took almost all of his earnings. He would be rich if she hadn't done that."

"Yeah. That's how he's homeless."

"I saw it all on *King of the Haunt*. He did a big expose´ on it once he found out the guy who lived here thought he had been filming him, when really he had been filming-"

"Can you just stop?" Stephen said sharply. His mask of

professionalism finally slipped from his face. "Even if any of that was true, and I'm not saying that it is, but *if* it was do you really think that this is something to be gossiped about and celebrated? You're talking about real people. Real people with real lives."

Neither woman had an answer for this. With an obvious air of disappointment, they climbed into their car, put on their seatbelts, took a final picture of the house's exterior and then began their long journey back to the south where they would never think about the house again.

Stephen stood in the driveway for a while. A dull ache started to spread across his head, settling uncomfortably behind his eyes.

He took his phone from his pocket and dialled Harry's number. Harry picked up almost immediately.

"Stephen? How did it go?"

"I'm sorry mate. It didn't go well."

Wind whipped down the phone line. "Did you tell them about the reduced price?"

There was a hopelessness in Harry's voice that went some way toward breaking Stephen's heart.

"I did mate. I made the price very clear."

"OK" Harry said. "Drop the price again. I'll take forty-five thousand. Furniture included."

"Harry. Come on. You don't need to do that."

"I just want rid of it" Harry said.

Stephen pressed his fingers into his eyes. It did nothing to numb the growing ache at the back of his skull.

"Are you absolutely sure that you won't just stay here while you try to sell it? Surely it can't be any worse than where you are right now. This all seems so crazy."

Harry pulled his blanket around himself tightly as the wind whipped across the broken down old High Street. He leaned forward to look at the coffee cup that sat in front of him. It was half full. There was probably enough loose change in there to get him into a hostel for the night.

"I'm not going back into that house."

"Then at least give Lisa a call" Stephen said. "If she knew how you were living, surely she would see things differently."

For a moment the line was quiet, with only the sound being the wind that whipped at the receiver filling the reflection between the two men. When Harry spoke again there was a thin gleam of determination in his voice

"Drop the price" Harry said. "Forty thousand. There has to be somebody out there willing to buy that house. If we drop the price enough someone is going to move in and take a chance on it. There has to be someone out there who hasn't seen that footage."

Stephen ended the call, desperately hoping that Harry was right.

A MESSAGE FROM THE AUTHOR

I wanted to take the opportunity to thank you for reading my book. If you enjoyed *Our Haunted Home*, it would mean a lot to me if you could rate it positively on Amazon and leave a review telling others why you enjoyed it.

Thanks again, and I hope you'll read my other books once they are released.

Matt

Printed in Great Britain
by Amazon